THE
FINALISTS

ALSO BY DAVID BELL

THE FINALISTS

DAVID BELL

BERKLEY
New York

BERKLEY
An imprint of Penguin Random House LLC
penguinrandomhouse.com

Copyright © 2022 by David J. Bell
Penguin Random House supports copyright. Copyright fuels creativity, encourages diverse
voices, promotes free speech, and creates a vibrant culture. Thank you for buying an authorized
edition of this book and for complying with copyright laws by not reproducing, scanning,
or distributing any part of it in any form without permission. You are supporting writers
and allowing Penguin Random House to continue to publish books for every reader.

BERKLEY and the BERKLEY & B colophon are registered trademarks of
Penguin Random House LLC.

Library of Congress Cataloging-in-Publication Data

Names: Bell, David, 1969 November 17- author.
Title: The finalists / David Bell.
Description: New York : Berkley, [2022]
Identifiers: LCCN 2021057351 (print) | LCCN 2021057352 (ebook) |
ISBN 9780593198698 (hardcover) | ISBN 9780593198704 (trade paperback) |
ISBN 9780593198711 (ebook)
Classification: LCC PS3602.E64544 F56 2022 (print) |
LCC PS3602.E64544 (ebook) | DDC 813/.6--dc23
LC record available at https://lccn.loc.gov/2021057351
LC ebook record available at https://lccn.loc.gov/2021057352

Printed in the United States of America
1st Printing

Book design by Daniel Brount

In memory of my father-in-law,
R. Michael McCaffrey, 1942–2021

THE
FINALISTS

PART 1
MORNING

1

THE HOUSE SITS ON the far eastern edge of campus, nestled in the woods among the sycamores, the maples, and the white oaks, all older than the college. Older than Kentucky itself. To reach it by car, one must turn left off the main road that circles campus and onto Ezekiel Hyde Lane, a narrow, winding strip of asphalt that cuts through the trees, enters the clearing, and ends in the small parking lot on the side of Hyde House. On foot, the house can be reached by way of the numerous paths that cut through the trees and give the campus its natural beauty.

I step out of my car and look back up the road I just traveled, and it's easy to believe the world doesn't exist even though the rest of campus is just a third of a mile away. Standing on the Hyde House grounds can feel like standing in another century, which is exactly the way Ezekiel Hyde, the founder of the college and its first president, wanted it to stay.

The sun is bright, and its rays hit the windows of Hyde House, reflecting the light, capturing the morning glow.

Is it weird to say the sight of that house still lifts my spirits?

It's eight fifteen, and I'm early. Which is good. I want to be here before the students. More than anything, I want to be here before Ezekiel Hyde's great-great-great-great-grandson, Nicholas, arrives.

I climb the portico steps to the Neo-Federal structure. Up close the brick is more weathered than I realized. I reach for the brass knob, which is tarnished. The heavy black door needs to be re-painted. For years, the college's board of trustees has wanted to renovate the house, but the money is never there. The college has a list of projects that never get done.

I pull on the knob and, not surprisingly, find the door locked.

I step off the right side of the portico, my shoes sinking into the soft soil, and press my face against the window. I've been in Hyde House many times for college events and know the layout well. I'm staring into the music room, the space where Major Hyde, his family, and subsequent generations of Hydes came to listen to recitals on the piano. The piano originally moved to the house by Major Hyde fell into disrepair and was sold in the 1990s, but a music stand remains along with a bust of Major Hyde's favorite composer, Wagner.

The sun warms the back of my neck. I wait on the lawn in front of the house. In the distance, the campus is quiet on a Satur-day morning in April. The students sleep off the night before. Purple hyacinths bloom in the flower beds, and I catch their over-whelming scent. A robin chirps in a nearby tree.

I want to call Rachel, apologize for our fight earlier. Money. We only fight about money. We have to decide whether to get new windows or a new roof, and we disagree about which is the higher priority. Our household is like the college—there's never enough money to go around.

But before I can hit the call button, the phone rings.

"Shoot," I say, then answer. "Hello?"

"Hey, Troy. It's Grace."

"Hey, Grace." I try to keep my voice buoyant and not let any irritation show, even though my boss—the president of the college—is calling to check up on me. But she's not just my boss—she's my friend. She and Rachel belong to the same book club, and just last weekend Grace and her husband, Doug, came over to our house for drinks. "How are you on this fine morning?"

"Is he there?" she asks. She cuts to the chase. Today is about business. On another day, we would talk about our kids—Grace's oldest son, Michael, is in the same grade as my oldest daughter, Rebecca—but I know Grace has other things on her mind.

"If by 'he' you mean Nicholas Hyde, then no, he isn't here yet. No one is."

"Damn it. When did you talk to him last?"

"It's been about a month. And that was just a short e-mail."

"Yeah." Grace sounds defeated. She never sounds defeated. "I can't get ahold of him either. Did you know he left Kentucky and moved to California?"

"He did? I thought he was still living in Lexington. He didn't tell me."

"He's lost both his parents in the last year. That's a terrible blow for anyone. And I know he was close to his mother. Very close."

"Maybe that's why he moved to California. His mom was his last real family tie here."

"I'm worried about this, Troy. He's not connected to the college or to Kentucky the way the Hydes always have been. You know as well as I do his father would never have left us twisting in the wind."

"You're absolutely right. I'm worried too. Nicholas is pretty much the only living heir of Ezekiel Hyde. Certainly the only direct descendant. And he controls the estate."

"And they've been giving us less and less every year. For the last decade. And it's been coming to us later and later every year, which makes it harder to budget and plan. Is it too early for a drink?"

"A bit. But if you want to get one tonight, you know our patio bar is always open to you and Doug."

A car comes down the main road and turns onto Ezekiel Hyde Lane. It makes the slow, winding run in my direction and pulls up and parks next to mine. An older model with a dent in the fender. A middle-aged man steps out, trim and tall. He wears a dark suit with a white shirt and a thin black tie.

"The students are starting to arrive. I think this is—"

"Troy," Grace says, "remember what we talked about."

I know right away what she means. The 100 More Initiative I've been working on for the past two years.

"I think it's fantastic you want to increase the number of minority and first-time students at the college. That's why we promoted you to this position. It's not just because you're my friend and a nice guy. It's to raise money. But we've been falling short. *You've* been falling short. The Hydes are giving less, so we need to raise more from other sources. And the board is—"

"Nicholas promised us the money for One Hundred More. Two million dollars. We shook hands on it."

"Do you know how much a handshake is worth?" Grace asks. "Don't let him leave without getting a real commitment. Okay?"

"That's my plan."

"I'm sorry, Troy. You know I am, but I don't have to remind you of what's at stake. For the college or for you personally."

"I get it, Grace. We'll toast our success tonight, have a drink around the fire."

The man in the dark suit comes my way, almost marching. Back straight as a flagpole. A chin made of granite. His heels clack off the pavement, and his hair is cut close to his head.

"Grace, the students are—"

"Wait, Troy. There's one more—"

The man reaches me, extends his hand. He doesn't seem to notice or care that I'm on the phone.

"Vice President Gaines, sir. It's a pleasure to meet you. I'm James Stephenson. Retired, United States Army. Thank you for the opportunity to compete for this scholarship, sir."

We shake. My hand feels like it's been slammed between two bricks.

"Sir, I know no Black student—indeed, no student of color— has ever won the Hyde Scholarship. I'm intent on being the first, and I want to thank you for the chance."

"Well, it's not me. It's the Hyde family and their board—"

"Sir, I was wondering if I could express some concerns to you before we begin—"

"Troy, are you there?" Grace asks.

"Just a minute, Grace. Can we speak in a moment, Mr. Stephenson?"

"Call me Captain Stephenson, sir."

"Okay, Captain Stephenson. Can we speak in a moment?"

"Yes, sir."

He remains in front of me, hands folded behind his back. Parade rest. His shoes are so polished and clean, they reflect the sky like the windows of Hyde House.

I hold up my index finger. "Just one moment."

I walk fifteen feet away and switch the phone to my other ear. "Okay, Grace, I'm back. But you don't have to tell me again that I've missed my fundraising quotas two years in a row. I'm well aware—"

"No, Troy, not that. Something else. Something about the scholarship process today. I'm afraid we have a situation brewing there. And you need to be ready for it."

2

BEFORE I ASK GRACE what is going on—and before she is able to tell me—two campus police cruisers turn off the main road and come down Ezekiel Hyde Lane. They stop at the boundary of the grounds of Hyde House, a couple of hundred feet from where I stand.

Two officers step out of each cruiser, and a cool wave of relief passes through me.

"Grace, don't worry about it. The campus police are here, and I see Chief. He'll let us in now. Problem solved."

"Troy, that's not it."

The four police officers open the trunks of the two cars and pull wooden sawhorses out. They stand them up across the entrance to the Hyde House grounds, creating a barricade that shuts off vehicle traffic. Even Captain Stephenson has turned away from staring at me and fixed his eyes on the activities of the police.

"What's going on, Grace? The cops are making some kind of perimeter at the edge of the lawn. They've never done that before."

"That's what I'm trying to tell you, Troy." Grace speaks to me in the way I speak to my daughters when they are slow to understand something. "We've received word there are going to be protests during the process today. A number of students are going to gather, so I notified the campus police. We want them to keep the protestors back as far as possible."

"They're protesting *against* their fellow students competing for a big scholarship?"

"No, it's not that."

A couple of students come walking toward the house from one of the paths that cuts through the woods from the south. A man and a woman. They appear to be having a passionate conversation. The young woman—who is tall and lanky like an athlete—seems to be trying to convince the guy—who is almost strutting like he's in a movie—of something. He's listening, nodding his head as she speaks. Captain Stephenson has noticed them as well and turns in their direction.

"Then what's the problem, Grace?"

"It's the Hyde family they're going to protest. They want us to divest from the Hyde family fortune. You know they think money made in coal is blood money."

"I thought the Hydes settled that. They have a plan to move away from coal to green energy during the next two decades."

"You know that's not nearly fast enough for the students," Grace says.

"What good does it do to block the road?" I ask. "Can't someone reach us by one of the paths?"

"They met outside the student union. Then they're marching over to Hyde House as a group. We know which way they're going."

The police appear to have the sawhorses all in place. And just in time. About thirty students carrying signs and chanting approach Hyde House from the direction of campus. They walk down the main road, the one I just drove over to get here, and then turn down Ezekiel Hyde Lane, heading in the direction of the police barricades. It's hard for me to make out the chant from this distance, but I can kind of read one of the signs, which a student holds high in the air. It's written in red paint—at least I hope it's paint—on white poster board.

NO BLOOD MONEY!

Captain Stephenson turns his whole body in that direction, facing the protestors. "I don't like the looks of that," he says, shaking his head.

For a moment, I worry. What will happen when they reach the cops? I don't want anyone to get hurt. And I don't want any arrests or fights. The police are outnumbered, but I know they're armed. The cops tense, their bodies primed for action. They all stand with hands on hips, but I know that puts their hands closer to weapons—pepper spray, Tasers, guns.

The protestors continue to chant as they approach the edge of the lawn, their faces angry and determined.

"Grace, I think we . . ."

"What is it, Troy?"

My body tenses like I'm about to brawl.

But the protestors stop behind the barricade. They don't appear interested in pushing their way through or making any more trouble. They chant and wave their signs, but there's no actual trouble.

I breathe a sigh of relief.

"It's okay, Grace. They stopped. They're facing the cops, but they're not too loud. Once we're inside, the students should be able to concentrate. The house is old and keeps sound out pretty well. But they are blocking the driveway to the house."

"The cops are going to take care of that," she says. "They can protest, but they can't block traffic."

The young man and woman continue their discussion off to the side. They stand close together. The woman wipes at the corner of her eye. A tear?

"Grace, I think I need to go. The students are arriving."

"There's one more thing."

"What else could there be?"

"Can you read any of the other signs?"

"I can try, but you're testing my middle-aged eyesight. They're kind of far away." I watch, squinting as the signs move up and down. Someone beats on a tambourine, making an oddly discordant jingling. "I think there are a couple about blood money. One about paying for education with coal. Another about killing Mother Earth. Oh, and one nasty one about slaughtering the innocents. I guess it has a nice biblical touch. You can tell the protestors I appreciate the large type they're using."

"*That's* the one I was worried about," Grace says.

"What about it?"

Grace sighs into the phone again. "Well, we were trying to keep this under wraps until we could fully investigate the claim, but word leaked out on social media this morning. It's about Ezekiel Hyde's service in the Civil War."

"You mean *Major* Ezekiel Hyde."

When I say the word "Major," Captain Stephenson looks my way. He raises his hand like we're in a classroom, reminding me he still wants to talk. I hold up my index finger again and then point to the phone.

"Yes," Grace says, "*Major* Ezekiel Ellis Hyde. This is courtesy of Charlie Porter in History." She sighs. "Oh, Charlie. He's uncovered something about Major Hyde's service in the Civil War."

"What could possibly be uncovered? Everyone knows that Ezekiel Hyde served with the Union Army."

"That's what we say on the tour when everyone goes past the statue of Ezekiel on his horse Lancer by the campus gates. But . . . Charlie uncovered something in his research."

"You mean something not related to the family destroying the earth with their coal?"

"It's about the Palmyra Massacre."

"The what?"

"Exactly. Not many people remember it, but the Union Army massacred ten Confederate troops rather than take them off as prisoners. A horrific atrocity." I can hear Grace shudder through the phone. "There was always speculation that Ezekiel was there, but no proof. Well . . ."

"Charlie found the proof."

"He did." Grace sighs. "Ugh. He posted about it on his blog and tweeted about it. And he's writing a book too. So not only has the Hyde family made their money off coal—and continue to do so. Now everyone knows that Ezekiel Hyde, founder of our beloved college, participated in a slaughter. How do you think the students feel about that?"

"Not good. Is there a statute of limitations on mass slaughter?"

"Troy. That's not funny."

"Sorry, sorry. I'm just not sure what we're supposed to do. Dig Ezekiel and Lancer up and scold them?"

"You need to know that the mood on the campus is tense because of these things."

A dusty black Ford pickup turns down Hyde Lane and approaches the protestors and the police barricade. It looks like trouble, like someone from town has shown up intending to counterprotest. Someone who remains a big fan of Major Hyde. The pickup truck looms large and intimidating, like a vehicle of destruction.

But the protestors move aside, and the driver—a guy in a cowboy hat—leans out and speaks to the police. The cops move the barricade, letting him through. The protestors increase the volume of their chants as he maneuvers his vehicle onto the Hyde House grounds, but no one tries to run through in his wake, and the cops quickly shut the opening.

The truck approaches my position, its muffler rumbling, the large tires squealing slightly. Once it's parked, a slender, muscular young man wearing pointy-toe boots and the aforementioned cowboy hat slides out, the ornamental clasp on his bolo tie glinting in the sun.

"I'm glad to know this, Grace. Once all the students arrive, we'll go inside and get started. The protestors will get bored or hungry or tired, and they'll go home."

"I don't think Nicholas knows about the stuff concerning Ezekiel."

"You've met Nicholas, Grace. He's a wealthy playboy. He struggles to remember my name, and I've had several meals with him. I don't think he's going to be upset about the . . . What did you call it? Palmyra Massacre?"

"I mean the protestors. He's going to see that when he arrives. There's no other way for him to drive in except right past them. What if that makes him pull all the money from the school?"

"You could tell Charlie to put a lid on his research."

"Yeah, right. He has tenure. You know the administration can't muzzle the faculty. You used to be a professor, remember?"

"Barely. I sold out for money. My fault for having three kids who want to go to college. Look, Grace, it's all going to be fine. Nicholas likes me, even if he isn't sure of my name. He's a baseball fan, and so am I. When we get together, we talk about the Reds and the designated-hitter rule and how defensive shifts are ruining the game. We have *rapport*. I'll smooth any ruffled feathers, I promise. I'll nail down the One Hundred More donation, and we'll all be in fat city. Okay?"

"Okay, Troy. I *do* believe in you. I know the board is putting a lot of heat on you. They're putting heat on the whole administration. Shit, you know my contract is up this year. We're all facing the reality of how hard it is for private colleges to survive. It's daunting, Troy."

"I know. But Hyde College is a special place. It's been here for a hundred fifty-two years. It's like these oak trees I'm standing by. Strong. Powerful. Unbending."

"You really believe that, Troy?"

"I'm suffused with the Hyde spirit."

"Okay. Let's concentrate on something good. One of those six students is going to win a really nice scholarship."

"That's right," I say. "And more of them are arriving, so I'd better go."

"Thanks, Troy."

"Try to enjoy your Saturday," I say.

Before Grace can answer, a fat red bird comes streaking through the sky, heading right for me.

3

EXCEPT IT'S NOT A bird.

It's heavy and falling fast.

"Incoming!" Captain Stephenson shouts.

He ducks, and so do I. And the brick that one of the protestors threw whistles past the side of my head so close I can feel a rush of air as it goes by. The brick bounds against the pavement and makes a scraping noise as it skids across the parking lot and stops only after striking one of the fat tires on the cowboy's pickup.

"Hey!" He starts to move toward the protestors. "That hit my truck."

Captain Stephenson moves to stop him. "Easy now. That's not a solution."

Two of the police officers leap over the barricade and wade into the crowd. The chanting grows louder, and nearly every one of the protestors has a phone out recording the actions of the police, who quickly identify the culprit and place him in handcuffs.

I slide over and move next to Captain Stephenson and in front of the cowboy, holding up my hands like I'm a cop. "He's right. Let the police handle it."

"That brick almost hit you right in the head," the cowboy says. "It would have done serious damage."

"I know. And I appreciate your concern. But it didn't hit me. That's the good news. And the police are taking care of it. Okay?"

"Who are those punks?" the cowboy asks. "They should be taught a lesson."

"Let's go back, okay? Come on, guys."

I herd them back toward the house, displaying a calm I really don't feel. The skin on the back of my neck crawls, and adrenaline is making my heart do backflips. The cowboy is right—the brick came dangerously close to my head. And if it had hit me . . .

"Why don't we all stand on the portico there? It has some cover."

"The what?" the cowboy asks.

"The portico. The porch."

They start to move that way.

"What's your name?" I ask the cowboy.

"Duffy Mansfield," he says. "Are you Mr. Hyde?"

"No. I'm Troy Gaines, vice president for institutional development at the college."

"Oh, you work here?"

"I do. I'm an administrator, so I don't get to know the students as well as I once did. I used to be a business professor, but I moved on up. Like the Jeffersons."

"Thomas Jefferson?" Duffy asks.

"Never mind."

The young man and woman who were having the intense discussion earlier have already huddled under the protection of the portico. They try very hard not to touch each other, even though they're standing side by side. They're wide-eyed and scared as we join them under cover.

"Did you see that?" the guy asks. He wears a black blazer over a T-shirt emblazoned with the letters "BLM." His long hair is swept back behind his ears, and he appears to have doused himself with a healthy amount of cologne or body spray, which is strong enough to overwhelm even the scent of the hyacinths. "That almost hit you."

"Maybe we should all leave. I don't feel safe here," the woman next to him says. She's wearing a sundress and Birkenstocks. Her straight brown hair is piled on top of her head, and a spray of freckles decorates her nose and cheeks. "I mean, I didn't think any of this would be happening when I was invited here. Right?"

"Why don't we all introduce ourselves to one another?" I say. "You're the Hyde Fellows for this year. You were selected to participate and compete for the Hyde Scholarship, and you were all chosen partially for your outstanding academic ability."

"Partially?" the guy in the BLM shirt says. "What else is there?"

"There's financial need."

"And *who* picked us?" the woman in the sundress asks. "There are plenty of students on this campus who are smart and also have financial need."

"That's true," I say.

"Did you pick us, sir?"

"Oh, no. Not me. It's handled by the Hyde family and members of the Hyde Corporation board of directors."

"How do they do that?" the captain asks. "It seems like an invasion of privacy."

"Well, it's above my pay grade, but they work with the college president to make selections. What do you say, since we're going to be together all day, we learn one another's names if you don't know one another already? And we can ignore what's happening out there."

The protestors have grown somewhat quiet. The police stuff someone into the back of one of the cruisers. The siren lets out one *whoop* and then the cruiser drives off through an opening in the barricade. The protestors jeer more as their brick-throwing compatriot is taken away.

"I hope he learns a lesson from this," Captain Stephenson says. "That was a foolish act."

"I agree," Duffy says. "That brick hit my truck."

"Dude, it hit your tire," the guy in the BLM T-shirt says. "And it's free speech. They have the right to protest."

"I'm not sure throwing a brick is free speech," Captain Stephenson says.

"I mean, the protesting is free speech."

"Easy, guys," I say. "Remember? Introductions?"

Someone has stepped onto the portico behind me and stands very close to my back. I almost jump, thinking a brick is about to come down on my skull.

But a quiet voice asks, "Is this Hyde House? Is this the location of the scholarship process?"

I turn and a short woman in an oversized gold cardigan sweater stands there. Her eyes are so large they seem to occupy half of her face. And they're the deepest brown I've ever seen. Her curly dark hair reaches the tops of her shoulders.

"Yes, you're in the right place," I say. "All the fellows were just going to introduce themselves to one another. Would you like to start?"

The woman stares at the ground. Beneath the giant cardigan, she wears dark jeans rolled up over heavy-looking black lace-up oxford shoes. Her white shirt is buttoned to her neck, and her nails are painted a dark blue.

"Or someone else can start. Just name, major, that sort of thing. Captain?"

No shyness. Captain Stephenson's posture becomes even more erect than ever, and he clears his throat. "My name is Captain James Stephenson. I'm a history major, and I served twenty-five years in the United States Army as a Ranger. I guess you could say I'm a nontraditional student who took a circuitous path to being here. I also have a wife and two children, and I'm originally from Los Angeles."

"LA?" the tall, slim woman says. "That's so cool, James. Or do you prefer Jim?"

"I'd prefer to be called Captain."

"Right," I say. "Captain it is." I think the guy in the BLM T-shirt makes a low noise that might be mockery, but I plow ahead. "And you said your name is Duffy, right?"

"That's right." He touches the brim of his hat. "I'm Duffy Mansfield. I'm an ag major from Whitley County here in Kentucky. I grew up raising cattle." He points at the woman in the sundress. "Hey, I know you, Sydney. Remember? Business writing?"

"Oh, yeah." Sydney smiles for the first time. "That class. Aren't you roommates with Steve Roth? He used to date my roommate, Nikki."

"That's right," Duffy says, adjusting his hat.

"Okay, see?" I say. "We're all coming together here as one big Hyde family. Sydney, why don't you go next?"

"Oh, okay. Yeah, so I'm Sydney, obviously. Sydney Mosley. And I'm a marketing major from Plainfield, Illinois. I guess I'm kind of nervous about being here. You know, locked in a house all day. Right?"

"I hear you," Duffy says.

"Okay, cool. Well, I'm also on the volleyball team, so you might have seen me out there playing." She mimes spiking a ball, and when she does, a tattoo on the inside of her left forearm shows. One word in dark blue script: *Persistence.* On the inside of her right arm, another one in the same dark script: *LJM RIP.* "And yeah, that's it."

"Great. The Lady Lancers volleyball team had a good year." I point to her friend in the BLM T-shirt. "How about you?"

He cocks his head to the side and speaks in a low James Franco basso profundo voice. "Cool. Yeah, I'm Milo Reed. I'm an art major. From Louisville. And my politics are really important to me. So. Yeah."

"And?" Sydney says.

Milo's eyes cut toward her. "What?"

"And you're, like, the best student at the school, right?"

Milo tries to look embarrassed, but he clearly enjoys the praise. "Well, I don't know—"

"No, I heard that too," Duffy says. "Not only do you have a perfect GPA, but . . . what was it? The IQ test. Didn't you get a one sixty-three or something like that? My roommate told me."

"It's no big deal, man," Milo says.

"Oh, it is," I say.

"I agree," says the captain. "Although those exams contain an inherent bias in favor of the white and the privileged."

"Well, if I were privileged, I wouldn't be here taking this exam because I needed the money," Milo says, "would I?"

I quickly turn to the latest arrival, the woman in the cardigan sweater built for two. "And can you tell us your name?" I ask.

She still stares at her heavy shoes, but her voice—a combination of the ethereal and the formal—says, "I'm Natalia Gomez, and I'm studying biology. Cellular biology to be exact. I'm kind of from

Columbus, Ohio. I'm an honors student." She lifts her head and focuses on Milo. "You were in my sophomore honors seminar last year."

Am I imagining it, or do Milo's cheeks flush?

"Was I? Oh, yeah. That was a cool seminar. Tough prof, though. That final paper nearly did me in."

"Well, Dr. Wyland is a stickler for citations and research."

Now I know. Everyone can see it. Milo's face flushes. He says, "I didn't think Wyland communicated what she wanted clearly. She was vague and not very approachable."

"She was eminently clear about how to use sources," Natalia says, her small, acne-dotted chin thrust forward.

I'm not sure where the conversation is going, so before Milo or anyone can say anything else, I say, "Great. I'm glad we're not strangers anymore—"

"Excuse me, sir," Captain Stephenson says. "Aren't we supposed to have one more fellow?"

I take in the little group jammed under the portico roof. "You're right, Ja—Captain. There are supposed to be six fellows here. Plus, we're still waiting on Nicholas Hyde."

I check my watch. Eight forty.

"What's going on over there?" Milo points toward the protestors.

I turn and see another commotion at the barricade. A lot of gesturing and some booing.

And then one of the police officers moves a sawhorse aside, and a young woman comes walking through, head held high, and starts toward our spot on the Hyde House portico.

4

ONE OF THE POLICE officers walks with the woman. It's the campus police chief, Lonnie Rogers. He's built like a fireplug, and his head is shaved, which makes it resemble a bullet. He's closing in on sixty and has worked at Hyde for more than thirty years. Students and faculty alike call him Chief.

"He's arresting her," Milo says, shaking his head. "Chief gives no quarter. Guy's all over everybody."

"No, no," Duffy says, "he's *escorting* her."

"Chief will have a key to the house," Sydney says. "He can let us in. Right?"

"Good thinking," I say. "Chief has a key to everything."

"That's Emily Paine," Natalia says. "She's an English major. Creative writing, to be more precise. We both lived in Collins during our freshman and sophomore years."

"Oh," Duffy says. "Emily."

"What does that mean?" Sydney asks.

"Nothing. I just kind of know her."

"Then that's our last student," I say.

Emily Paine wears glasses so big they obscure most of her face. She's wearing a short-sleeved black dress and Doc Martens boots. Every exposed inch of her wiry, muscular arms is covered with tattoos, so many that I can't tell where one ends and the next begins. Or maybe they're all one giant image? The tattoo phenomenon among the students makes me feel older than my forty years.

"Vice President Gaines," Chief says, "this student is supposed to be here with you in Hyde House. She came walking up by those miscreants back there, so I decided to help her."

Chief stands with his thumbs hooked into his belt, like a marshal from a Western movie. Tough, capable, noble. "I'm sorry about that brick business. The perpetrator is being taken down to the city jail. We're going to move these protestors back to the main road about a hundred yards so there won't be any more trouble."

"Did they resist at all?" Captain Stephenson asks.

"No, sir," Chief says. "Just a kid who got carried away. Mob mentality does that to people. They make decisions they wouldn't otherwise make."

Captain Stephenson nods along to every word Chief speaks.

"What about freedom of speech, Chief?" Milo asks.

Chief studies him for a moment, eyes squinted. "Reed, right? *Milo* Reed?"

"That's me."

"It's been, what, about a year? I remember you. I saw your name on the list of fellows."

"The college dismissed your charges against me on appeal. I guess you can't just go into any party without permission and start hassling students."

"Hassling, huh? Is that what you call it?"

"Emily, why don't you . . . ?" I wave at her, and she steps up onto the portico with us. "Emily, we understand you're a creative writing major. Anything else we need to know about you?"

Her owlish glasses have slipped down her nose, and she knuckles them back up. "I guess someone was talking about me." She looks at Natalia, who stares at her feet again.

"Actually," I say, "I had a report on all of you from the college. Where are you from?"

Emily is slow to answer, but then she says, "Montgomery, Alabama."

"Very good. And now that Chief is here, he can let us in."

"Rock on, Chief," Duffy says.

But Chief is shaking his bullet head back and forth, still staring at Milo, his lips pressed into a thin line. "No can do, friends."

"But you have a key to everything," I say. "You probably have a key to my house and car."

Chief's mouth turns up on one side, his version of a smile. "I do have a key to Hyde House. Of course. In fact, I was here early this morning letting campus catering inside. Then I locked the house behind them."

"So then let us in, Chief," Sydney says. "I mean, like, you saw that giant brick come flying at us. Right?"

"They won't throw a brick when I'm standing here," he says, his voice a tough-guy rasp. "And the bad apple has been plucked. Besides, as you know, Vice President Gaines, the Hyde Scholarship bylaws prohibit anyone from going inside the house until the arrival of the presiding member of the Hyde family. This isn't my first rodeo and can't any of us go against what the Hyde family wants. Especially today." Chief checks his watch and sighs. "So . . . we wait."

I turn to the students. "Hold on one second. I need to ask the chief something."

Chief nods his head, and I step off the portico and walk about twenty feet into the yard with him. His leather gun belt creaks as we move, and I feel exposed and think again about flying bricks and Molotov cocktails. But the chief's broad, stern presence eases my mind.

We stop, and I say, "Chief, you've been here a long time. You know everybody. What are you hearing about Nicholas Hyde?"

Chief nods sagely, his blue eyes cool and opaque. Like most police officers, he's slow to reveal information. "I know he's the sole heir now. His father, Theodore, died last year, of course. Ted was a stand-up guy."

"Indeed. The last four years when I've overseen the process, Ted was here representing the Hyde family. Now it's going to be Nicholas."

"And he was close to his mother, and he lost her this past year too. A damn shame for him. We only get one mom. I never met Olivia Hyde. Did you?"

"A couple of times, but she didn't have much to do with the college since she was divorced from Ted."

Chief nods again. "I guess I hear what you hear about Nicholas. He's young, about thirty. Rich, of course. Not married. No significant other. Kind of . . . What's the word I'm looking for?"

"'Immature'?"

"'Entitled.' Like some of our students."

"You mean Milo? Is he a troublemaker?"

"We busted him at a party. Underage possession last year. Disturbing the peace. It went to the college disciplinary board, and he won on appeal. Said we didn't have permission to go into the apartment."

"Oh."

"We used to run a tighter ship around here. Now the inmates are in charge."

"So back to Nicholas Hyde . . ."

Chief's voice is lower than before, even though there's no way anyone can hear us. "You've seen his social media feed, right? Twitter?"

"I have."

"I try to keep an open mind about people," Chief says. "My policy is to get along with everyone, regardless of their political views. I'm sure Theodore Hyde wasn't the most enlightened guy in the world, but he kept those views to himself. I guess I'm old-school, but young Mr. Hyde has spilled a lot of crazy conspiracy theories all over his feed this past year. It's—how should I say this?—different."

"He's young, like you said. He has time to grow out of it. That's how I view the students."

Chief doesn't seem convinced. "I wouldn't be surprised if there were some substance-abuse issues there, Troy. Drinking. Drugs. Whatnot. That's what my sources tell me about Nicholas Hyde."

"Really?"

His sources? I imagine Chief meeting shadowy figures in dark parking garages to learn about campus intrigue. Signaling with flowerpots and chalk marks on mailboxes.

Chief nods once again. "You've no doubt seen what's been in the papers, right? About the Hyde Corporation?"

"You mean that it's hemorrhaging money?"

"Sure. Look at these protestors. The fossil fuel industry is yesterday's news. I used to own stock in GM, but I sold it. You were a business professor. You must have seen the writing on the wall."

"Yeah, sure. But the Hyde family has moved away from fossil fuels. They've branched out into a little of everything over the years. Retail, green energy, some manufacturing."

"Some would call that being overextended. Or overleveraged."

The protestors seem to have lost some steam. A few continue to chant. Others talk or look at their phones. One stands off to the side, exhaling a plume of smoke from a vaping pen. The two police officers manning the barricade appear relaxed, almost bored.

"You know, it won't be good at all for the college if the Hyde family money disappears," Chief says. "They're about all that's keeping this place propped up. And if it's in the hands of someone . . . let's say . . . unreliable . . ."

"You're right about that. I'm not crazy about the whole house of cards being built on the efforts of one partying thirtysomething. I wish I had a better read on him."

Chief's voice is even lower now. I lean closer to hear what he says and catch the scent of coffee and cigars.

"Keep this under your hat, but I'm thinking of retiring soon. Like I said, it's not like the old days, when we all received a little more respect. You know, the college is talking about trimming pension benefits. I've been here too long to take a hit on that. Those catering folks I let in today, some of their colleagues have been laid off. Groundskeepers, maintenance crews. A lot of people aren't happy about the way things are going."

"The administration is doing everything it can to keep the school operating." I hear the defensiveness in my voice. And I know Chief does too.

"I mean no offense. And I know you're one of the good ones, trying to look out for the employees and the students. But President Chan . . . she's sharpening up that budget scalpel. Everybody's going to get a haircut. And it seems to disproportionately affect the folks who do the dirty work around campus. The landscapers, the cleaners, the cooks, the cops."

"It's not that, Chief—"

"Hey, my two boys are finished with college, the house is paid off, so my work is done."

I get a jealous twinge in my chest. My house is nowhere near being paid off. My daughters—all three of them—haven't even started college. And I can't conceive of a way to pay for them all to go unless I win the lottery. The discount I'd get as a Hyde employee is only fifty percent. Fifty percent of private college tuition times three is still a lot.

"Sounds like you have it all figured out, Chief."

"I see bad things rising around here. I'm trying to play a stronger hand."

"Do you know anything else about . . . ?"

My voice trails off. Chief is staring past me in the direction of Hyde Lane. He lifts his chin, and I turn that way.

A jet-black BMW pulls up to the barricade, music thumping from behind its tinted windows.

"Looks like our guest of honor has graced us with his presence," Chief says.

5

THE BARRICADE PARTS, AND the black car rolls through and heads our way.

As it pulls into the small parking lot, I leave Chief behind and make a beeline that way, where the music continues to thump, and the door of the BMW stays closed.

The students remain on the portico, and six sets of eyes follow me as I approach the car. When I get there, I wait.

The door is still closed. After a few moments, the music stops—mercifully—but the door stays shut. Chief has taken up a position near the students, thumbs hooked in his belt Old West–style again. His posture says, *Don't look at me for help on this one. I can handle brick throwing, but not wealthy donors.*

Finally, the door opens a crack. Then Nicholas Hyde places an expensive brown leather boot against the door and kicks out, and the door swings all the way open. He glances up at me, an astronaut just splashed down to earth. His face is pale, his thick dark hair in disarray. He squints.

"Man, it's bright," he says.

"It's good to see you again, Nicholas."

Nicholas places his hands on either side of the doorframe and, after a moment's pause, pushes himself out of the car. He wears a blue suit and a pink shirt, the collar open with everything wrinkled as though he drove a long way or slept in the clothes. He's an inch taller than I am, and since the last time I saw him a year earlier, he has developed a sizable paunch that spills over his belt. Stubble dots his face, and I want to believe it's a fashion statement and not slovenliness. But I can't tell.

He holds out his hand, and we shake. His skin is clammy, like a dead fish.

"Nice to meet you," he says, his voice full of a wealthy man's hail-fellow-well-met jauntiness. "And you are . . . ?"

"Troy Gaines," I say, assuming my name will trigger a look of recognition. Which it doesn't. "Vice president for institutional development for the college. We toured campus together in the fall, and you might remember we discussed the One Hundred More Initiative."

Nicholas studies my face for a moment, then nods. "Right, Gaines. Yes. You sent me an e-mail or something."

"I did. I sent you quite a few."

"Right. You and the president . . . What's his name again?"

"Her. Grace Chan."

"Yeah, she wrote to me a lot too."

The wind has shifted slightly, blowing from behind Nicholas. I catch a whiff of recently smoked cigarettes, and alcohol appears to be oozing out of his pores. He's looking over my shoulder, so I turn.

"Ah," he says, "Hyde House."

From where we stand, the house shows only its glory. We're too far to see the fading bricks, the chipped paint. The tarnished knobs and ancient wiring.

"It's quite a legacy your family has created here," I say. "I was hoping to speak to you about some—"

Nicholas Hyde brushes past me and goes to the rear of the BMW. He opens the trunk with the key fob, which makes a high-pitched beep, and reaches inside, bringing out a sleek leather briefcase. He also removes a phone from his pocket.

"We spoke in the past about the One Hundred More Initiative," I say, "and I thought if you're free for dinner—"

He's tapping at his phone. "Okay, yeah . . . I think this is all okay now. . . ."

"—if you're free—"

Nicholas's face contorts with concentration. He lets out a deep breath. "Yeah . . . okay . . . I think this is ready to go."

"Did you need help with something?"

He tosses the phone into the trunk and slams the lid. "Not anymore."

"Did you hear what I said about dinner? If you're—"

This time I'm interrupted by shouting from behind the barricade. The protestors have apparently figured out who Nicholas is, and they have resumed their chanting—and it's even louder than it was before when it reached its crescendo with the thrown brick.

Chief gestures to his fellow officers, but I don't know what anyone can do about the noise. I agree with Milo—the students do have the right to protest and say whatever they want. Even if they're making it that much more difficult for me to do my job and schmooze with the college's most important donor.

Nicholas is past me, walking toward the house and the students, so I hustle to catch up. "I'm sorry about the protestors over there. It's a small number of students and doesn't reflect the way the college community feels about your family and their contributions to the campus."

Nicholas nods toward the barricades. "What's that?" he asks.

"The students. The protestors. Actually, I doubt they're all students. They think . . . Well, never mind."

"Is that about the coal stuff? Or the Civil War stuff?" he asks.

I pause a moment before I answer. But I can't bring myself to lie.

"Both," I say.

Nicholas watches the protestors for a moment. They press against the barricade, shaking their fists in his direction.

I'm able to make out a few words.

Bastard . . . Killer . . . Asshole.

Nicholas says, "I hope it makes the little freaks feel better."

6

MOVING TOWARD THE HOUSE calms me.

Everyone is present, and once we go inside, the noise and the thrown objects will be in the past, and we can turn our full attention to the process we've all come here for.

We're almost to the house when something else comes flying through the air. It doesn't come close to us but shatters against the front walk. A Bud Light bottle. Student beer.

The police start pointing fingers into the crowd, trying to identify the culprit. I quicken my pace for the portico.

But Nicholas Hyde seems not to have noticed the bottle breaking twenty feet away from us. He walks steadily, briefcase swinging in the morning light, looking very much like a man without a care in the world.

As we reach the portico, Chief stands with his body facing the protestors, staring them down. I wouldn't be surprised to see lasers shoot out of his steely eyes and zap the party guilty of throwing the bottle.

"Chief?" I want his attention. I want his *key*. "Chief?"

He turns back to me reluctantly. He lifts his eyebrows.

"The door," I say. "Can you unlock the door for us so we can get inside?"

But Chief doesn't move. His eyes track to my right and land on Nicholas Hyde, who has stepped up onto the portico alongside the students, who all scoot back a little, out of his way. He doesn't say anything or introduce himself, but there's something about the man that gives off an air of confidence and authority.

It's strange, given that he looks like an unmade bed.

But then I understand exactly what gives him that authority.

Money.

I step up next to Nicholas and point to the door. "What do you say we head inside? Chief Roberts has a key."

Nicholas nods at Chief. "Hey, man, what's up?"

"Sir," Chief says, his lips pressed into a thin line.

"Nicholas," I say, "inside?"

But Nicholas shakes his head. He spins the combination dial on the lock and then fumbles with the clasps on his briefcase with his clammy pale hands, and when he gets it open, he reaches inside and quickly brings out a thick well-worn leather book tied with a black ribbon. Nicholas places the briefcase on the portico floor, rests it between his legs, licks his index finger, and slowly unties the ribbon.

Things appear to be heating up even more with the protestors. They wave their signs high in the air.

They're saying two words in unison now. Over and over again.

Kill-er Hydes! Kill-er Hydes! Kill-er Hydes!

I look at Chief, who rolls his eyes. What can he or anyone else do about it?

He could move them back, like he promised. But Chief is with us, and the other officers don't go to the bathroom without Chief's permission.

I just want to get inside *as soon as possible.*

Nicholas opens the book like he's presenting holy writ to the masses. The students watch, eyes wide and curious. He reaches into the inside pocket of his jacket and pulls out a sleek black pen.

"This book of bylaws has been in my family since Major Ezekiel Ellis Hyde founded the college. Everything about the Hyde Scholarship process is written down in here, codified in the handwriting of the presiding officers." He lifts the book higher. "This is the only copy that exists. The *only one.* There's no backup. No duplicate. It has never even been photographed, even though I once suggested to my father that it should be. He wasn't a fan of my suggestion."

Nicholas's face colors, and he looks wounded.

"It's not on the cloud?" Duffy asks, breaking the awkward moment.

Everybody laughs, even Nicholas. "Nope," he says. "You may not know this, but every year the presiding member of the Hyde family signs their name at the front of this book. And this year, it's my turn to add my name. For the first time."

He turns the book around and holds it up like we're a class of kindergartners. Signatures scroll down the page, almost like hieroglyphics. I spot his father's name at the bottom.

"I want to make sure I do *everything* right." His tone shifts, becoming arch. His right eyebrow goes up. "My *father* cared very much about doing these things right, and I don't want to let *him* down. So here we go."

He uncaps the pen, turns the book back toward himself, and writes. The pen makes a light scratching noise against the paper.

Come on, come on. Couldn't we do this inside?

When he's finished writing, Nicholas clears his throat. "You know, I think I need to learn your names."

"We did that already," I say.

"But I wasn't here."

"Can we do that inside?" I ask.

Nicholas purses his lips like he's making a big decision. "I guess so."

"Great. Chief? The key?"

"First, a word from our sponsors," Nicholas says, before beginning to read from the book. "'The Hyde family bylaws, amended in 2006 and approved by a simple majority of members of the board of the Hyde family trust and forwarded to the Hyde College board of trustees for their consideration, state that all students, faculty members, staff, and members of the Hyde family who attend the process that leads to the . . .'" Nicholas squints and blinks his eyes a couple of times. His body wavers, like he might fall, but then he steadies himself and goes on. "'. . . to the awarding of the Hyde Memorial Scholarship on the third Saturday in April, that in addition to surrendering all personal items such as purses and backpacks, they absolutely must surrender all personal electronic devices, including but not limited to cellular phones, computers, BlackBerrys, pagers, beepers, or anything else the presiding member of the Hyde family decides could allow a student to reference or engage with online resources. Said electronic devices are to be surrendered to the chief of the campus police force or, in that individual's absence, the highest-ranking police or security official present for the process.'"

When Nicholas is finished, he seems satisfied. I'm not sure if it's the message he's delivered or his ability to read it all while in the grip of what appears to be the mother of all hangovers.

And I know he's right. Every year I've been here presiding over the process, the students—and I—have handed over our phones, computers, and Apple Watches to Chief. In fact, we encourage the students to leave most, if not all, personal items like backpacks and purses at home, and they do for the most part. But it's tough to ask a college student to go anywhere without a phone.

I want to hang on to mine. I want to finally put through that call to Rachel and talk about our skirmish this morning, but there's clearly no time. Especially since protestors are hurling projectiles at us.

From somewhere on his body, Chief produces a black canvas bag with a zippered lock on the top. He opens it and steps forward, nodding at the bag, and the students dutifully but regretfully hand over their phones.

All except Milo, who stands with his phone in his hand and a defiant look on his face. "Is this legal?" he asks. "I mean, what if I need my phone for some kind of an emergency?"

I'm about to speak, but Chief says, "Do you see this as a violation of your rights?"

Milo shifts his weight forward. "I know what you all do while we're taking the exam."

"Process," Nicholas says. "It's a two-part *process*. Written exam and personal interview."

"Whatever you want to call it," Milo says. "I know the cops and everyone else stay back and out of the way. A guy I met once said he participated in the process. He lost because he's a terrible writer, but he said the cops are nowhere near the building. If there'd been any trouble—"

"We keep a weather eye on Hyde House," Chief says. "No one is ever in any danger. I thought you students liked it when the police stayed out of your business. And didn't, you know, *hassle* you. Besides, you can't believe every rumor that goes around campus about the scholarship. We ask the students who participate to keep as much of the process to themselves as they can."

"And the bylaws are the bylaws," Nicholas says. "We must adhere to them."

"I get it," Captain Stephenson says. "Rules are rules."

Everyone is watching Milo now, and I wonder if this is what he wanted all along. He's the star of *this* moment of the process, getting a little bit of the spotlight even before we've gone into the building.

Milo smiles a little, his eyes twinkling in the morning light.

"Okay," Milo says. "*Rules.* It's bogus, but I'll go along." He reaches out and drops his phone into Chief's bag with a clunk. "I'll go along because I need the fucking money. Hard."

"Okay, great," I say.

And Chief says, "All clear on devices."

He nods at me, and I know what I'm supposed to do.

I step closer to the students and ask each of them to hold their hands out. I'm required to check all of their wrists, making sure that no one is wearing a smart watch. It feels . . . strange . . . to be examining everybody's arms.

Chief nods, satisfied.

"Okay," I say, "can we go in now?"

Nicholas reties the ribbon around his leather book. His nails are long, and a few have dirt under them, like he was digging in a garden or changing the oil on his Bimmer. He picks up the briefcase and slides the book back inside and then turns the clasp with a crisp metallic snap. He spins the combination dial, locking the briefcase.

For a moment, Nicholas looks like he might turn around with his briefcase and bylaws, jump in his car, and leave us all alone.

But then Nicholas nods.

"Okay, Chief," he says. "Let's do it."

7

WE FILE INSIDE HYDE House, entering the large foyer.

The group bottlenecks here, all eyes trailing around and taking in the scenery.

Most if not all of the students have never been inside Hyde House. It is used only for special events—guest lectures, meetings of the board of trustees, a home for visiting artists and writers—so students wouldn't find themselves here unless they were invited.

Just as I felt a thrill when I first saw the house earlier this morning, I get the same tingle seeing the inside of the house through their eyes. As much as possible, the college has gone to great lengths to preserve everything the way it looked when Ezekiel Hyde and his family resided here in the 1870s. Much of the furniture and decor is original, and where the original wasn't available, the college studied old photos to reproduce it.

A marble-topped wooden table stands in the middle of the entryway with a fresh bouquet of flowers—goldenrod, the official flower of Kentucky—on top in a decorative porcelain vase, which helps compensate for the slightly musty odor of the house. I know the roof leaked earlier in the spring when the area was hit with heavy rains. I also know goldenrod blooms naturally in the late summer, so these were grown in a campus greenhouse.

The wallpaper is a reproduction, I've learned, but replicates a popular floral pattern known as Dresser from the 1880s. A wooden staircase leads to the second floor, the ornate newel post and bannister polished to a bright finish. Above us, high up at the top of the foyer two stories in the air, light slants in through a circular window. When the home was built, it was a stained glass window designed by Major Hyde himself. It was a replica of the seal of the great Commonwealth of Kentucky, Ezekiel's beloved home state, which shows a buckskin-clad frontiersman clasping hands with a suit-wearing statesman. The two men represent the frontier spirit of the commonwealth meeting the spirit of government and law.

The state motto was highlighted as well: *United We Stand, Divided We Fall.*

But the stained glass window was smashed in 1969 when a group of students protesting the Vietnam War occupied Hyde House. The higher-ups at the college deemed the window too expensive to replace and went with something that lets in more light.

The students soak in their surroundings, while I sidle up to Nicholas. "It must be a thrill every time you come in here," I say.

He's staring at the shaft of light from above. "I've never actually been in this house."

"You haven't? Oh, I'm sorry. When you were here in the fall, I could have—"

"My mom had just died when I was here. It was a short visit."

"Right. That must have been a tough time."

"My dad did most of the business with the college. My parents split up when I was five, and I was with Mom a lot. We lived in Lexington, near her family. Dad was . . . well, he was busy with the company. That was his focus."

"Oh, I didn't know—I mean, I knew your dad pretty well. But I didn't know much about his personal life."

"He was dedicated to work," Nicholas says. "The company. And the college."

"Yes, he was."

"And he found a new girlfriend after the divorce. A series of them, in fact."

I'm not sure what else I can say. My mind changes gears ever so slightly, and I see Nicholas Hyde in a slightly different light. No longer is he simply the rich playboy who shows up late and smelling of booze on the day of his most important duty to the college and his family's legacy. Now he is a child who didn't get to spend as much time with his father as he wanted.

And here he is doing his level best to live up to the spirit of a man who is dead. In a way, he's trying to live up to the spirit of generations of Hydes who are long gone—from his father all the way back to Major Ezekiel Hyde himself.

"Well," Nicholas says, "I guess we're supposed to have tea now. In the parlor."

"Right."

Cooler air brushes against my back. Chief remains in the doorway, the canvas bag of electronic devices in his hand.

"Chief, we're going into the parlor for tea. Would you like to join us?"

But Chief is shaking his bullet head. "Now, you know I can't do that, Vice President Gaines. It's time for me to lock this place up so you all can get to work. If you don't need anything else from me."

"No, Chief, we don't. And you're right. I know you have to lock up."

Chief shifts his bag from one hand to the other and looks at his watch. "You all are starting a little late, but that's okay. There's some extra time built in at lunch." He lifts his eyes to mine. "I know for a fact every door and window is locked. Upstairs and down. I inspected this morning when I let the caterers in. And once I lock this one from the outside—" He points to the inside of the door, where there's another tarnished knob, a twin to the one on the exterior of the house. "See, there's no way to unlock it from in here." He nods toward Nicholas. "Per the Hyde family bylaws."

"Right. Of course." I laugh, but I sound nervous. There's something ominous about being locked *inside* a house. "I guess I should remember all of this from previous years."

Chief lowers his voice, leans close so I can smell the cigar again. "Well, you had a firmer hand guiding you in the past."

I know he means Theodore. But now I think of Theodore in terms of being an absent father, and his memory becomes more complicated.

"We're ready to get to work, Chief," I say. "And be careful out there. Those protestors aren't pulling any punches."

"They'll settle down now that you all are inside." He winks. "And we're going to move them back down Hyde Lane to the main road. I've dealt with a miscreant or two in my time here. Like the ones you have inside. I know how to take care of them, but that's one part of the job I won't miss."

Chief steps back, hand on the exterior knob, and pulls the door shut with a whoosh. I hear a key enter the lock with a metallic rustling, and then the turning of the cylinder and the bolt slamming into place.

And with that, we're locked inside Hyde House.

It's time for the process to begin.

8

BY THE TIME I turn around, Nicholas Hyde has taken control.

"It looks like the parlor is over here," he says.

He is guiding the students through an open entryway on the left and into the room where we will be having tea. I follow along and am the last one to come into the room, which is small and comfortable. A silver tea service is set up on a parlor table on the right, and the students, who rarely drink tea and never out of porcelain cups decorated with hand-painted roses, stand around awkwardly, uncertain of where to begin.

I'm about to show the way, but Nicholas steps forward again, reaching for his briefcase.

"Let's get those names first," he says, pointing at the students.

Milo goes first, and they go around the semicircle repeating their names and their majors. Sydney is the last, and when she's finished, Nicholas says, "You're so tall and lithe. Do you play a sport here?"

Lithe?

"Volleyball," she says.

"No doubt. You have that look. What position?"

"Outside hitter."

"Deadly," he says. "You look like you could get up high and punish the ball. And your opponents."

"Well, I try to. . . ." Sydney's face flushes.

Duffy sighs.

"Did you all have a good season?" Nicholas asks. "I have to be honest: I don't follow women's sports. But maybe I should."

"We were runner-up in the conference."

"Excellent. I bet you're doing your off-season conditioning—"

Duffy sighs again. Louder.

"Maybe we should get to the tea," I say. "So we stay on track."

Nicholas looks over at me like he's forgotten I was here. "Okay. Rules are rules, as somebody said earlier." Nicholas undoes the lock and clasp on the briefcase. "Just trying to get to know the students."

"*One* of the students," Emily says.

"We're supposed to have a wee dram of bourbon at lunch," Nicholas says, "but I was thinking . . . well, life is short, so maybe there's no time like the present. Would anyone care for a quick shot?"

The students look more awkward, and their eyes trail to me, seeking guidance.

Do I think it's a good idea for college students to drink before an important exam?

"Well, Nicholas," I say, "I mean . . . maybe we should stick to the plan and drink later. We want the students sharp now. Right?"

Nicholas freezes, his hands on the clasp of the case. For a moment, it looks as though he's going to go ahead, ignoring my plea for sobriety. And if he does, what can I do? He holds all the cards.

Nicholas exhales a breath and straightens. "Okay. Sure. I wouldn't want to violate Great-Grandfather's wishes. He clearly liked to follow the rules."

Nicholas moves over to the tea service, where he pours himself a cup. As he pours, his back to the room, he explains to the students why we're all doing what we're doing.

"Speaking of my great-great-great-great-grandfather Major Ezekiel Hyde, the man who built this house and founded the college . . . he started every morning with a cup of black tea. He believed it was essential for his health and gave him a burst of energy early in the day. Caffeine, you know. I'm sure you all can relate to that."

They laugh, and some of the tension we feel eases.

Nicholas turns with a teacup in his hand. "My mother drank Earl Grey every morning. Milk and two sugars." Clearing his throat, he looks to his right, past Milo, who is standing closest to him. "Sydney, why don't you pour tea for everyone? That will make everyone's day."

Sydney hesitates a moment, then shrugs. "Okay, yeah, sure. I warn you—I can be kind of klutzy when I'm not on the volleyball court. My grandma won't let me touch her nice dishes. I broke her gravy boat one Thanksgiving, and, like, she didn't talk to me for a month. Plus, I'm kind of nervous about being locked in here. It's . . . weird. Right?"

"Don't you think we can just each pour our own?" Emily says. She stands with her hands on her hips, her black dress sleek in the faint light. "I mean, why does Sydney have to do it? Why not Milo?

Or *Duffy*?" She places an unusual emphasis on that name, and Duffy gives her an unsettled look. "Or you?"

Nicholas laughs at Emily's comment. "Sure. Why not? Everybody pour their own." He winks at Sydney. "Maybe a beautiful girl like her shouldn't bother with that kind of work, right?"

Sydney blushes, and Emily rolls her eyes.

"I might vomit," Emily says.

"Easy, dude," Duffy says, his cheeks flushed a deeper red than Sydney's. "Let's be respectful."

Nicholas shrugs. "This isn't bourbon, but it will do the trick, I guess. It really doesn't matter what we drink now. . . ."

The students shuffle forward and pour. While they do that, Nicholas's eyes trail around the room, taking in the decor.

"This is quite a place," he says to no one in particular. And to everyone. His eyes are half closed now, almost like he's about to fall asleep standing up. "Can you just imagine what it was like to live here one hundred fifty years ago? How quiet it would have been. How peaceful. Just the sound of the trees and the wind."

No one speaks, so I provide an answer. "It's magnificent, isn't it?"

Nicholas nods. "A little worse for wear, if you look closely. Probably needs a roof, wiring. HVAC."

"Well, we try to keep the house in good repair," I say. "But it is expensive."

"The past isn't what it used to be. Probably full of termites and rodents."

"I'm not sure," I say.

"Maybe I'm the pest," he says, "or the big bad wolf."

As each student gets a cup of tea, they move away from the service and stand in a semicircle around Nicholas. Their eyes trail up and around the room, taking in the sights—the camelback sofa, the parlor chairs, the ornate mantel. And over the fireplace, a giant portrait of Major Hyde in his Union blues, sword at his hip, his hand resting on a book-littered desk, dark eyes staring back with greater intensity than I thought a painting could summon. And next to the portrait, Major Hyde's actual sword in its scabbard, the one he wore during the Civil War. It gets polished regularly by the cleaning crew and gleams brightly in the morning light.

A large glass-fronted bookcase sits on the left side of the room, and I know it displays books that belonged to Major Hyde, including several volumes of his own writings detailing his time in the military and the origins of the Hyde Corporation. While I've never read any of them, I now know he skipped over some key details, like the massacre of prisoners at Palmyra.

I also notice the gas sconces. Over the years the other gas sconces in the house have been converted to electric and are simply decorative. But the ones in the parlor still run on natural gas, and they cast a warm yellow glow over the room.

I'm the last to go up and get a cup of tea, and now everyone is holding one. I let the steam waft past my face as I add two lumps of sugar and brush the residue off the tips of my fingers.

"Well, this is great," I say.

"Before we drink, I want to explain about the food." Nicholas still wears a remnant of the dreamy look on his face. "There are croissants there," he says, pointing to another table. "Does anybody know what those other items are?"

"They look like cucumber," Emily, our English major, says. She has one hand on her hip, and one of her tattoos is Virginia Woolf's face. "I took a seminar on Victorian literature. Everybody was always eating cucumber sandwiches with some chopped mint. They pair it with tea. And those are biscuits."

"Those aren't like any biscuits I've ever seen," Duffy says.

And everybody laughs.

"When they say 'biscuit,' they mean cookie," Sydney says. "Right? We talked about this in my British history class. I think that was the one . . . or maybe it was sociology."

"These aren't the kind of biscuits you put gravy on, Duffy," Captain Stephenson says, and everyone laughs again.

"I've never had tea before," Duffy says. "I usually throw back a Coke in the morning. But if I'm going to drink this tea, I might as well have one of these cook—biscuits. And hell . . . is it really a cucumber sandwich?"

"It is," Emily says, trying her best to disguise her disapproval of the philistine in our midst.

"You only live once," Duffy says, stepping forward and taking a cookie and a sandwich in his rough-looking hand. "We used to grow cukes, but I never liked the taste that much. Unless they were pickled."

The others follow Duffy's lead, and the eating, drinking, and conversing begin, even though one or two students make faces when they bite into the food or swallow the tea. At least they're broadening their horizons. Exactly as Major Hyde intended. I've glanced at the bylaws for the process—the ones Nicholas carries in his briefcase—once or twice, but only briefly, since they stay in the possession of the Hyde family. But I do know Major Hyde scheduled tea at the beginning of the process so the students who were participating would get to know one another and relax just a bit before the written exam began. Major Hyde was a big believer in fellowship and community—perhaps as an outgrowth of his military service and love of education—and the tea portion of the morning provides our little group with an opportunity to experience both.

Sydney and Duffy begin to talk. Milo moves closer to Nicholas, who holds his teacup halfway to his mouth. He desperately wants to drink from it and enjoy the restorative effects of the caffeine, but Milo is asking him questions and preventing him. Emily wanders across the room, pressing her owlish glasses against the front of the bookcase, squinting as she tries to read the titles on the volumes inside. Natalia stands by herself, lifting a teacup to her mouth and shifting her weight from one foot to the other. I want to go talk to her, to make sure she's not the only person in the room being left out of the conversation, but Captain Stephenson appears in front of me. And I remember he wanted to talk to me about something outside, although, for the life of me, I can't imagine what I can do for him.

"Sir," he says, "would you have a moment now that teatime is underway?"

"Sure, Captain."

But I look past him to Natalia. I want to find a way to encourage her to talk to somebody else. Maybe Emily, who is continuing to stare inside the bookcase?

Natalia's brown eyes are boring in on Milo and Nicholas, and I remember her veiled comments outside about the honors seminar and research. Was she just fumbling to make conversation with a fellow student who is obviously more confident and popular than she is? Or was she implying something?

Milo remains close to Nicholas, explaining something to him in great detail and gesturing with both of his hands, which are empty. Nicholas places his cup down and begins to mimic Milo's hand gestures. Is Milo teaching Nicholas some new dance?

It seems like they might have known each other already. Or they're developing the world's fastest friendship.

Then I hear what Milo is saying. "This is what they call a crimp grip, with your hand like this. Dude, you're seriously going to spend two weeks doing nothing but climbing in Mexico and Central America?"

"That's the plan," Nicholas says. "I know a guy with a guide—"

"Sir?"

I turn my attention back to the captain. "Okay, right. Why don't we step out into the foyer?"

We leave as Milo is demonstrating something called a pocket grip to Nicholas, and Natalia eases my mind a little by making a move toward the two of them. She says something I can't hear, and the captain looks in her direction but keeps walking out of the room.

A tinge of regret passes through me. As an administrator, I don't get to know the students anymore, and I miss having the kind of conversation Milo and Nicholas and Natalia are having. I've learned about a lot of things from my students over the years—music, movies, social media. That part of my life evaporated with my promotion.

The captain and I stand close to the front door. He holds his teacup, which shrinks like a child's toy in his massive hand. I hold mine as well, and since I left the house in a rush—and spent most of the morning talking with Rachel—I missed my coffee. So the small shot of caffeine from the tea gives me a pleasurable rush. Major Hyde was right about that.

"What's on your mind, Captain?"

"It's this, sir, and I'm only speaking to you now because I have a lot of respect for your high position in the college. I have a lot of respect for achievement and authority."

"I appreciate that, but my authority here is limited."

"It's this, sir—the political winds in our country have shifted. I feel as though a guy like me—a little older, a military veteran, a family man—doesn't quite fit in around here. And then that demonstration outside, the disrespect for Major Hyde's military service in a war that saved our country—well, it just confirmed what I already feared. The deck may be stacked against me here."

"I'm trying to understand, Captain. Maybe I'm slow. Are you saying you think you can't win the scholarship because . . . because of something about who you are?"

"That's right. There aren't a whole bunch of students who look like me. In so many ways."

"We're always trying to recruit more nontraditional students. And military veterans. And students of color."

I'm surprised by what the captain is telling me. He seems overeager, like most nontraditional students. I can picture him sitting in the front row of every class he attends, raising his hand to answer every question. But faculty love having those students in their classes—it's such a pleasant change from undergraduates who can't be bothered to buy a textbook, let alone bring one to class or read it.

"I know the college is trying to do its best," he says.

"I'm sorry you feel uncomfortable, Captain."

"Thank you. I know some things are stacked against me. I've paid the Black tax before."

"What happened outside is unfortunate, but in no way does it reflect the way the college or our students as a whole feel about military veterans. As a matter of fact, my grandfather went to Penn State on the GI Bill."

"Was he an army man?"

"Yes. Europe. World War Two. He fought in the Battle of the Bulge as a tank commander."

"God bless him, sir."

"Thank you. He's been dead for fifteen years."

"May he rest in peace. Look, sir, I hope it doesn't seem like I'm grade grubbing or working the refs here."

It does. But I continue to listen.

"People assume because I'm a veteran that my tuition is completely paid for by Uncle Sam, and that's just not true."

"I know that. It wouldn't be enough to pay the tuition at a private school like Hyde."

The captain snaps his fingers. "Exactly. And, see, I can't leave this area to attend a public university due to certain family obligations, so I have to attend Hyde. It's the only four-year college within eighty miles of here. Therefore I do have financial need."

"No one's questioning that."

"I know you're involved with the selection process here. And making the final decision about who gets the scholarship—"

Now I hold up my hand. I want no misunderstanding.

"I'm sorry, Captain, but I have to stop you there. The Hyde family selects the Hyde fellows based on academic ability and need. That's the six of you who are here today. And it's Nicholas Hyde in there who will select the winner of the scholarship after today's events. I'm just here as a liaison for the college. And to try my best to make the trains run on time. If I can."

"So you're saying you think I have as good a chance as anybody? I wasn't born with a silver spoon in my mouth like these kids."

"None of them were. We're never exactly sure how the Hyde family selects the fellows to participate, but we do know that every student who comes in here on the third Saturday in April has significant financial need. And student loans. That's the only real criterion I can suss out."

Captain Stephenson lowers his voice. "And that joker in there is going to wield all that power and make such a big decision?"

"That's a little harsh," I say.

"Okay, you're right, sir. I shouldn't jump to conclusions about others if I don't want others to do that to me. I learned that in Sunday school. But I saw the look on your face when he was late. And when he rolled up in that Bimmer and barely acknowledged you. Very disrespectful, sir, if you don't mind my saying so. You might be too polite to say it, but I will."

"Nobody's perfect, Captain. And I'm going to give Nicholas a chance."

"You're right, of course. But I've been reading up on the Hyde Corporation. Some of their subsidiaries have outsourced a lot of jobs. Do you want to be involved with a company like that? I'm all for free enterprise, but that practice rips the heart right out of our communities."

A faint sound reaches us from the parlor. A clinking. Over and over.

"What's that?" Captain Stephenson asks.

"You're married, aren't you?"

"Yes."

"Do you remember your wedding reception? I think somebody is about to make a speech. And I think it's your friend Nicholas Hyde."

9

WE STEP BACK INTO the parlor, where the students are moving closer to Nicholas, who still stands by the tea service.

Milo is by Nicholas's side, and for all I know, the two of them will be departing on a climbing trip together as soon as the process is complete.

I'm relieved that Natalia has now joined Emily at the bookcase. They are both pointing inside the case and having a spirited conversation about something. They walk over to Nicholas side by side and even appear reluctant to stop talking. Emily is shaking her head, and Natalia glances at Milo like he's something stuck to the bottom of her shoe.

It's some sort of victory for Major Hyde's process, even if they've bonded over disdain for the Hyde family. I expect to see his portrait smile, but it maintains its stoic reserve.

Nicholas is holding his leather book again, his teacup set aside. I let the students go close, and I stand back, happy to see the Hyde heir taking the reins and apparently enjoying himself. The tea appears to have perked him up and taken the edge off his hangover.

He clears his throat.

"Good morning, Hyde Fellows, and welcome to your day. It is my great honor to welcome you to Hyde House for the . . ."

Nicholas pauses, brow furrowed. For a moment, I become indispensable.

"One hundred fifty-second," I say, knowing the exact piece of information he is scrambling for.

"One hundred fifty-second awarding of the Hyde Scholarship," he says, brow unfurrowing as he returns to the ceremonial welcome originally drafted by the major himself, revised over the years, and meant to be read by succeeding generations as they oversee the process. "One hundred fifty-two years ago, Ezekiel Hyde founded this college on this very spot. My great-great-"—his lips move as he counts—"great-great-grandfather believed in education as the key to a life well lived. He also believed in a love of country and service to others. The six of you men—" Nicholas lifts a fist to his mouth, and his cheeks puff as he stifles a burp. "I'm sorry. When were women admitted to the college?"

Six sets of eyes turn to me.

"Women were first admitted to Hyde College in 1941," I say.

The students turn back. Emily is the last, her lip curled in a sneer over the college's tardiness in admitting women. Her anger would increase if she knew the board of trustees did it only because all the men went off to the war, sending enrollment plunging.

"When were students of color first admitted?" Natalia asks. "Specifically, Latinx students?"

Again, six faces swing my way.

"Well, I think a little later than the forties."

"Nineteen sixty-one, sir," Captain Stephenson says. "The first Black student enrolled at Hyde College in 1961. Her name was Myra Lott. She majored in education and spent her life teaching here in Bluefield. Quite a remarkable woman, really, if you read about her life. My mother-in-law attended the same church as Ms. Lott."

"Thank you for knowing that, Captain," I say.

"I don't know when the first Latinx student was admitted. Do you, sir?"

"Well . . ."

Nicholas saves me by going on. "The six of you men and women have been selected from among your peers to be Hyde Fellows. Just by being here, you have *already* been awarded the prestigious Hyde Fellowship worth five thousand dollars toward your senior-year tuition at the college."

Nicholas looks up from his book and nods.

No one gets the cue, so I start to clap. Then the six students clap as well.

A pleased Nicholas continues. "But today is the biggest day of all. And I mean—really big. Today, you compete for a chance to win the Hyde Scholarship. As you already know, the Hyde Scholarship provides the following for one student every year." Nicholas lifts his right hand off the book and uses it to point while he enumerates the components of the award, a gesture he probably learned in a course on public speaking. "Free tuition. Free room and board. Free books. The award also guarantees the recipient an entry-level job with the Hyde Corporation upon graduation from the college. And there's one more key part of the award." He turns to me. "What year was this added, Mr. Gaines?"

"Fifteen years ago," I say. "Actually, it was your father, Theodore Hyde, who insisted on the addition of this part of the scholarship. He really cared about access to college."

Nicholas nods absently as though I just paid a compliment to a complete stranger. "The winner of the Hyde Scholarship will also receive repayment of any and all student loans they have taken out during their first three years in college up to the amount of one hundred thousand dollars."

At one time, the college was able to keep the details of the Hyde Scholarship hidden from the students, so they learned this information for the first time when they were standing in the parlor. Given the social media age we live in, the information inevitably leaked out. But despite already knowing what the award is worth, hearing it said out loud and directly to them by the man who controls the access to those funds causes a ripple of excitement to pass through the room.

The back of my neck tingles, and it's not just from the caffeine. After all this time, it's still hard for me to wrap my head around the size of the award and the leg up on life it will give to one of these students. Tuition, loan repayment, a job. All at a time when it's harder and harder to acquire those things. While I'm happy for the students in the room, my thoughts turn to my three girls, ages eleven, thirteen, and sixteen. What kind of world will they enter as they get older? How much help will I be able to give them if I lose my job or the college closes?

"As you all know," Nicholas says, "the Hyde family selects the six participants every year based on a combination of superior academic achievement and financial need. We try to offer this opportunity to a diverse group of students in order to reflect the tenor of the times." He clears his throat, a long, wet gurgling. "Major Ezekiel Hyde believed in making higher education accessible for everyone." Nicholas studies his book for a moment and then glances up. "That's the overview. It almost sounds too good to be true, doesn't it? Are there any questions before I tell you about the process itself?"

Past experience has told me there are rarely questions at this stage. The students are eager to hear about the process. If anyone asks questions now, it's usually about something mundane like where the bathroom is or what time lunch is served.

Nicholas is about to go on when Natalia's small hand goes up.

She's been so quiet so far, I'm surprised, and I wonder if she's just stretching. She's so short I'm not sure Nicholas can see her.

But her hand is up. With a question.

Nicholas notices and nods in her direction.

All eyes turn to Natalia. I wonder if she'll just say, *Never mind*, and let her question go. But she clears her throat, her hand placed against her chest, and speaks up.

"I did read something on Twitter this morning, a post by one of my professors," she says. "I'm trying to see if there's a delicate way to say this, but I don't think there is. . . . Is it true that Major Hyde was some kind of a war criminal?"

10

"A WAR CRIMINAL?" WHEN Captain Stephenson turns toward Natalia, tea sloshes over the rim of his cup. He points at the portrait. "I think you're mistaken. He was a patriot who served his country."

"What do you mean, Natalia?" Duffy asks. "Was he a Confederate?"

"I, like, heard the same thing," Sydney says, turning to Milo. "Remember? I told you when we were walking up. Right?"

Milo is nodding. Smirking.

All the students start talking at once, and I fear the situation inside is about to get as ugly as the situation outside.

Emily comes right up to me, owlish glasses reflecting the light. "Are you telling me I'm in a home that belonged to someone who owned *slaves*?" Her words are pointed, like she thinks I held influence over Major Hyde's life. "Other things about this day are bad enough, but I just can't, okay?"

"Hold it," I say to the group. "Hold it."

But they keep talking.

A shrill whistle cuts through and above everything.

Nicholas Hyde has stuck his thumb and middle finger—dirty nails and all—into his mouth and blown. The sound is so piercing everyone stops talking at once. They turn their attention back to him.

"Sorry for the noise," he says. "I learned to do that when I was on the wrestling team." His eyes pass over everyone, an authoritative glare. Even I find myself feeling like a scolded child. "If you just give me a moment, I can address those rumors about Major Hyde."

He waits again. And while we anticipate his explanation, I picture the windows of Hyde House opening and piles and piles of Hyde family cash blowing out and going away, leaving the college with nothing.

But Nicholas addresses the room with great calm. "Major Hyde served in the Civil War. That's true. Everyone knows that. He did serve in the Union Army, not the Confederate."

"Wait," Milo says. "Wasn't Kentucky in the Confederacy? This is the South, after all."

"Kentucky was officially neutral during the war," Captain Stephenson says. "It didn't secede."

"But people did, like, own slaves here," Sydney says. "Right? I took a class about it with Dr. Porter."

"Porter," Captain Stephenson says. "That man pushes his own agenda more than he teaches."

"One second, please," Nicholas says. "I had something to say, remember?"

Captain Stephenson nods at him as if giving him permission to continue.

"Major Hyde served in the Union Army. And, yes, he participated in the massacre of Confederate prisoners at Palmyra," Nicholas says.

Emily puts her tattooed arm to her forehead like she's about to swoon. If she does, we could easily find her a Victorian fainting couch around here to land on. "I can't believe that," she says. "I knew this was a mistake."

"It's called the fog of war, Emily," Captain Stephenson says, his voice carrying a calm authority. "It's regrettable, and no one likes it. Good soldiers always strive to protect and give quarter to prisoners. That's why we have the Geneva convention. But I don't know enough about the situation Major Hyde faced in Palmyra to render judgment. Maybe he was given an unjust order."

"But he was on the right side of the war," Duffy says. "Right? So that's pretty cool, isn't it?"

"You can't just massacre people, even if you're on the right side, can you?" Sydney asks. "I mean, that's not cool. No offense, Mr. Hyde."

"None taken."

"It's not cool," Milo says, daring to risk his budding bromance with Nicholas by criticizing the major. "Not at all."

"I really did just have my curiosity piqued," Natalia says. "That's why I asked."

"Like I said," Nicholas says, "the family has known about Major Hyde's actions in the war for a long time. And now everyone is finding out. And I'm not condoning what he did one hundred fifty-five or so years ago, but I understand that it might make some people uncomfortable. If anyone would like to leave, they are welcome to go. We can summon the chief, and he can unlock the door for us."

Everyone shuffles their feet, waiting for Emily to speak up. She opens her mouth, but before she can say anything, Nicholas goes on. "And let me remind you, the bylaws are very clear—if anyone steps so much as one foot out the door, they are disqualified from any consideration for the Hyde Scholarship and all its attendant perks. And in case you're wondering, you lose the five-thousand-dollar Hyde Fellowship as well."

Emily's mouth closes. And no one else speaks either.

"Okay," Nicholas says, "back to the task at hand. We're on the clock here."

11

NICHOLAS LOOKS AT HIS watch and shakes his head ever so slightly.

It's a comforting sign that he's concerned about keeping us on schedule. And we are about fifteen minutes behind.

I take a deep breath. Chief is right. Extra time is built in for lunch.

I know I'm just eager for the students to begin the exam because I want to talk to Nicholas more.

"As you all know," Nicholas says, "the process has two main components. First, we will have a written exam in the formal dining room. That will take up the morning. We'll have a break for lunch, and then the afternoon will consist of a personal interview with me and Vice President Gaines. The winner will be—"

I'm surprised—no, shocked—to hear my name.

It's not in the bylaws. And every year in the past, the interviews were between the representative of the Hyde family and the student. Never me.

"—announced on Monday morning. Is something wrong, Mr. Gaines?"

I don't play poker. Apparently that's a good thing.

"Oh, I'm sorry. But I know this is your first year overseeing the process. The interview has never included me."

"I'd like your help and input in choosing the winner," Nicholas says. "Is that okay?"

"Yes, of course."

My face flushes. Is this a good sign? Does he trust me that much? Does this mean I have a better shot at nailing down the 100 More Initiative?

"As I was saying, the winner of the Hyde Scholarship will be chosen based on three factors—comportment, presentation, and communication. Communication through the exam. Presentation through the interview. And comportment . . . who knows what I mean by 'comportment'?"

It's like being in a classroom. No one wants to guess. No one wants to be wrong.

Captain Stephenson's hand goes up. "'Comportment' means your manner, your behavior. How you conduct yourself. How you treat others."

"Right," Nicholas says. "It's a nebulous thing, but one we'll be looking at today."

"How exactly did you choose us?" Milo asks.

"It's a combination—"

"I know that," Milo says. "But how did you get that information about us? Did the college cooperate?"

"There's been a long partnership between the college and the family."

"But that seems like, well, what the captain said outside. An invasion of privacy."

The students shuffle their feet more. Milo looks a little green around the gills as he gives the side-eye to Sydney. I remember the way they were talking as they approached the house, the awkwardness of the way they stood next to each other on the portico.

"As I already said, now that you're inside, you can't leave without forfeiting everything. But if you choose to stay the entire time, I think you'll find it to be a rewarding experience. Or at least a memorable one. My family . . . well, my family . . ."

Nicholas wobbles again, tips to the left, and then straightens. Is there a provision in the bylaws covering the member of the Hyde family passing out from the aftereffects of a bender?

When he continues, he seems to be off script. He's not looking at the book anymore.

"Earlier, Mr. Gaines said something about this house and my family's legacy. And he was right. My family has built quite a legacy here at Hyde College. Quite a legacy. And being here today after so many years . . . well, it feels somehow like coming home. Like a circle being completed. For me. Finally. After a long time away. My mother. . . . if she were . . ."

Tears well up in Nicholas's eyes. He sniffs.

The students are all listening. But they're not sure what to do or say.

Neither am I.

Nicholas clears his throat. "Well, there is just one more thing to do before you all go into the dining room and start to write. The bylaws state you all must repeat the Hyde College motto, which was coined by Major Hyde and is inscribed on the statue of my great-great-great-great-grandfather at the entryway to the college. If you would all raise your right hands and repeat after me."

The students do as they've been told. Six hands go up in the air.

"'In duty, there is freedom,'" Nicholas says.

An awkward pause settles over the room.

Captain Stephenson says, his voice booming off the walls, "'In duty, there is freedom.'"

"Good," Nicholas says, "but you all have to say it as one. Ready?"

Six voices join together: "'In duty, there is freedom.'"

12

THE DINING ROOM IS nearly filled by a fourteen-foot-long ma-hogany table, which sits on an ornate area rug. Heavy red drapes, faded from years in the sun, cover the windows, and the light comes from a bronze-finished chandelier decorated with elaborate floral scrollwork.

Ordinarily, sixteen chairs surround the table, but the campus staff removed ten of them so the six students can spread out and have plenty of room to write. At each chair, a lined composition book and several pens have been placed, requiring the students to write without the aid of a computer or any of the research materials that would be available to them on the Internet.

A couple of students groan at the setup. They settle into their seats.

There are only five. One is missing.

I do a quick inventory. Emily. No Emily.

Maybe she's in the bathroom? But I know Nicholas is going to start laying out instructions, and we're already a little behind. In the front of the house, I find Emily in the music room on the opposite side of the hall from the parlor. She has her face pressed against the window, knocking her glasses slightly askew.

"Emily?" I say.

She turns to me quickly.

"Is everything okay?" I ask. "Mr. Hyde is going to be giving you all instructions about the exam. You don't want to miss them."

"Oh, okay."

But she doesn't move.

"Are you sure you're okay? Are you still thinking of leaving?"

"It's just his . . . superiority. And conspicuous wealth."

"You mean Mr. Hyde?"

She nods. "I don't know how you can stand to work with him."

"His family has done a lot for the college."

She starts to object, and I raise my hand.

"I know. It's all very complicated. And sometimes you have to work with . . . certain people . . . for the greater good."

"Ugh."

"Are you worried about something else?"

"No. It's just . . ." She makes a vague hand movement toward the window.

"Is it the protestors?"

"Yes, that's part of it."

"What else is there?"

"It's just . . . someone here . . . one of the other students . . . I'm not a fan of theirs."

"I'm sorry to hear that."

"It's— Well, it is what it is."

"Do you feel unsafe?" I ask.

"I don't. I'd worry about someone else in here."

"Who?"

"It's fine," she says. "I just need to do my job."

Chief has been true to his word—the protestors have been pushed all the way back to the spot where Hyde Lane meets the main road circling campus. Instead of being at the edge of the Hyde House lawn—a few hundred feet away—they are now a few hundred yards away. Well out of throwing range. And far enough away that we can't even hear them.

"Chief is out there, and he'll be out there all day. If I know Chief, he won't even take a lunch break. I don't think those protestors can hurt anyone now."

Emily exhales a short breath. "And the police can't really hear or see us, can they?"

I see her point. Which is a bit unsettling. "Chief said he'd keep an eye on things."

"Will he, though?" Emily asks. "I mean, he's so far away. It's almost like he wants us on our own in here. He didn't even step inside. He seemed happy to lock us in."

"Do you want to come to the dining room?" I ask.

I know I sound like I'm speaking to a small child, but I'm continually struck by how young and vulnerable the students seem. It's always a mistake on my part to look at them and assume they're living happy, carefree lives. They have pressures too, ones I need to be aware of.

"Yes," she says. "Okay."

"Try to block out the stuff about the Hyde family and their past," I say. "And if you don't like one of the other students, focus on this opportunity."

"Yeah, that's what I want to do."

We go into the dining room, and Emily takes the last open seat at the far end of the table.

The students are still discussing their primitive writing implements. All except Natalia. She stands at the front of the room, talking to Nicholas Hyde. I should say, she stands there *listening* to Nicholas Hyde. He's explaining something to her, ticking points off by touching the index finger of one hand against the fingers of the other. Natalia is scowling, her large eyes narrowed and her cheeks flushed, but she stands in place while he talks.

Just as I start over, Natalia turns and goes to her seat, saying, "Why should that matter?" She continues to scowl, and no one says anything to her once she's sitting.

"I can't even read my own handwriting," Duffy says, and the others laugh.

"That's okay," Nicholas says. "I'm the same way. We'll manage."

"Are we able to get up and use the restroom?" Milo asks. "That tea . . ."

"Of course," I say. "Everything is carefully controlled but not sadistic." I laugh, but no one else does. "The restroom is out in the hallway near the kitchen. At the back of the house. There's another near the front."

I expect Milo or someone else to avail themselves of the facilities, but they don't. They remain in their seats, pens in hands, faces eager and tense.

Nicholas places his briefcase on a marble-topped side table. He opens it and reaches in like a magician, bringing out a stack of papers and the book of bylaws. He opens the book and scribbles something in the back of it, his jaw set hard while he writes. Should he be writing in that book at all, other than signing his name? Isn't it like defacing a Bible?

Then again, it's *his* Bible. And I suppose there's something powerful about a book being passed from one generation to the next, about everything being written down in plain pen on paper. I can't name a single one of my great-grandparents, let alone go back a century and a half.

When he's finished writing, he grabs the stack of papers and turns to the room, saying, "Every year the Hyde family writes a new prompt for the exam to reflect our ever-changing world. This year's prompt is a simple one." He clears his throat and squints at the page. "'Please write an essay in which you explain your feelings on the future of education in twenty-first-century America. Give specific examples of technologies you think might play a role in future learning processes.'"

"Technologies?" Sydney says like she's never heard the word before.

Captain Stephenson's hand is up. When Nicholas nods at him, he asks, "Sir, how long is this essay required to be?"

"As long as it takes to make your point," Nicholas says.

Captain Stephenson looks unsatisfied with the answer. Emily's face scrunches as well. She shakes her head. Milo's mouth is twisted like he's trying to solve a vexing puzzle. Duffy taps his pen against the table.

"Are there other questions before you begin?" Nicholas asks.

Natalia raises her hand. "We may refer to other works or sources we know about, but because we don't have them with us, we can't utilize the correct citation. Will we suffer a penalty if we can't precisely cite the source?"

Milo's mouth twists even more.

"Don't worry about that," Nicholas says. "We understand the constraints you're working under."

"So we *have* to use outside sources?" Sydney asks. "I'm not sure I'm clear."

"No," Nicholas says. "Just do your own thing. And write your best essay." He quickly moves on before anyone else can ask a question. "Great. Why doesn't everyone get started?"

He looks at his watch, and his eyebrows go up when he does. Is it later or earlier than he thought? "It's now nine eighteen. Lunch is served at noon, so you have more than two and a half hours to write. Make the best use of that time. Okay? And you're off."

13

THE STUDENTS BEGIN TO write.

The sound of pens scratching against paper fills the room.

I allow myself a sigh of relief. The process has started. Events are underway. All the other stuff—the protestors, the brick, the tensions among the students, Ezekiel Hyde's ugly war record—fades away.

Nicholas slides his papers and book back into his briefcase, shuts the clasp, and spins the lock. He leaves the briefcase on the sideboard and comes over to me. His speechifying is finished for the moment. He has performed his duties on behalf of the Hyde family. Year number 152 of the scholarship is underway. Shouldn't it all be downhill from here?

But his lips are pressed in a tight line as he walks over. He scratches his head with his pale fingers.

"I need to go get some more tea," he says. "I expected it to have cleared away my cobwebs by now, but it hasn't. You want anything?"

"I'll go with you."

Nicholas checks the scribbling students. "Are we . . ."

"They'll be fine," I say. "I don't think the bylaws say we have to watch over them every second. Besides, your dad and I used to slip out for some tea when he ran the show."

"Oh, really?"

"Sure. Call it another tradition."

Nicholas shrugs, his face slightly irritated by my desire to tag along. *Can I get a moment of peace?* he seems to be thinking.

His father is dead, so no one can catch me in the lie I just made up. Ted and I never went out for tea during the written part of the process. But I'm fighting for my job—and the college's life—so I'm willing to try anything.

ABC. *Always be closing.*

I let Nicholas lead the way. The students barely raise their eyes as we leave the dining room and go back to the parlor. Dirty tea-cups litter the area around the tea service, so Nicholas reaches for a clean one and hands it to me. He offers to pour again, and I accept, the liquid still steaming as it comes out. Then he pours for himself and reaches out for one of the remaining cucumber sandwiches and stuffs it in his mouth. He chews methodically, his mouth slightly open, his lips making a mild smacking sound. I hate cucumbers with a passion and settle for one of the cookies.

"Well," I say, lifting my cup, "here's to a successful start."

"Cheers," he says. "I guess we'll still do our bourbon shot later. I wanted to have already drained one."

"That's right. Buffalo Trace. A Hyde family tradition."

Nicholas stuffs another sandwich into his mouth. A smear of butter clings to his upper lip.

"Was Natalia okay?" I ask. "You two seemed to be having quite the conversation."

"Who? Oh, her." He shakes his head. "She's quite the little firecracker, isn't she? I had to set her straight about a few things."

"Was it the war-criminal stuff?"

"Among other things. Do you know her very well?"

"Not really. I don't get to know the students as well as I did when I taught."

"These kids." He waves his hand, dismissing a whole generation not much younger than himself. "They'll learn. Maybe the hard way, but they'll learn. That's the thing, though. You want the right kind of person to win the award."

"'The right kind'?"

"Well, it's a big honor. The person represents the college. The family. Someone like that Sydney, you know? She seems like the real deal."

"The students are all impressive."

"Sure, but some are more impressive than others."

"Speaking of those kids . . . I just wanted to use this time to remind you about the One Hundred More Initiative. We talked about it back in the fall, and the whole administration is really excited about it."

"The what?"

"The One Hundred More Initiative." I wait for recognition to interrupt his chewing. It doesn't. "The scholarship program designed to bring one hundred additional students from underrepresented groups to campus. Our enrollment is currently just under one thousand as a college. If we could add one hundred more students and if they were from underrepresented groups, then the college would win on multiple fronts. More students. More diversity. We'd probably get a lot of positive national attention, and then the number of students applying would grow. It would all feed on itself. Plus, it would be the right thing to do."

"The right thing to do?"

"To try to bring about greater equality of opportunity."

Nicholas swallows but doesn't wipe the butter off his lip. And I desperately want him to. I decide it would be poor form for me to reach out and do it like I'm his mother.

"Sounds good to me," he says.

A speck of food flies out of his mouth when he says this and goes over my shoulder. Better than dodging bricks and bottles.

"Great. I'm glad you feel that way. President Chan is really eager to meet with you about it. She told me she's free for dinner tonight or anytime you're in town this weekend or next week."

He takes a big swallow of tea and picks up yet another sandwich. But he doesn't throw this one into his mouth. "Can I ask you something?"

"Of course."

"Those protestors outside, what do you think of them?"

I drink my own tea, hoping to buy time. I sense I'm being tested. And I'm not sure of the right answer.

"Well," I say, "they're young, as you pointed out. They're passionate about their causes, and they want to express themselves. Hyde College has always believed in educating the whole person and encouraging students to think for themselves."

"Critical thinking, right? That's one of those education buzzwords."

"Right."

He points to me with the hand holding the cucumber sandwich. "It's different if it's your family being protested against. I mean, how would you feel if someone lobbed a brick at your relative's house? Or your own house?"

"I see your point. Of course I'd obviously be upset. But those protestors are a very small minority of our student body. Look at those six students in there. They're the best and the brightest of Hyde College."

"Would you give money to the people who lobbed a brick at your relative's house? See, that's the position I'm in." He continues to gesture with his sandwich. And he continues to have the butter smear on his lip. "I'm in charge of the family now that Dad is gone. And I'm inundated with letters and e-mails and calls from charities and worthy causes. And this is the only place where they throw bricks at me. It's the only place where one of the employees—and now one of the students—is calling my great-great-great-great-grandfather a war criminal. So maybe the college doesn't want our money anymore."

I manage to keep my grip on the teacup steady, even though everything is loose and shaky inside. *Comportment.* I try to manage my own comportment.

I nod, putting on the sympathetic look I break out for recalcitrant donors. The nod says, *I hear you. I see you. I understand.*

"These are certainly tough times for everyone. Economically. Socially. We live in a complicated world. That's why a legacy like Hyde College matters so much. It's built out of solid rock. Like a granite mountain."

Nicholas's eyes narrow. He isn't sure how to take me. Am I putting him on? Or am I making a sincere sales pitch?

Both, I think. It's always both.

"Your name is on this college. Your family's name." It's my turn to point. "And you are going to be the guy to guide your family through the bulk of the twenty-first century. That's your personal legacy."

He studies me for a moment. Mercifully, he lifts his index finger and swipes the butter off his upper lip. Did he know it was there the whole time? Was he leaving it there to torment me? To distract me?

"I understand what you're saying," he says. "I do. And I know how much this place meant to my family . . . to my dad anyway. I get it."

"I figured you would."

A measure of relief passes through me like a cooling wave.

Nicholas extends the finger that wiped the butter off his lip in my direction. "But I don't give a good goddamn about—"

Something crashes to the floor in the dining room.

We both spin.

"What was that?" I ask.

"Sounds like a chair broke."

"Just—let me go—"

I take one step, and Duffy's at the parlor door.

"It's Milo," he says. "He's on the floor. He's having a seizure or something."

14

I SPRINT INTO THE dining room first, and Nicholas is right behind me.

Milo is on the floor, his body seizing. His legs kick, and his torso spasms.

Captain Stephenson is kneeling next to him. He's tilted Milo's head to keep his airway clear.

The other students stand back, giving them both room and air. Sydney has her hand to her mouth, tears in her eyes. Natalia stands next to Emily, her arm around Emily's back.

I drop to my knees. "What happened, Captain?"

"We were writing—he jumped up, grabbed his throat. Then he went to the floor. Seizing." The captain lifts Milo's wrist. "He's not wearing a medical bracelet or anything like that."

"Do any of you guys know? Does he have a medical condition?"

My eyes land on Sydney, since she and Milo walked up together. She shakes her head. "No, he was totally healthy."

"No, he wasn't." It's Natalia. "He passed out in sophomore seminar one day. Just out cold on the floor. Somebody said he had an irregular heartbeat or something like that."

"He what?" Sydney asks.

"Is he high?" I ask. "Did he take something?"

Sydney shakes her head again. "Milo doesn't do drugs. I *know* that."

"Oh, God. Oh, God." It's Nicholas. He comes closer, stops on the other side of Milo, looking down at the captain and me. "What happened to him? He was perfectly fine. We were talking. . . ."

"It's a seizure of some kind," I say.

"Maybe . . ." Captain Stephenson is leaning closer to Milo, whose breathing is becoming more labored.

"Oh, no. Look," Duffy says. "His face . . ."

I see it too. Milo's skin is changing color, slowly becoming blue as his eyes roll back in his head. His lips move as a wet, choking sound comes from his throat.

"He's dying," Emily says.

"No." It's Sydney. *"No no no no no no."*

Frothy white liquid starts to come out of Milo's mouth. The movement of his chest slows . . .

And slows . . .

. . . and then stops completely.

Captain Stephenson leans forward. He places his hands on Milo's chest, one on top of the other, and starts compressing.

I lean in as well. I slap Milo's cheeks, one side and then the other. Harder and harder.

"Come on, Milo. Come on. Stay with us, okay, buddy? Stay with us."

I slap and I slap.

"Can you hear me? Milo, say something. Can you hear me?"

I don't know how long the captain compresses Milo's chest. Or how long I lean over him and try to revive him.

At some point, Nicholas hands me a glass of water, and I dash it into Milo's face, trying to shock him back to life.

Like we're in a movie.

If only we were in a movie . . .

"Oh, God, oh, God, oh, God. How did this happen?"

The captain keeps going. Sweat beads on his face, a drop running down to the tip of his nose and falling onto Milo.

Onto his body. Because that's what he is now.

A body.

There's no more movement. No choking or breathing or gasping.

His eyes are half closed, the whites showing.

"Milo, come on," I say, but my voice is faint. Empty.

"Damn it all to hell," Duffy says.

"Oh, God, oh, God, oh, God."

The captain finally stops. He leans back on his heels and lets out a deep breath of resignation. He wipes his forehead with the back of his hand, like he's just run a race.

"I'm sorry, sir. We've lost him. I tried . . . I wish . . ."

Milo is so young. So promising. As they all are. Not much older than my own daughters. Could his life be extinguished before our very eyes like that?

My eyes start to burn with tears. I think about Milo's parents. His family. His friends.

What will they do when they hear the news? What could devastate a parent more than this? They'll be broken.

But I need to take control of things. I need to be the strength here. The leader.

The students need me.

I wipe my eyes and prepare to stand.

"Sir?"

"Yes, Captain?"

"I think we have a problem. I mean, a bigger one than just this young man dying."

"What could be bigger than a young man dying?"

Captain Stephenson points to Milo's face, the froth coming out of his mouth.

"I believe he was poisoned, sir."

15

THE WORD HITS MY ears but doesn't register.

It's like Captain Stephenson is speaking in a foreign language. *Poisoned.*

No, it doesn't make sense.

It can't be.

"What are you talking about, dude?" Duffy asks.

"I think it's poison," Captain Stephenson says. "The way he collapsed and started seizing. The frothing at the mouth. It's the only explanation. After all, why else would a healthy young man with no known medical condition just drop dead? It doesn't add up."

"What about the irregular heartbeat?" Nicholas says. "You heard her. He fainted in class once."

"Why didn't he tell me about his heart?" Sydney asks. She's sniffling and wiping at her nose with her hand. She stands alone, no one else close. "I thought he was healthy."

"People keep medical conditions secret all the time," Nicholas says.

"Old people do," Emily says. "Like my grandma. She had a stroke, and she didn't tell anyone for six weeks. She was limping around, and she told my mom she'd sprained her ankle. Young people share that information with their friends."

"Okay," I say, standing up. "We don't know what caused this. And it's useless to speculate. They'll do a— They'll examine him and figure it out."

Captain Stephenson is still down next to Milo, studying him closely.

"What exactly are you doing?" Natalia asks. Her eye makeup is smudged from crying.

"I'm checking for any sign of poisoning." He straightens up as well and tugs on the ends of his suit coat, tidying it. "If it were cyanide, there would be a cherry red color on the lips. Also the scent of almonds."

"His lips *are* red," Duffy says.

"They're always bright red," Sydney says. "Like, they naturally look that way."

"Could be strychnine," the captain says. "Maybe thallium. Potassium chloride does the trick as well if you inject it. Maybe someone stuck a needle in him. Certain rat poisons are highly toxic. And herbs can kill. You know, it would have been easy to add poisonous herbs to the tea. You'd just have to be able to recognize them and pick them. They grow out in the country."

"I thought that tea was unpleasant," Natalia says. "I'm a coffee drinker myself. Could it have been expired? Everything is so old here."

"It was bitter," I say, "even with sugar."

"Who are you, with all this poison knowledge?" Emily asks the captain. "Hercule Poirot?"

"Who?" Duffy asks.

"I did some Special Forces training in the army. Covert stuff I'd prefer not to talk about. But we learned about poisons. It's tough to use those to take down a target, but sometimes it works. Putin clearly likes it. A lot of it depends on how fast it acted, and we don't know that. Some poisons can take hours to act. We drank our tea—" He checks his analog watch. "We started drinking less than an hour ago. That could be right."

"Or he ingested something deadly before he got here," Natalia says.

"Could be," Captain Stephenson says. "If he ate or drank anything in his room, someone could have slipped it to him. Or injected him. I'm guessing most of us didn't eat before we showed up since we were told we'd be fed here. Ultimately, of course, an autopsy will tell us what really happened. Poison. A heart condition. Accidental drug overdose."

"He doesn't do drugs," Sydney says. "Okay?"

"People try things for the first time. It's college," the captain says.

"That's true," Duffy says. "My best friend from home snorted coke at a party once. He ran naked down the middle of the street."

I look at Sydney again. "You walked up with Milo. Had he eaten or drank anything? Do you know?"

All eyes in the room turn toward Sydney. A flush spreads across her cheeks.

She wraps her arms across her chest like she's cold.

I immediately regret my question. I've put her on the spot.

"I'm sorry, Sydney. If you don't know, it's—"

"I don't know. We just, like, ran into each other on the way here. I don't know what he was doing this morning."

"And that's okay. I understand."

"Wait," Duffy says. "If he was poisoned here, then that means we all might be poisoned. We all might be about to collapse."

"We all drank the same tea and ate the same food," Natalia says.

"Shit," Nicholas says.

"Hold on," Captain Stephenson says. "It's true we all consumed the same items out there. But I noticed something about Milo while we were in the parlor. He kind of had a funny look on his face, like he didn't feel well. I thought he just didn't like the tea. Or maybe he was hungover or something. Does anybody else feel sick? You'd likely know something by this point. You'd be starting to feel it."

We all look at one another. And I'm scared. If one of them so much as has a stomachache or nausea, I don't know what I'll do.

"Anything?" I ask.

Natalia clears her throat. "I'm a little light-headed, but that's my ADHD medication. It always has that effect on me. It's a stimulant."

"How could anyone even get poison in here when we were all searched?" Duffy asks.

"We weren't looking for poison," I say. "Just electronics."

"It could be a very small amount," Captain Stephenson says.

"That's solved easily enough," Emily says. "Just go check the teacups and the food. See if it smells funny."

"That's a fine idea, Emily," the captain says, "but some poisons are odorless. That would be more sophisticated stuff. But you never know what you're dealing with. I can go have a look—"

"Shouldn't it be someone impartial?" Natalia is looking at her feet again, but her voice comes through loud and clear. "We all have a stake in this. The students, that is."

"What are you saying?" the captain asks.

"Shouldn't it be one of the adults?" Natalia asks. "I mean, I know you're an adult. You're somewhat older than anybody here."

I wince a little on the captain's behalf.

Natalia goes on. "But you're a student too. Shouldn't it be one of these gentlemen?" She points to Nicholas and to me.

"I can go," I say, and take a step forward.

"Well, hold on." Sydney rubs her arms again, one hand going over the word *Persistence*. "No offense, Mr. Gaines, but you do, like, work for the college. You're not exactly impartial. Maybe it should be Mr. Hyde. He's the outsider here."

Sydney's words have a strange effect on me. She's right and shows a great deal of wisdom. But I'm still stung by not being the guy to handle the problem. I only want what's best for the students and the college too.

"Fair enough," I say.

Nicholas is nodding his head. "Okay, I'll check. And then I'll come right back."

"Don't worry," Duffy says. "We won't go anywhere."

Nobody laughs.

We all stand around. Waiting. With a dead body in the middle of the room.

"So nobody's sick?" I ask.

I'm met by silence. A silence I welcome.

"Okay," I say. "Okay. Good. If anyone starts to feel sick, please let me know right away. Don't keep it to yourself."

"Maybe it was the people who work here," Emily says, adjusting her glasses. "They made the food and tea and put it out. Have you seen some of the people they hire to work on campus?"

"Geez," Duffy says. "Blame the regular workers, why don't you?"

"It's not that. We found out there was a convicted sex offender working as a maintenance guy in our dorm."

"Ewww," Sydney says. "That's so creepy."

"Did you report it?" I ask.

"Eventually they fired him. But it took forever. It's amazing the things they let go around here."

"That's disgusting," Captain Stephenson says. "To have someone like that around young women."

My conversation with Chief comes back to me. He told me the staff is unhappy, disgruntled because of layoffs and pay cuts. I'd never admit it out loud, but I know Emily's right. The college has hired some questionable staff—and faculty—members over the years. Who's to say who might have had access to the food or the house this morning while it was being set up? How many people might want to strike a blow against the Hyde family or the college?

We try to maintain a good relationship with the town. And the college is by far the largest employer in the area. But that doesn't mean there aren't tensions. Many in town perceive the student body as a bunch of rich kids drinking and partying in a camplike setting. And in some ways, that's not wrong.

Nicholas Hyde enters the room again. Everyone turns to him expectantly.

"I didn't see or smell anything unusual," he says. "The tea, the food . . . I think it's okay."

"But you're not sure?" Duffy asks.

"How can I be sure?" Nicholas asks. "But I feel pretty strongly it's okay."

"Isn't it obvious what's going on here?"

It's Captain Stephenson. He stands with his hands on his hips, his chest out.

"What are you talking about?" Nicholas asks, his face paler than when he first pulled up and emerged from his car, when the sun made him react like a wounded vampire.

"Everyone seems to know Milo is the best student in this group. Best grades. Best writer. Highest IQ even. It seems like you all expected him to win, didn't you?"

No one answers, but a few heads nod.

"And now he's dead," Captain Stephenson says, his voice laced with a weary sadness. "And it's a tragedy he's gone. It's heartbreaking. Isn't it clear someone killed him to get him out of the way of the competition?"

16

"IT'S TRUE." SYDNEY USES her pinkie finger to dab at the corner of her eye. "He is the best student here. Maybe the best at the school."

"Dude was supersmart." Duffy's voice is full of admiration.

"Let's not get too carried away with our hagiography."

Everyone turns to look at Emily, who stares back through her giant glasses.

"What's that?" Duffy asks. "A poison?"

"It means, don't turn him into a saint just because he's dead," Emily says.

Sydney continues to wipe her eyes. "He's not a saint. Right? But he is smart."

"Was," Captain Stephenson says.

"Jesus, Captain," Duffy says. "That's kind of harsh."

"You're right. I'm sorry. I forget where I am sometimes. It's just that I've seen guys die in front of me before. It's a soldier's mentality to try to go on as quickly as possible. I know I shouldn't expect that from all of you. And . . . Well, look, I understand. I have children just a little younger than Milo. I get it."

"You're right, though." Natalia is looking away as though she can't bear the sight of Milo's lifeless body on the floor. I can't say I blame her. "I mean . . . what does happen to the examination now? We were already started."

"You can't think of—"

Something rustles to the right, cutting off Sydney's words. I turn that way. It's Nicholas. He's slumped against the mahogany credenza. A pitcher of water and a set of glasses that rest there rattle as his weight leans against the heavy piece of furniture. He's sweaty and pale.

"Nicholas? Are you feeling ill too?"

He braces himself with two hands, then manages to shake his head. "I'm okay. . . . Just . . . this is all so terrible. . . . There's been so much death."

I make sure he isn't going to fall to the floor. When I think he's safe, I pour a glass of water for him and hold it out.

"Should we drink *anything*?" Duffy asks. "I mean, shit."

I hold the glass up to the light. It's crystal clear liquid inside.

I sniff it. Nothing.

"We have to trust at some point," I say. "I think Milo was poisoned before he got here. If he was poisoned at all. We don't know that."

"But—"

I cut the captain off. "We don't know anything for sure, do we? It could have been his heart."

The captain shakes his head like he doesn't believe me.

"Here." I hand the water to Nicholas.

His hand shakes as he reaches for the glass, but he manages to lift it to his mouth and gulp it down. Some water spills out the side and runs down his neck and beneath his shirt.

"Okay, that's better, isn't it?"

Nicholas keeps drinking. When he's emptied the glass, I pour more. And he drinks. He steadies himself like he's going to be okay. And with that under control, I turn my attention back to the group.

I'm here representing the college, so I need to be worthy of their trust.

"Look," I say, "it's obvious what we have to do. It's going to be very tough for anyone to concentrate on the exam now. So I'm going to go to the front door, and I'm going to try to signal Chief somehow. Like he said, he's keeping an eye on the place. I can get his attention, and he can unlock the door with his keys. The police will take control of the situation, and we can reschedule the exam for another time. I promise you can all come back and try again."

A few of the students nod. I assume the ones who don't are in shock. Or just aren't sure what to think.

I can't blame them—neither am I.

"Okay, I'll go now."

"Wait."

The voice stops me. I turn and see Nicholas Hyde pushing himself up to an erect position against the credenza. Some of the color has returned to his face. He looks like someone injected steel into his spine.

"What's the matter?" I ask.

"You can't do it," he says. "You can't call the chief. Or anyone else. It's simply an impossibility at this point. There's far too much at stake."

17

NICHOLAS GOES TO HIS briefcase, works the lock, and undoes the clasps.

They snap like firecrackers in the quiet room.

He brings out the leather book again and starts thumbing through. His hands shake as he does, but not as much as earlier when he looked like he was going to slump to the floor.

I move closer and speak so the students can't really hear me. "Nicholas, we have a dead student here. Our first priority has to be making sure everyone is safe."

He continues to riffle through the book. He licks his forefinger and keeps turning the pages with sharp snaps. Finally, he reaches the page he's been seeking. He stabs it with his moistened index finger. One with a dirty nail.

"Here we go," he says.

He turns to the students with the book open and held in his two hands. He licks his lips.

"Remember what we said earlier, when there was that little

upset about my great-great-great-great-grandfather being a war criminal. If anyone leaves, they are disqualified. Not just from the scholarship but from the fellowship as well."

"We know that, Nicholas. But this isn't about one person leaving because they are upset or offended about Major Hyde's activities in the Civil War."

"Or the fossil fuel money," he says. "That was the other thing."

"Yes, that too. But this is about something different. I'm talking about *all* of us leaving. And regrouping. And then holding the process another day. If you're concerned that you won't be in town for it, we can work something out. I mean, there's always Zoom if you want to appear. Or we can do it quickly while you're still in town. Maybe you want to spend a little time in Bluefield. This town meant a lot to your family."

"These bylaws were written by Major Hyde when he created the Hyde Fellowships and the scholarship. And they've served the family and the college well over the years."

"What are you talking about?" I ask.

"Look here," Nicholas says, pointing at the book. "The process *must* take place on the third Saturday in April." He looks up. "Major Hyde liked the idea of the process happening in the spring when the seasons were changing. April is also the month that General Lee surrendered to General Grant at Appomattox Court House. Major Hyde was a big admirer of General Grant. Did you know General Grant visited Hyde College once?"

"I did know that. But these bylaws and the date for the process . . . This is an emergency. We can bend them."

Nicholas reads from the book again. "'If the Hyde Memorial Scholarship is ever not awarded on the third Saturday in April during a given year, then the award shall cease to exist for all subsequent years. All funding for future Hyde Fellows and Hyde Scholars will be discontinued, never to be restored. Thus, the completion of each year's process ensures the enduring and everlasting continuation of the Hyde family legacy, an unbroken chain from generation to generation.'"

"I've never noticed that before," I say.

Nicholas holds the book out to me, his finger marking the spot. It's right there in ancient quill-and-ink handwriting. Major Hyde's handwriting, which I've seen many times.

"But Major Hyde wouldn't want the students to suffer this way," I say as though I'm talking about my next-door neighbor or my close friend and not a man born in the nineteenth century who has been dead over one hundred years.

"He didn't want anyone to suffer, that's true," Nicholas says.

"Except those soldiers he massacred."

When we all look, Emily stares back, her mouth a tight line.

The captain shakes his head.

"But," Nicholas says, "Major Hyde placed these provisions in the bylaws because he believed in brotherhood and community. In other words, he believed that the actions of one generation or one cohort of students affected the lives of the next generation or cohort. Hence, that continuous unbroken line."

"But that—" I say.

"The process has taken place every year. During world wars, civil unrest, the Great Depression. It's always gone on. And we can't stop it today."

"What about—" I say.

Nicholas turns to the students. "If we leave now, then no student will ever again be a Hyde Fellow or a Hyde Scholar. Not only will the five of you lose the chance to get this great gift, but no

Hyde College student for the rest of time will be able to. It will be over. I know that's a tremendous burden to bear, and I'm not sure you want to be responsible for that. Do you?"

And then he turns back to me.

"Do you want to see this portion of the Hyde family's money removed from the college forever? I know it makes for quite a recruiting tool to tell students they might someday have the chance to compete for such a giant scholarship."

He's right. Of course.

We use the scholarship as a recruiting tool—a giant carrot we can dangle before the wide eyes of prospective students and parents. I can only imagine how Grace Chan and the board would react if the money for the Hyde Scholarship goes away. Forever.

Nicholas's eyes bore into mine. It almost seems like a dare. Does he hope I will insist on having everyone leave so that he can withdraw that portion of his family's wealth from the college?

Nicholas is smart to turn it back on the students the way he has. I may be somewhat removed from day-to-day contact with them, but I know this generation doesn't like to deprive anyone of anything. Perhaps more than any other generation, they believe in equality and fairness and equity. The idea that their actions would take scholarship money out of the hands of future generations of Hyde College students is going to be a tough one for them to swallow.

"You guys," I say, "we don't know about this. There might be ways to work around the bylaws. We can take it to the board."

"When do they meet next?" Nicholas asks.

"I guess they're scheduled for June. But we could try for an emergency session."

"That might take forever," Natalia says.

"Okay," I say. "Maybe Nicholas can make an exception."

He's shaking his head, but Sydney says, "I think Mr. Gaines is right. I think we need to go. I don't, like, feel safe here. Right? And with Milo dead . . ."

"Thank you, Sydney," I say. And I allow myself to believe that she has spoken for all the students, that her attitude is the prevailing one.

Then Captain Stephenson speaks up. "Look, I'm going to speak freely here and offer my opinion. It may be out of step a little, but I feel compelled. Mr. Hyde is right, and so was the major. We need to tough things out sometimes. We need to endure. I understand if someone wants to leave, but I'm staying. And then the odds for those who choose to stay will be better."

18

THE ROOM DEVOLVES INTO chaos and cross talk.

The split between the students quickly becomes apparent. Captain Stephenson, Natalia, and Emily are arguing—at various volumes—in favor of staying and finishing the process. Duffy and Sydney are arguing back, saying the process should be halted in honor of Milo's death.

"Hold it," I say. "Hold it."

But the arguing goes on.

Coherent snippets reach me through the noise.

It's the right thing to do—

What about the money—

Somebody is dead—

We're all sorry but—

I decide I have to raise my voice. Like I'm back in the classroom settling an unruly bunch.

"Can we please stop? Can we please *stop* the yelling?"

My voice echoes through the dining room like a cavalry bugle. The students stop arguing and turn to me. Eyes wide.

"We're not going to get anywhere if we yell," I say, my voice back to its normal volume, although I hear a slight quaver in it and I hope no one else does. "Remember, Mr. Hyde mentioned comportment earlier. Let's comport ourselves like Hyde College students. We have a legacy to live up to. All of us."

The students nod. I've struck the right note, played the right card. It's tough to do as a teacher. I never know if I'm doing or saying the right thing, so when it works, I'm always relieved.

And I'm really relieved this day.

"Now," I say, "everyone has a valid point. And everyone has a right to be heard. I would remind you that Milo is one of your fellow students. And he has a family. Parents. Maybe siblings. I don't know."

"He's an only child," Sydney says. "And he never knew his dad."

"Okay. That's information I didn't know."

"His mom is bipolar, and she really can't work. That's why Milo had to pay his own way through school and take out loans. He wasn't rich or privileged. He works forty hours a week as a dishwasher in the cafeteria. He has a little bit of a scholarship, but it's not enough. He's pretty much on his own."

"Then his mother is going to want to know," I say.

"Okay," Emily says, "that's a really good point. To mention his mother. In fact, it's a good emotional argument. You're relying on our sense of pathos. You're considering your audience."

"I'm what—"

"But we all have to think of the greater good here," she says, going on. "There's Milo and his mother. Okay. That's one side of the equation. And then on the other side, there are all of us and *our* parents and *our* need to pay for school. Right?"

"Emily's right," Captain Stephenson says. "This is a tragedy, and his mother will be devastated. As a parent, well, I can't imagine that. But we *all* have families and obligations to fulfill. We all have things weighing on us. Commitments." He points at Sydney. "That word on your arm is important. 'Persistence.'"

"And then there are all the students who are going to come after us," Emily says, clearly enjoying her moment in the spotlight. She sounds like a lawyer from a TV show making a closing argument in favor of acquittal. "Mr. Hyde says the money goes away forever if we all leave. So what about all of those people who won't ever have the chance at this money? And their families? That's a lot of people lining up on the other side."

I've had plenty of students like Emily in class before. Smart. Articulate. Disarmingly able to sound like they're making more sense than I am.

"I understand that, Emily," I say. "But if we all agree to leave . . . I promise you . . . I mean, the college, the Hyde family, they would all understand why we did it."

"Those bylaws sound pretty ironclad," Natalia says.

"Truth." Duffy stands with his hands on his hips, staring at the floor. "My mom once worked for a Hyde subsidiary company. They're hardcore."

"Duffy?" Sydney turns to him, her mouth turned down, her hands raised in supplication. "I thought you said . . ."

Duffy looks perplexed. "I don't know. Can't we compromise somehow? Between the two sides?"

"There aren't *sides*," Sydney says. "Right?"

"Yes, Duffy, we should try to meet in the middle and accommodate everyone," the captain says. "But I think the people who want to go can go. The people who want to stay can stay." He points to the floor. "I'm sorry for Milo. I really am. But we can honor him by staying."

Duffy adjusts his stance, lifts one of his hands, and scratches his head. "I don't get you, Captain. You seem awfully eager for the rest of us to go. And you sure seem to know a lot about poison. I mean, you were on that right away. How do we know you aren't the one who killed Milo? After all, you're so worried about him being the best one. And now he's out of the way."

"I'm sorry—are you questioning my integrity?"

"He did perform CPR on him," Natalia says, her voice surprisingly firm.

"That's right," the captain says. "And we all poured our own drinks because we didn't want to be sexist. Either the whole pot is poisoned or just one cup was."

"Well, I'd do CPR on someone if I murdered them too," Duffy says. "I mean, that's pretty good cover."

Nicholas Hyde moves on my right. He steps forward, clearing his throat, the bylaws still in his hand. "I understand what you all are saying, but the bylaws aren't going to change. You can back me up on this, Mr. Gaines, but when someone creates a scholarship like this and they encode it so carefully, those words can't be broken or violated. It has the force of law." He turns to face me. "Isn't that right, Mr. Gaines?"

"I wouldn't say it has the force of law. The law is the law and bylaws for a scholarship are something else."

"But on this campus, Major Hyde's words have the force of law, do they not? All of this came from him. It's his legacy, as you so correctly pointed out to me earlier."

Now *he cares about the legacy,* I think. *Cares enough to invoke it.*

But what does his invocation mean? Is it another reminder that he holds the purse strings and I'm just the beggar waiting for a scrap?

"Duffy, you talked about a compromise," Emily says. "Do you have one?"

He scratches his head again. He's still staring daggers at the captain, who is giving the look right back. "No, I sure don't. I guess I'm just not that smart. Not like some people who seem to know all the answers."

No one speaks for a moment. The silence hangs over the room like a shroud.

Milo's body remains on the floor. Still as stone.

"I think I know what we can do," Natalia says.

19

WHEN THE ATTENTION OF the room turns to her, Natalia doesn't shrink.

Her giant eyes remain fixed on all of us. And everyone waits to hear whatever wisdom she is about to impart. Even I allow my hopes to rise. More than anything else, I want a way out of the spot I'm in. Something that appeases Nicholas Hyde but also manages to protect the interests of the students as much as possible.

Natalia points to the grandfather clock in the corner. Its pendulum moves back and forth. Eternal motion ticking off the seconds.

"See that?" she says. "It's ten thirty."

"So it is," Captain Stephenson says.

"We're supposed to write our essays until noon, correct?"

Nicholas Hyde nods.

"What if we all finished our essays?" Natalia says. "That's only another ninety minutes of writing. We all got the prompt and started and made some progress."

"I think I see where you're going," Emily says.

"We could reevaluate at noon," Natalia says. "We can finish the essays, and then if anybody wants to leave, they can. There's a natural break, and . . . I don't know. Maybe people will see things differently then."

"That's okay with me," Nicholas says. "But the bylaws remain in place. If anyone leaves at that time, they are disqualified. And if everybody leaves and no award is given, all of it goes away."

"I think we understand that by now," Captain Stephenson says.

"I think this is a good idea," Emily says. "Natalia's right. It provides a nice break for everyone to reevaluate what they want to do. And why waste what we've written so far?"

"Oh, my God." Sydney turns angry eyes on each of us. "Are you really going to act that way after someone died? Seriously?"

Duffy turns to her. His face becomes suffused with compassion, with understanding. "Look, Sydney, I know you're upset. And if you want to go, then you should go. In fact, if you go, I'll go right with you. I will."

Sydney sniffles, genuinely moved by Duffy's offer.

I find his offer moving as well. He's making a good case for being old-school chivalric man of the year.

"But here's the thing," Duffy says. "We can't really help Milo now, can we? And we can *hurt* all those people who want to get this scholarship in the future." He turns to Sydney again. "What does the greatest possible harm? And what does the greatest possible good? That's how I look at it when I'm caught between two tough things. I learned that in my ethics class with Dr. Zollinger."

Sydney nods. She's taller than Duffy, tall enough to spike a ball down the throats of the most fearsome competitors on the volley-ball court. But she looks young and small now.

They're all so young. Except for the captain.

Young and vulnerable. And in need of help. And yes, that in-cludes financial help.

"I can't ask you to leave, Duffy. Right?"

"But I will. I promise."

Sydney wipes her eyes again. She reaches up and pats her hair, even though it's in perfect shape.

"My parents don't have any money," she says. "My dad . . . well . . . they just don't have any money." She looks at Duffy. "My little sister wants to be a doctor. She needs to go to school, and I'm afraid I won't be able to help her. My brothers . . . they can't or won't help."

"I know," Duffy says. "Well, not really. My little brother is a dumbass. He's never going to be a doctor."

Everybody laughs a little. The mood in the room is clearly shifting in one direction.

"I think you've all shown a great deal of maturity by reaching this decision," Nicholas says. "I know it's hard. And I promise you the Hyde family will do whatever we can to help Milo's family when this is all over. That's a promise from me."

"I think that's very honorable," Captain Stephenson says.

Natalia has her small hand up. "Will it be taken into account that we had this long delay?" she asks. "I mean, when the essays are evaluated, that will be taken into account, right?"

"Everybody's in the same boat," Emily says.

"I know, but some of us have more anxiety than others. Mine's really bad."

"Yes, we will take today's circumstances into account," Nicholas says.

I can't just let everyone go back to writing the exam. Not that easily. I worry that peer pressure is winning the day.

"Are you all sure that's what you want to do?" I ask. "We can discuss other options."

"I think we have," Nicholas says. "And this one is the winner."

The students start to move back to the table, but Sydney's voice cuts through everything.

"Wait."

Hope lifts inside me. She's going to reverse and stand firm. If one of them resists, maybe more will. Duffy. Maybe others . . .

"What is it?" I ask.

"Can we . . . can we just, like . . . take him out of here?" she asks. "So we don't, like, have to look at him while he's . . . dead and everything."

Everyone looks at everybody else.

Captain Stephenson says, "This is a crime scene. The police are going to want to see everything that's going on in here."

"Did you learn that in the army too?" Duffy asks.

"No. *Law and Order* reruns."

"What do you think, Mr. Gaines?" Nicholas asks.

I remember my call with Grace Chan. My fight with Rachel over money that morning.

I know the difference Nicholas Hyde and his family's wealth can make to a school like ours. The 100 More Initiative. Generations have graduated. Generations more still can.

I sigh.

"Grab his feet, Duffy," I say, bending down. "There's a sofa in the music room."

We awkwardly shuffle with Milo between us out into the hallway and toward the front of the house. We turn left and bring Milo into the music room.

"Over there," Duffy says.

A dusty-looking sofa with pink upholstery sits against the wall, a spot from which anyone could comfortably watch the piano player and applaud their musical ability.

We swing Milo onto the sofa. His feet land on the edge of the cushions, and the body starts to slide toward the floor.

"Look out," I say.

We manage to grab him in time and gently work him into place on the sofa. His arm dangles off the side, so I lift it and place it across his chest. Then I take the other one and fold it over his chest as well.

"Is he stiff?" Duffy asks.

"Too soon, I think."

Milo's eyes are still half open, which creeps me out. And one side of his mouth is up, almost like he's grinning. I press down on the eyelids, trying to close them like people do in the movies. They kind of close. Kind of don't.

So I remain unnerved.

Duffy looks queasy.

"Here," he says. In the corner of the room sits a wooden rocking chair, and a quilted blanket is draped over its back. Duffy picks it up, beats some of the dust off it, and hands it to me. "That'll do the trick."

I unfold the quilt and place it over Milo's body, just as though he's cold and I'm trying to keep him comfortable. Except I pull the quilt up all the way and cover his face.

Duffy removes his hat and holds it in his hands, which are folded at his waist.

"It's a damn shame, isn't it, boss?"

"It is."

"My mom always says not to speak ill of the dead, but I've always heard Milo was kind of a prick."

"Really?" I ask.

"I'm not saying he deserved *this*. Whatever happened. Whether it's his heart or drugs or poison."

"Sure." We stand here a moment. "Duffy, do you think staying until lunch is the right thing?"

He purses his lips, hat still in hand. He seems to be giving my question more thought than I expected him to.

"I had to read this Shakespeare play last year for a lit class. I hated the professor, but some dude in the play says, 'Uneasy lies the head who wears the crown.' Or something like that. Did you ever read that play?"

"I don't think so."

"It was one of those Henry plays. The Fourth or the Fifth. Or was it the Sixth? I'm not sure. The point is when you're in charge it's tough to make a decision that will keep everybody happy. I mean, say you're the president of the United States. You could give everybody vanilla ice cream, and half the people would hate you because it isn't chocolate. Or fudge ripple. Or whatever. You know what I mean?"

"I think I do. Thanks."

Duffy puts his hat back on. "I grew up on a farm. Stuff died all the time. Sometimes we had to kill it. I've hunted and slaughtered stuff. Not people, obviously. But I kind of get what the captain's saying. Life goes on, you know? For the living it does."

"Yeah, but . . ."

"Family farms aren't what they used to be. And my family's been hurting for years. It's . . . We've had a rough go of it."

Duffy tells a story similar to ones other students have shared with me. Five years earlier, one of my best business students dropped out of school when her family soybean farm went belly-up. She came to my office in tears, facing the prospect of stopping her education and saying good-bye to all of her friends and professors—everything she'd grown to love about the college. But her family needed her. And they couldn't come close to making tuition payments.

Nothing has ever made me feel so helpless. Nothing has made the Hyde Scholarship and the 100 More Initiative more important to me. I hate the thought of any student leaving their education because of crippling financial need.

"To be honest," Duffy says, "I kind of took Sydney's side out there because . . . Well, you know. I've . . . for a while . . ." His cheeks flush. "We're kind of in the same big friend group, but I don't think she was very aware of my existence."

"I get it," I say. "I was a young single guy once."

"And I really do feel bad for her. I think she's taking Milo's death pretty hard. But I wanted to keep going on the exam."

"Why's that?"

"Shit, boss, because I owe sixty thousand bucks in student loans. And I need all the help I can get. This Hyde dude . . ." He jerks his thumb toward the dining room. "He's what my mom would call 'a piece of work.' And damn, he sure is wedded to all of us staying in here no matter what. He's pretty inflexible."

"But other times he's not," I say. "The bylaws spell out when we drink the bourbon, and he wanted to change that. I don't know why."

"Maybe he had a hankering for a drink. Hair of the dog, from the looks of him. Besides, a rich guy like him, he can enforce the rules any way he wants. If it suits him, follow the book. If not, screw it. That's what money allows someone to do."

"He's trying to do his best," I say. "Like all of us."

"You think so?"

"I hope so. It's odd that he rolled up here like a plastered frat boy, but that's the hand we were dealt."

"Well, I hate the Hyde family's fucking guts, but I'll take their blood money if they're handing it out."

PART 2

MIDDAY

20

THE STUDENTS WRITE FOR ninety minutes.

During that time, it's easy to believe everything is normal, that one of their classmates isn't lying dead in the other room covered by a quilt.

While the students write, I have no official duties. Nicholas keeps his distance from me. He stays on one side of the room, his book of bylaws open. He pages through them, continually licking his finger, as though he expects to find something particularly fascinating inside.

I watch the students. The room is silent except for the scratching of pen against paper, the occasional cough or sneeze or cleared throat. Students shift in their chairs or sigh, but they keep writing.

Duffy's words rattle around in my head. Why would *he* hate the Hyde family? I get it from the staff and even the faculty of the college who have seen pay and benefits cut. But can those things be strictly laid at the feet of the Hyde family? Yes, they're the college's biggest donors, pretty much single-handedly bankrolling most of the operations of the school. But it's the administration and the board of trustees who make the actual decisions.

Unless it's simply convenience. Decisions at the college are made in a diffuse fashion. Layers of bureaucracy. Faculty, staff, administrators, the board. It's tough to find any one person who could be blamed for any one thing.

But the Hydes? They loom larger than the college in some ways. The name is everywhere. The house we're in. The statue that greets everyone as they arrive.

The conglomeration of companies and subsidiaries that employs thousands throughout the state. Duffy is right. *Uneasy lies the head . . .*

The bigger you are and the greater the power and influence you have, the more people hate you.

My thoughts send a shiver through me as the students continue to write. Am I a potential target of whoever poisoned Milo? Was the brick that just missed my head an accident? The bottle thrown in my vicinity?

The poison?

Was it for Nicholas? Or for me?

Was it a giant fuck you to the whole college?

When the grandfather clock hits noon and starts chiming, Nicholas Hyde steps forward, putting aside his book of bylaws.

"Okay, everybody, you need to stop writing and put your pens down. That's the end of the written portion of the process."

A couple of students have already finished—Emily and Captain Stephenson. Some are still writing, and others appear to be proofreading, but they complete their tasks and stop when Nicholas asks them to. The students let out deep breaths and stretch while remaining in their seats.

"Mr. Gaines, do you mind collecting the exams?" Nicholas asks. "We need to collect them before we move on to the next step in the process."

While I circle the table, gathering the exam booklets, Nicholas is opening his briefcase.

"We're going to have lunch now," he tells everyone. "But before we do that, there's a tradition prescribed by Major Hyde that we must uphold, one I referred to earlier. And I think this one is going to be something you really like. Maybe more than the cucumber sandwiches and even the biscuits. And to be honest with you, I think we all deserve what we're about to partake in."

I know what comes next. And Nicholas is right—we all do deserve it.

I'm not even a big drinker, but the thought of a shot of bourbon makes my mouth water.

But I'm shocked by what Nicholas pulls out of his briefcase. Shocked because, while I've heard about it many times, I've never actually seen one in person.

21

I KNOW TRADITION DICTATES a shot of bourbon before lunch is served.

Major Ezekiel Hyde had a favorite bourbon—and it's the brand always used during the process. In fact, it's the brand of bourbon always served on campus as a tribute to Major Hyde and his tastes: Buffalo Trace, created by the oldest continually operating distillery in America. Made not far from here in the capital of Kentucky, Frankfort.

It's good bourbon, reasonably priced. Somehow it always seems to fit the image of Major Hyde—a link to the past, not too flashy. Always reliable.

The bottle Nicholas has pulled from his briefcase isn't Buffalo Trace. It lacks the familiar green top, the black-and-white image of a buffalo, animals that were hunted to extinction in Kentucky by the time the nineteenth century began, which was around the time the first batch of Buffalo Trace was made.

Nicholas might as well be holding up the Holy Grail itself, if

I'm seeing what I think I'm seeing. Gold foil decorates the top of the mostly full bottle, and the label shows a sepia-toned image of a bespectacled fat cat in profile smoking a cigar. The black script looks almost Gothic.

Nicholas holds the bottle in the air, letting everyone take it in.

I'm not sure all of the students will recognize the magnitude—or the value—of what's in his hand.

But Captain Stephenson quickly does. "No way. Absolutely no way."

"Do you all know what this is?" Nicholas asks.

"That's Pappy 23," Captain Stephenson says.

"That's right. Pappy Van Winkle Family Reserve. Aged twenty-three years. One of the rarest bottles of bourbon in the world."

"No shit," Duffy says. "My papaw used to talk about that. He had it on his bucket list to have one taste before he died."

"Did he get to?" Sydney asks.

"No. His tractor overturned on him ten years ago. Crushed his aorta."

As if we haven't seen enough death today, now we all have that image in our heads for a moment.

Nicholas quickly goes on. "Well, his grandson is going to fulfill the wish for him, because that's what we're going to toast with before lunch."

"What's the big deal about this?" Natalia asks. "I don't drink alcohol. No one in my family does."

"What's the big deal?" Captain Stephenson is ready to explain. "Mr. Hyde is right—that's one of the rarest bourbons in the world. And because it's so rare, it also happens to be one of the most expensive." He points at Nicholas. "That bottle right there can go for five thousand dollars. Or more."

"I paid sixty-three hundred and change for this one," Nicholas says, making it sound as casual as paying five dollars for a fancy cup of coffee. "I know a guy who knows a guy."

Emily's eyes narrow behind her glasses. Her pupils look like tiny polished stones. She says nothing.

Nicholas doesn't notice. Or doesn't care. Likely the latter. "The bylaws written by Major Hyde dictate that we have some before we eat. Major Hyde believed it sharpened the appetite and was good for digestion. Who am I to argue?"

"No argument from me," Captain Stephenson says.

"Mr. Gaines? I think there were some shot glasses on a tray out there in the parlor. Did you see them?"

Did I see them? He means, *Will you go get them?*

I kind of hate myself, but I do it. If Nicholas Hyde said jump, would I ask how high?

I go out to the parlor, and sure enough, a silver tray with eight shot glasses sits on a sideboard near the tea service and food in question. I lean close and sniff at all the teacups, but I smell nothing. Who do I think I am? Hercule Poirot? I look up at the portrait of Major Hyde, but he simply offers a stern glare back and offers me no help.

I grab the tray and walk back to the dining room, the glasses gently clinking against one another as I go. When I return, everyone is gathered around Nicholas Hyde, studying the bottle of Pappy—everyone but Emily, who stands to the side examining the now electric sconces like she's thinking of buying the house. I try not to think about the number of textbooks or computers that could have been purchased for the college for sixty-three hundred dollars. I focus on the tradition, the greater good. Would I trade sixty-three hundred dollars for the scholarship money to be handed out this weekend? For the 100 More Initiative?

I'd make that deal every time. I might grit my teeth, but I'd have to do it.

I put the tray of glasses down on the table, and the group breaks up as Nicholas brings the bottle of Pappy over. I should keep my mouth shut, but I need to ask a question.

"Don't the bylaws say we drink Buffalo Trace?" I ask. "If the bylaws are so rigid and strict, so much so we can't stop because someone died, can we change the bourbon choice of Major Hyde?"

Nicholas looks at me like I'm a centipede that just crawled across his bowl of oatmeal.

"Well, Mr. Gaines, you're right that the bylaws can be pretty rigid about the larger picture. But since this is my first year in this position, I wanted to bring a special treat. I thought maybe you all would indulge me. Is that okay?"

And what am I supposed to say?

Nothing. I'm going to say nothing.

"Sure," I say. "I've always wanted to try Pappy."

"Wait," Emily says. "Just wait."

She's leaning against the wall with her arms crossed.

"What is it?" Sydney asks.

Emily lifts her head and clears her throat now that she has the room's attention. Virginia Woolf stares sternly at all of us as well from a canted angle on Emily's arm. "I thought we were going to decide if we wanted to stay here at all. I thought this was the time we were going to vote on who stayed and who left."

22

A HUSH FALLS OVER the room.

Everyone exchanges looks, but no one speaks.

Nicholas holds the bottle of Pappy by the neck, and the pendulum in the grandfather clock swings back and forth with a faint tick, marking the time.

"We've all finished the written exam now," Natalia says. "We're halfway through. . . ."

"What are you saying?" Nicholas asks.

"It seems like if we're halfway through, it would be pretty easy to finish," Natalia says. "You know, just continue on."

A couple of students nod—Captain Stephenson and, surprisingly, Emily, who proposed the vote-taking compromise. And who has seemed all along like she couldn't wait to get out the door, scholarship or no.

Inevitably, everyone ends up looking in Sydney's direction, waiting to hear from her. She's rubbing her hands together but not speaking.

I decide to give her time to think. And a little help.

"Conversely," I say, "everyone is in the exact same place right now. You've all finished the written part of the exam. There's a natural stopping place here, like Emily said earlier. We could just call it a day."

Duffy's face is puzzled. "But then we'd be blowing it for future generations. We already covered that."

"I think . . ." Sydney's voice makes us all turn to her again. She continues to knead her hands together and doesn't look up, even though all eyes are on her. "I think there's, like, something you all should know about Milo. Something important."

We all wait. And I brace myself for a disturbing revelation.

Sydney goes on. "It's just . . . Well, his politics were very important to him. He really cared about other people and doing the right thing. That kind of thing mattered to him. He wanted to make a difference. That's why he wore that shirt. Right?"

She stops talking. She raises her thumb to her mouth and nibbles on a loose piece of skin none of us can see.

"I know that about him, Sydney." Duffy tries to help her out. If this were a volleyball game, he'd be setting her up for a spike. "All Milo's friends know that."

Sydney smiles in a forced way. "That's why I think we should stay. He wouldn't want everyone else to stop just because he . . . well, because he . . . you know . . ."

"Passed away," Captain Stephenson says.

"Yeah," Sydney says. "Passed away."

Everyone nods, solemn as church deacons.

Nicholas steps forward. "I guess we don't have to vote, then. We know how everyone feels—"

"I think we should still vote," I say. "I think it's important to go on record with what we all think."

Nicholas takes a step closer to me. He speaks in a low voice that the students can no doubt hear. "Are you sure you want to do that?"

"We agreed to take a vote, and I think we should take one. So show of hands. Who wants to stay and finish the second half of the process?"

For a moment, no hands go up. Nobody moves.

Then Captain Stephenson's hand goes up. Followed quickly by Nicholas's.

Then Natalia, Emily, and Duffy raise their hands.

Finally, Sydney lifts hers. And since she has the longest arms of anyone in the room, it looks like she's almost reaching the ceiling.

Every eye in the room turns to me. It doesn't matter. I'm clearly outvoted. But I did say everyone should go on record with what they really think.

The students stare at me, waiting. But it's not them I notice. It's Nicholas. He's watching me, his face hopeful. His eyes are wide, his face encouraging. He wants me to join in, to be one of them. To do what everybody else is doing.

I might have received a call from Grace Chan that morning, and she spoke to me like she's my boss. But I know who I really work for. And why.

It's simply a no-brainer.

I lift my hand.

The process continues.

23

NICHOLAS WASTES NO TIME.

As he fiddles with the bottle, I decide to make conversation. "How did everybody feel about the written portion? Do you feel good about your essays?"

Duffy runs his hand down his bolo tie. "Writing was never really my strong suit. I'm better at digging in the dirt, making things grow."

"It was a good question." Captain Stephenson rocks back and forth from his toes to his heels. "It gave us all something to sink our teeth into."

Emily adjusts her glasses. "Milo was the best writer in the school. Remember he won that award last year? The one given by that local group?"

"The Optimists' Club," I say.

"I think he won five hundred dollars for that," Emily says.

Natalia makes a sound like she's clearing her throat, but she doesn't speak.

"What was that?" I ask.

"Nothing," she says. "I remember he won that prize. I entered too and finished second."

"Really. Congratulations."

"Thanks." Natalia is looking at Emily. "English is my second language, so I've had my struggles, but you're an English major, so this is right in your wheelhouse, writing an essay."

"I guess." She adjusts her glasses again, even though it seems hard to believe they moved at all in the few seconds that passed since the last adjustment. "I just got honorable mention in that Optimists' Club contest. When I told my parents about it, my dad said honorable mention is like kissing your sister."

"Harsh," Duffy says.

"But you did have a poem published in the campus literary magazine. Right?" Sydney turns to the rest of us. "Emily and I took creative writing together freshman year. The professor hated all of my poems. I wrote about volleyball a lot. I guess it, like, could have been boring for someone who's not a fan."

"I don't know," Duffy says. "Volleyball poems. That could be a unique thing. A niche, right?"

Sydney smiles at Duffy, glancing at him from the corner of her eye. Her freckled cheeks flush. "Well, maybe. I remember that poem you wrote, Emily. The one about starting college and how exciting it was. It perfectly captured how I felt too. Right? I guess that's what makes a great poem, when you can tap into what other people are feeling."

But Emily is shaking her head. "I hate that poem."

"Why?" Sydney seems genuinely hurt by Emily's denial of her own freshman-year poetry.

"It's so . . . I don't know. Naive. Simple. Like I just used to believe everything everybody told me. I was so dumb back then."

"Weren't we all as freshmen?" Duffy says.

Everybody nods, and Captain Stephenson says, "I was a dumb freshman too. And I was forty-two years old with two kids and a wife."

"No, seriously," Emily says. There's an urgency to her words as if she really needs to say this to all of us. Here and now. "I was such a product of who everybody else wanted me to be. My religion, my politics. It all came from others. I was a little drone. A worker bee. I'm glad I'm not like that anymore."

Today's students are tomorrow's alums. And donors. So I never miss a chance to extol the virtues of Hyde College. "We aim to educate the whole person. I'd hate for any one of you to be the same person when you leave Hyde as you were when you came in. That's progress."

Emily turns away. Maybe my little commercial is too much. Or maybe she doesn't think Hyde College had anything to do with her transformation. Sometimes fundraising requires a great deal of patience. Donors can be courted over the course of many years. And alums can take a long time to be in a position to donate anything back to their college.

I know my time with Nicholas is short. I can't be too patient. Not with Grace and the board breathing down my neck.

As if on cue, we all hear the sound of the cork being pulled out of the bottle of Pappy. It makes a satisfying pop. Then Nicholas is pouring the amber liquid into the glasses I ferried in from the other room. The gurgling of the bourbon refreshes me. When he's finished, he returns the cork and smacks it into place with the palm of his hand.

"It's time for our toast," he says.

Captain Stephenson rubs his hands together. And I have to

admit, I'm excited too. I've always wanted to try this most famous and most rare drink. And I'm about to have my chance, thanks to Nicholas Hyde.

"I know you're all twenty-one," Nicholas says. "So feel free to give it a try."

"If you don't feel like drinking or don't want to, you don't have to," I say. "That's okay."

"Unless the bylaws require it," Duffy says, laughing to himself. "Heck, I hope those bylaws let me go to the bathroom at some point."

I expect a laugh from Nicholas, but he's irritated. "It's okay if someone doesn't want to drink. The bylaws require a toast, but I guess they don't specifically *require* that everyone drinks in the wake of the toast. There's toasting and then there's drinking. Still, I don't know why anyone would pass up this rare chance. Given the cost, it's once in a lifetime. For most of you."

Natalia shrugs. "I said I don't drink. I'm not *opposed* to it. Besides, this sounds like something I may want to try."

"That's the spirit," Nicholas says, and he starts handing out glasses of bourbon to each of us.

24

DUFFY RAISES THE GLASS to his nose and takes a few sniffs.

"Mmmmm."

Captain Stephenson swirls the bourbon in his glass, which I always thought is something you do for brandy or cognac. But I'm no expert.

I can't help it. I follow suit and bring the glass up to my face, taking a few sniffs of the most valuable liquid I've ever held in my hand. It smells . . . a little like maple syrup. A little like vanilla. A little like the white oaks that stand outside. I know it's aged—for twenty-three years—in oak barrels.

My mouth waters like a dog's. The bourbon actually smells like money.

Nicholas has his book of holy writ out and places it on the dining room table. Everyone is spread around the perimeter. Nicholas takes his own glass, and his hands shake. With his free hand, he finds the correct place in the book and stabs the page with his index finger.

"Before we drink," he says, "a few words in honor of Major Hyde."

Everyone grows mildly impatient with the insistence on ceremony. Even Captain Stephenson looks like he's ready to disregard the rules and throw back his shot. I too wish we could skip this part. Theodore Hyde used to rush through it as quickly as he could, knowing that everyone was hungry and the summary of Major Hyde's life did little to move the students. But Nicholas insists on reciting every word.

"'When Major Hyde returned from the Civil War,'" Nicholas reads, "'he found himself possessed of an intense desire to matriculate at the University of Kentucky to complete his education in the classics. But the pain and terrors of the late unpleasantness had left his family's finances in grave tatters, and his beloved father, Clement Hyde, found himself stricken with a series of ailments that rendered him unable to care for either the family or the property. Alas, Major Hyde was faced with a nearly impossible choice. Attend college and fulfill his own long-delayed dreams of higher education. Or forgo that crystalline vision and care for his family.'"

Nicholas scans the students in front of him. "Which option do you think he chose?"

"Spoiler alert," Emily says. "He skipped college and took care of his family."

"That's right," Nicholas says, either unaware of or ignoring the trace of snarkiness in Emily's tone. Nicholas appears to be off script now. He's speaking his own words to the group and not reading out of the book.

"I didn't know all of this until very recently. I always assumed Major Hyde attended college, and that gave him his interest in education. But it turns out he didn't go. He worked, and as he became successful, he paid for his younger brother, Rodney Hyde, to attend medical school and become a doctor." He turns to me. "Did you know that, Mr. Gaines?"

"I did. That's why the building that houses the biology department is called *Rodney* Hyde Hall. In honor of the major's brother."

"Oh, that's who Rodney Hyde is," Natalia says. "I always wondered."

"He founded the hospital here in Bluefield," I say. "And it's still going."

Nicholas finds his place again with his finger and completes his toast. "'This exemplary commitment to family, community, and education is why Major Ezekiel Hyde created the Hyde Memorial Fellowships and Scholarship. He wants others to have the educational opportunities he never had.'"

Everyone seems relieved. And really ready to drink.

But Nicholas goes on.

"You know," he says, "it's funny. All these years I thought about Major Hyde going to college, and now I know he didn't. He's a self-made man, one who pulled himself up by his own bootstraps without a formal education. The truth is, we're kind of missing that toughness as a country, that willingness to work and work to get ahead. As I've learned more and more about this process over the past few weeks, I've really started to ask myself about the value of higher education. It's so expensive these days, insanely so. And isn't that why you all are here? Because of the ridiculous cost of an education?"

A ripple of unease passes through the room. Perhaps they too recognize that Nicholas is off script and rambling.

"That's why we're all so grateful to Major Hyde," I say, hoping to move things along. "And your family."

"No," Nicholas says, "just think about it. All of this exists because of Major Hyde, but he didn't go to college. Many other successful people didn't. For example—"

"I know," Emily says. "Bill Gates. People always break that one out when they're trying to say you can make it without a college degree."

Nicholas stares back at Emily. He winces at his thunder being stolen. "Yes, he's one example. Of many. As another example, I never completed my college education. I started at Pepperdine but never graduated. I'm about three semesters short of a degree. And I don't think I'll ever finish. Fortunately"—his words stop like he's lost his train of thought—"fortunately, my mother never cared about that. . . . She supported me no matter my choices. . . ."

A moment lingers while no one speaks.

"What's Pepperdine?" Duffy asks.

"A college in California," Captain Stephenson says.

"Malibu, to be exact," Sydney says. "They have a volleyball team. The Waves. They're really good."

"Well, we are on a schedule—" I say.

Captain Stephenson interrupts me. "It's pretty easy to say forget about college if you're born into a certain kind of family. Isn't that right?"

No one says anything contradicting or supporting Captain Stephenson's statement, but I can tell from the body language they all agree. I agree as well and am glad he said it.

Nicholas stares into his glass. "Some members of my family haven't always held me in the highest regard."

"I'm sorry to hear that," Captain Stephenson says. "But all of us"—he makes a gesture toward the other four students—"all of us are here because we feel we need to go to college. And we need to find a way to pay for it without going bankrupt."

"And I'm glad all of you are here," I say.

"I guess I was just thinking that there's a big world out there," Nicholas says, "and there's more to it than Hyde College. I mean, even if one of you wins this, the rest of you would have to find a way . . ."

"We're all probably pretty skilled at finding a way," Natalia says, touching a giant button on her cardigan. "We've probably all been doing so for a while. I know I have. My family's been doing that as long as they've been in this country."

"Well," I say, "we probably shouldn't let this good bourbon just sit here. And then we have a meal to eat."

"That's right," Nicholas says, lifting his glass. "Let's all drink a toast to Major Ezekiel Hyde. And the Hyde family. Whatever remains of it."

We all go ahead and drink.

25

IS IT POSSIBLE FOR bourbon to be better than sex?

Possibly not. But the Pappy 23 comes damn close. Damn close.

It's the smoothest bourbon I've ever swallowed in my life. Everyone else seems to agree with my assessment. Faces light up and cheeks flush as they swallow, even Natalia's.

"Wow," Sydney says. "I totally got sick on Jim Beam my freshman year. I mean, like, really sick. And I haven't touched brown liquor since then. But this is so smooth."

"I'm not sure what six thousand dollars tastes like, but this must be it," Captain Stephenson says.

Nicholas is holding his empty glass. A melancholy washes over him, and I immediately worry he's offended by the pushback on his comments about college. Even the world's most expensive bourbon can't go far enough to relieve my concerns about courting the college's most important donor.

I move next to him. "Did you want to say anything else?" I ask. "What did you think of the Pappy?"

Nicholas continues to contemplate his empty glass like it holds all the secrets of the world. "I don't have anything to say. Maybe we should all get moving toward lunch. I know we're on a schedule."

"That would be fine if you're ready."

"We just go load our plates in the kitchen and bring it back here?" he asks. "Is that how Ted did it?"

Ted? Not Dad. *Ted.*

"That's how he always did it," I say.

"Then who am I to argue?"

"Your dad always did read the menu to everyone," I say. "But if you don't want to—"

"Why don't you do it?" he says.

"Sure. If that's what you want."

"That's what I want."

The students are all looking at us. It reminds me of the times Rachel and I argue in front of the kids, and they stare at us like they aren't sure what to think. And that thought—and the one about bourbon and sex—makes me think of Rachel. And how I'm going to have to wait until four o'clock to talk to her again.

It's worth it, I remind myself. *I'm doing all of this for her. And the kids. For the future.*

I'll have to tell her about Milo—and the way we voted to stay and finish the process even with a dead student in the other room. The greater good. Always the greater good.

"Okay, everyone," I say, trying to sound like a cheery coach, "it's time we went in for lunch, which is waiting for us in the kitchen at the rear of the house. It's buffet-style, and the way we do it is everyone goes back and fills a plate with food. Then you bring it out here to the dining room, and we all eat together. Just as Major Hyde preferred. Would you like to hear the menu?"

"I'll eat just about anything," Duffy says.

But Emily and Sydney exchange a look, and Sydney says, "Are we sure it's safe to eat anything in this house? Whatever happened to Milo, if it was poison, it might be in that food. Right? I mean, what if someone wanted to poison all of us?"

"I don't think I'm eating anything," Emily says.

"I understand," I say.

Captain Stephenson raises his hand. He holds it high in the air until I nod at him.

"If I may, sir, I do believe Milo was poisoned. But if it was in the food and drink from this morning, then someone else would have ingested it. And if someone ingested it this morning, there's just about no way that person wouldn't already be feeling the effects. Or be deceased. And I'm assuming no one is sick?"

Everyone shakes their heads.

"I have to believe we're in the clear, sir," the captain says. "Whatever happened to Milo happened before he arrived here. Or he had a bad heart, which is why he passed out that time in class."

"I'm still not eating," Emily says. "I have a lot of allergies anyway. Gluten and dairy."

"No one has to eat if they don't want to," I say. "Just like drinking was voluntary."

I try to take comfort from Captain Stephenson's words. There's a logic to them. If Milo was poisoned here, why hasn't anyone else fallen ill? Couldn't he have eaten something before he arrived? And this is all assuming he really was poisoned and didn't suffer a seizure or an aneurysm or something else. Ten years earlier, when I'd been at Hyde College for only a few years, a student collapsed and died in a colleague's math class. The cause—an undiagnosed heart condition. Cardiomyopathy. Isn't it possible something like that happened to Milo? Something tragic but undetected?

"Who would like to hear the menu?" I say.

"I would." Duffy raises his hand.

"I'm hungry," Natalia says, holding her empty glass in the air. "Somebody told me once that drinking alcohol increases your appetite."

"So," I say, "the lunch menu has been the same for one hundred fifty-two years. It's a menu chosen by Major Hyde, consisting of some of his very favorite dishes. We're going to have rabbit, grits, wax beans, and, for dessert, buttermilk pie."

Nicholas stares into his glass.

Five students stare back at me, their faces somewhat blank.

"Rabbit?" Emily says. "Are you kidding me? You killed a rabbit?"

"Probably more than one to feed all of us," Duffy says. "It's pretty tasty, really. I'm not sure about the wax beans, though. Whatever those are."

"They're like green beans," the captain says.

"See why I'm not eating?" Emily says. "No real thought for vegetarians."

"We can—"

"Just eat the damn beans and the grits," Nicholas says. He slams his empty glass down on the table and walks out of the room. "I have to take a leak."

Everyone stands around with their mouths hanging open. Emily looks angrier than she has all day.

I decide that—for good or ill—Nicholas has provided us with a natural break.

"Why don't we all eat something?" I say. "And on the way, you're all welcome to take a bathroom break. There's one restroom by the kitchen and another by the parlor. I'll see you all when we're back here with our food."

26

I LEAVE THE DINING room and step into the hallway. Murmured voices reach me—the students chatting as they wait for the bathroom.

There's no sign of Nicholas. He must be in the bathroom, cooling off. Not a bad idea. I need to use the facilities and then get food for myself, but before I can, I hear something from the front of the house.

At first, I think it's the students waiting for the bathroom. Laughing or talking.

But the noise sounds more desperate. Sadder.

Is it someone crying? Or talking? Speaking in a low, harsh voice . . .

I think I know where it's coming from.

I go down the hall toward the music room, and as I approach, I think I make out the words being spoken.

I'm sorry.

Is that what's being said?

Sydney stands before the couch that holds Milo's quilt-draped body. She stands there with her arms folded across her chest, looking down at his shape.

It's an intensely private moment, but I can't just leave her here without asking if she needs help.

"Sydney?"

She turns quickly like a sleeper startled from a dream.

"Are you okay?"

She nods her head. Her eyes and cheeks are dry. "I'm fine."

I move farther into the room, closer to her side. "Is there something I can do for you? Anything you want to talk about?"

"Not really." Her eyes trail back to the shape on the couch.

"So, it seems like you and Milo were pretty good friends."

"Yeah, we were. I mean—yeah, friends. Or, you know, like that."

My daughter Rebecca experienced her first real heartbreak in the fall. She broke up with—or more accurately was dumped by—a guy she'd been dating for a few months. Rebecca cried for two days straight, and no amount of hugs or support from Rachel or me made a difference.

"Well, I'm sorry," I say. "What happened to him is terrible. And I promise you we'll find out why it happened. The college will get to the bottom of it."

"Have you ever known someone, but you could, like, only get to know so much about them? Like there was a wall or a barrier to what you could reach with the person?"

"I've experienced that before."

"That's what it was like with Milo. Only so far, you know? Like, did he really have a heart condition and not tell me?"

"Sometimes people are harder to get to know when they're

young. Maybe especially young men. They have more walls up because they're afraid."

She looks over at me. "You're saying young guys get better as they get older?"

"Some do. Most, maybe. I hope so."

"I should have just been patient."

Should have just been? Meaning—she wasn't?

"I just mean that as we all get older we look back on our past selves and we can see the mistakes we've made. And the ways we've improved. I've told my own girls that. So I'll share that wisdom with you. It's free for being here today."

"Thanks."

"Do you want to take another moment alone and then come and get something to eat?" I ask. "Unless the rabbit offends you."

"You have daughters?" she asks.

"Three of them. Just a bit younger than you. Rebecca, Robyn, and Rita. Rachel is my wife's name, so . . ."

Sydney uses the thumb and index finger of her right hand to twist a silver ring that circles her left middle finger.

"I wanted to leave earlier," she says. "When this happened to Milo."

"You don't have to stay," I say. "If you changed your mind—"

"My dad died when I was, like, twelve." She continues to twist the ring, then nods at her arm. "That's this tattoo, *LJM*. His initials. Actually, we think my dad was, like, murdered."

"Oh, I'm sorry."

"He was cheating on my mom. And I guess the woman's husband found out. The cops said he was drunk and fell, but my mom and I think he got beat up." She stops twisting and shrugs. "I guess it doesn't matter. Right?"

"Sydney, maybe all of this is too much. Maybe you need to go. I can try to get the chief, and we can open the doors."

"I want you to know that I stayed in here because of my little sister. Like I said, she wants to go to medical school, and my mom works two jobs. See, everyone thinks that because I'm on the volleyball team and have a scholarship that school is, like, free for me, but it isn't."

"I know that. Hyde doesn't offer full athletic scholarships. We're too small."

I also know Hyde offers a small scholarship of some kind—academic, athletic, artistic—to every student who applies. Most struggling private colleges are willing to knock a small amount off the tuition bill and call it a scholarship just to appeal to vanity and attract more students.

"My scholarship for volleyball is, like, two thousand dollars. That about pays for my books some years."

"I hear you."

"I'm staying for my family. Not because I don't care about Milo. My brothers, well, they just—they haven't really done anything with their lives." She shakes her head. "I thought they'd be taking care of my mom and sister once Dad died, but instead, they just, like, disappeared from the scene. My mom's boyfriend moved in, and he's . . . It's not good. He's a creep. Not good for my sister. I want to get her out so she can go to school. She's sixteen."

"That's a lot to deal with."

"It is, but I'm trying."

"I understand," I say. "These aren't easy choices. For any of us."

Sydney reaches out and places her hand on my arm. She grips it tight. She's strong—an athlete—and her fingers dig into my flesh.

"That's it," she says. "Choices. Everybody makes choices." She points at Milo's body. "He made choices, and so did I. You see? And I'm doing what I have to do to take care of my family."

"By staying?"

"By doing what I can to get that scholarship," she says. "That's what I have to do."

"Sydney?"

We both turn. Duffy stands in the doorway. "Sorry," he says. "I was looking for Sydney."

"I'm here," she says.

"I was going to get some food," Duffy says. "I think it's safe. And I thought maybe we could sit together. If you wanted."

"Okay, yeah, sure," she says. "I don't really want to be alone now anyway."

They both leave, and then I follow them.

27

I STOP IN THE bathroom, which is empty.

I wish I'd held on to my phone so I could call Rachel. But she knew I was going to surrender it—we've done this the last four years—and she won't be expecting to hear from me all day.

I'm then the last one in the buffet line, behind Sydney and Duffy, who are speaking to each other when I come into the room and clam up when they see me. I catch one word as I come in, and that's Duffy saying the word "hardcore."

He said that word earlier in reference to the Hyde family. And I remember what he said after we placed Milo on the couch in the music room. Apparently the most interesting conversations happen while standing over corpses. Duffy told me he hated the Hyde family but never explained why.

Now doesn't seem like the time to ask.

Duffy's face changes. A smile grows, like the sun emerging from behind clouds.

"Hey, Mr. Gaines, have you had rabbit before?"

"Each of the last four years. Right here. And once in Texas I had a rabbit burrito."

Sydney wrinkles her nose, but she has her plate filled. So does Duffy.

"What happens in these interviews we have to do?" Duffy asks.

"It's pretty standard really. You meet with Mr. Hyde, and he asks you questions related to the topic of the written exam. Or, I suppose, anything else he thinks is relevant."

"And we do that in the dining room? With everybody watching?" Duffy asks.

"Usually we do it in the—" I stop. "Maybe we can do it in the parlor."

When we're through the line, we return to the dining room. Natalia and Emily sit next to each other. Captain Stephenson sits by himself. Duffy and Sydney sit across from Natalia and Emily.

And there's no Nicholas Hyde.

"Where's . . . ?"

"We thought he was with you," Captain Stephenson says. "Maybe planning the rest of the day."

"No."

"Is he in the bathroom?" Emily asks, pleased with herself. "He seemed kind of pissed at me."

"He wasn't in the bathroom by the kitchen."

"I was in the other one," Natalia says.

"Maybe he . . ."

I put my plate down at the end of the table, leaving the spot at the head open for Nicholas. Something creaks above us.

"What was that?" Sydney asks.

"Is he upstairs?" Natalia asks.

"What exactly *is* upstairs?" Duffy asks. "Anything?"

The ceiling creaks again.

"Back in the old days," I say, "that's where all the bedrooms were. For the Hyde family when they lived here."

"How many of them?" Duffy asks.

"Major Hyde was married. And he had four children who lived to adulthood."

"What does that mean?" Sydney asks.

"It means it used to be a tougher world." Captain Stephenson doesn't really break his eating rhythm while he talks. The fork keeps going to his mouth. "This is delicious."

"Major Hyde and his wife, Mary, had seven children," I say. "But three died before the age of two. Scarlet fever and diphtheria."

"Oh, gosh," Emily says. "That's brutal. I hate to hear about children dying."

I'm still standing next to my empty chair, my hot food cooling in front of me. The creaking happens again. Maybe Nicholas just needs time to cool off. And it's best to leave him alone.

Upstairs.

"What's up there now?" Duffy asks.

"Just the bedrooms, like I said. With the original furniture. There's some stuff stored up there as well. Memorabilia. Things that belonged to the major."

"Things from the war?" Captain Stephenson perks up.

"Most of those things are in a museum in Bowling Green."

Surprisingly, Emily is digging into her food. Her plate is nearly clean already. "Maybe we can all go up and see the gun that slaughtered those Johnny Rebs."

Captain Stephenson shakes his head but remains quiet. He keeps working his fork.

The bottle of Pappy is gone.

"It's not here," the captain says. "He must have come back in and grabbed it before he went wherever he went."

The floor creaks above us.

"Maybe we won't have to stay all day," Duffy says, leaning in close to Sydney and laughing. "Maybe my boy is tying one on upstairs and won't be able to finish the rest."

"Sir, if that were to happen—"

I hold my hand up and cut off the captain's question.

"Why don't you guys keep on eating?" I say. "I'm just going to go upstairs and make sure everything is okay."

The sound of silverware scraping plates continues as I head for the stairs.

"At least try to bring back some of that Pappy," Duffy says. "I wouldn't mind having a little more."

28

THE STAIRS CREAK AS I go up.

My hand slides over the bannister, worn smooth as ice over the years. I can imagine the Hyde children—the ones who survived infancy—running up and down these stairs, their shoes clacking, their laughs and shouts echoing through the space. Just like my own children do in my house. How much did Major Hyde worry about the futures his children were going to have? Haunted by the Civil War and devastated by disease, did he worry more than a parent would today? Even though he quickly amassed a fortune, did that alleviate the fears all parents have?

When I reach the top, I hesitate and listen.

Straight ahead of me is a bathroom, which is clearly empty. Bedrooms surround the landing in every direction. One of them, the one on my immediate right, has its door closed.

"Nicholas?"

No response. I orient myself to the layout of the house, notice that the bedroom with the closed door sits above the dining room.

I move closer and lean in, the side of my face almost against the wood as I listen.

Silence. Then the sound of liquid sloshing.

"Nicholas?" I rap against the door with my knuckles. "It's Troy Gaines. Can I come in?"

"Sure." The voice sounds distant and small.

I push the door open. The walls of this room are painted a dark green. A large four-poster bed occupies most of the space, and to the right is a heavy oak dresser with a tarnished mirror. Nicholas sits in the corner, close to the room's lone window, in an antique rocking chair. He's staring out toward the campus—and the protestors in the distance—the bottle of Pappy in his left hand, the bottom of the bottle resting on his knee. I'm relieved to see most of the precious liquid remains. He hasn't thrown back too much of it.

The floorboards creak as I cross the room and sit on the edge of the bed. He keeps his face in profile, staring outside.

"Everybody's eating," I say.

"Hmm? Oh, good. Even the vegetarian?"

"She said she's from Alabama, so she can at least eat grits."

I hope to get a laugh—or at least a smile—out of Nicholas, but he acts as though he hasn't heard me.

"Is there anything I can do for you, Nicholas?"

He extends his hand, holding the bottle of Pappy in my direction.

"No, thanks," I say although my taste buds cry out for more. "Would you like to come downstairs and eat with the students?"

"What did your dad do for a living?" he asks.

"He was a college professor. He taught political science at the University of Missouri."

He turns to me for the first time. "So you're in the family business too?"

"I guess so."

"In fact, if you're an administrator, you're doing better than he did. Right?"

"I don't know about that. Maybe he was smart to stay in the classroom until he retired. He was good at what he did, and he stuck with it."

"You wouldn't want to let him down, would you?"

"No, I wouldn't."

"So you see why I need to stay here and do what I have to do today," he says. "Admit it—you didn't even think I was going to show up today, did you?"

"Well, I—"

"Just admit it."

If I'd known we were going to have true-confession time, I would have taken the bottle of Pappy when he offered it to me.

"You're right," I say. "I didn't know if you were going to show up. I haven't heard from you for a while, and then you were late. But you're here now."

He looks out the window and starts rocking back and forth gently. "Thank you for being honest with me. I appreciate that. I do."

"Sure. If you want more honesty, I think we should have left when Milo died. I don't think following the bylaws and proving you're not actually the black sheep of the family is more important than a young man's life. But I went along with it because everybody else wanted to. And I need my job. And your money."

I worry that I've gone too far, that I've so offended Nicholas he may storm out of the house entirely and turn his back on the whole endeavor. Instead, he laughs and turns back to me.

"Wow, I guess I really did open the honesty floodgates there."

"I guess you did."

He continues to rock, the Pappy on his knee. He points at me with his dirty pale finger. "You know what? I like you, Troy."

I conceal my surprise that he knows my first name. Then again, I did just say it when I knocked on the door. Maybe the reminder helped.

"My mom always told me to trust my gut, and I didn't always listen. But I like you. And that . . . What is it? Thousand More . . . What is it?"

"The One Hundred More Initiative," I say. "To get more underrepresented students into the college."

"Students like the guy who won't stop talking, Captain America or whatever? Or that Natalie, right?"

"*Natalia.* Yes, they both would have qualified when they applied."

"That's your pet project, isn't it? Kind of like a legacy thing. Right?"

"In a way, it is. I'm not without vanity. I want to help diversify the school and give all kinds of students the chance to come here and get educated. I think that would help everyone. But sure, I wouldn't mind having my name associated with it. You have a permanent legacy here." I gesture at the house and beyond—to the campus grounds. "Your name—and your family's name—can go on forever. Permanent. It would be nice if my daughters could someday say that their dad helped secure the money that allowed historically underrepresented students to go to college. Yeah, I think about that. I also think about being able to keep my job."

"More honesty."

"Just like you being honest and telling the students they don't really need to go to college," I say. "An odd approach for a guy whose family bankrolls a school."

"Hey, what do I know? I'm a child of privilege. Maybe my opinion shouldn't count. That's what the world seems to be saying about guys like me. And maybe even you." He points at me again. "But you know what? I like you. And I like that . . . One Hundred . . ."

"The One Hundred More Initiative."

"That's it. The One Hundred More Initiative for the— What am I allowed to call them today? Underprivileged students? Minorities? Poor? What's the correct term?"

"We're thinking of them as historically underrepresented students. That's what I said."

"Fancy term. Why don't you and I nail that down today? After all of this is over, we can talk about it."

Warmth spreads through me. It starts in my feet and moves all the way to my face, where I can't stop a smile from forming. "I'd like that. Very much."

"Maybe today's a day for both of us to nail down a legacy," he says.

"I agree."

Nicholas extends the bottle of Pappy toward me. "Maybe we should drink on it?"

"I like that idea."

Before I can take hold of the bottle, a voice calls up the stairs. I think it's Natalia.

"Mr. Gaines? I think you really should come down and see this."

29

I'M OFF THE BED so fast I almost fall.

I reach the stairs as my mind swirls.

Someone else is dead. Someone else is dead. Someone else is dead.

But as I descend the stairs, the students are gathered around the foyer. I do a quick head count. All five are there. All standing, none the worse for wear.

So then, what's the problem?

When I'm all the way down and standing among them, I ask, "What's the matter?"

"We believe our perimeter has been breached, sir." Captain Stephenson points to the front door. "We heard something shatter and then yelling."

"A window?" I ask.

"We don't know," Duffy says.

The stairs clack behind me. Nicholas's swanky boots against the wooden steps.

I go toward the front door and veer into the music room. The group follows along behind me, and when I enter, my eyes can't help but drift to the left, to the misshapen lump under the quilt.

Outside, through the surprisingly clear glass, the remains of another shattered bottle lie on the front walk, about ten feet from the portico steps. In the yard, it looks like a rugby scrum. Two protestors have broken through the police line and rushed Hyde House. One of them, a young woman in black jeans, a black leather jacket, and with hair dyed the same color as her clothes, yells at the house, her face contorted into a mask of rage. A campus police officer—a woman with her brown hair pulled back in a ponytail—has grabbed ahold of the woman and is either attempting to pull her away from the house and behind the barricade or is trying to get handcuffs on her wrists.

"I know her," Duffy says. "She was in my business law class. Kylie? Is that it?"

"Kylie Conway," Natalia says. "Her hair used to be fake blond."

The protestor's voice is muffled by the glass and bricks, and I can't make out what she's saying. I'm not sure it's necessary to know the exact words. She hates the Hyde family and all they represent, and she's letting it be known in no uncertain terms.

The officer, who isn't much bigger than the protestor but is clearly stronger and trained in restraining what Chief would call "miscreants," gains the upper hand and manages to turn the woman back toward the barricade. The protestor offers little resistance, satisfied perhaps with getting through and saying what she had to say to the front of the house.

The other protestor resists more. A young man, hair perfectly coiffed into an Elvis-like pompadour, wears two cops on his back as he lies spread-eagle on the lawn of Hyde House. He's also wearing dark clothes, and his horn-rimmed glasses sit askew on his face, which is being pushed toward the grass by one of the cops.

"I don't know that dude," Duffy says. "Anybody?"

"I think I talked to him at a party once," Sydney says. "Didn't he, like, flunk out?"

"He did," Natalia says. "Michael Braun. He still lives in Blue-field."

Chief mans the barricade by himself. I expect at any moment for all the remaining protestors lined up there to charge through the line like extras from *Braveheart*. Chief could do nothing if they made that break, and Hyde House might succumb to the onslaught of bottles and bricks and taunts, allowing the protestors to succeed in their desire to disrupt the process.

But none of the other protestors join the two runners before us.

While one cop pushes the bespectacled guy's face into the dirt, the other works a pair of handcuffs out of his belt and begins to apply them to the protestor's wrists. The man squirms on the ground, writhing his torso and kicking his feet, which makes it increasingly difficult for the cops to manage him. Finally, the cop with his hand on the protestor's head gives it a solid shove into the dirt, and the young man grimaces as though he's in real pain.

Someone gasps behind me. One of the women, but I can't tell which one.

"That's bullshit," Sydney says.

"He should stop resisting," the captain says.

"So it's okay to rub his face in the dirt?" Sydney asks.

"I didn't say that." The captain's voice is sharp. "The police shouldn't do that. Not at all. I just wish . . . I wish he wouldn't re-sist. It's all very complicated."

The protestor stops moving as much, and the cops manage to get the cuffs on him. Each cop takes one of the young man's arms, and they haul him to his feet. Once he's up, one of the cops—the one who shoved his face against the ground—actually steps in front of the kid and adjusts his glasses for him, making sure they won't fall off as they walk him away.

"Those cops are a mere twenty feet away," Natalia says. "If anybody wanted to knock on the window, you could get their attention. I mean . . . we could tell them about Milo."

Nobody turns, but we all know his body rests on the couch behind us.

And Natalia is right. The cops are within easy hailing distance for the first time all day. A good thumping against the window might just get their attention, and they could come over and let anyone out who wanted to get out.

Or they could take Milo away.

My right hand tenses. It forms into a fist, one that could easily knock on the window and summon the police.

But I also remember what I spoke to Nicholas about upstairs. He has a job to do as a member of the Hyde family. As the sole heir of the Hyde family.

And I have a job to do as well as an administrator of this college. If that door opens to the police right now, and they know about Milo, the whole day will be over.

And the Hyde Scholarship money might go. And the 100 More Initiative along with it.

My fist loosens and my hand remains at my side.

The police maneuver the protestor, one on each side, and start back for the barricade.

As they go, the kid looks back at the house and screams something.

And what he shouts becomes a problem.

30

THE PROTESTOR'S WORDS ARE hard to understand.

He's partially facing away when he shouts, and he's no doubt winded and overwrought from his encounter with the police.

"Memory," he shouts. "Screw it. Screw it."

"What?" Duffy asks.

As if the guy outside hears Duffy or understands our confusion, he looks back at the house again and shouts even louder.

"Memory! Blew it! Screw it!"

And then he's hustled away even faster, following in the footsteps of the other cop and the other protestor, who have already reached the barricade, which Chief casually opens for them. Clearly he has already decided no one else is going to run. Or maybe a stern talking-to and a laser-focused look from the chief have cooled any fervor to come at the house.

Or maybe seeing how quickly the police jumped on the two protestors—including the guy getting his face jammed into the dirt—has lowered tensions to a simmer.

We're all bunched together at the window, close enough to hear everyone breathe, and I want us to get back to the work at hand without any more issues.

And I want us to leave the room that holds Milo's body.

"Why don't we all head back to the dining room?" I say. "I haven't eaten. And I know Nicholas hasn't either. We should before—"

"Wait, wait, wait," Sydney says. "I want to talk about what that guy just said. The one they just dragged away in handcuffs."

"Can we discuss it while we eat?" I ask.

Sydney ignores me. "You all heard it, right? I mean, it was clear as day."

A tension fills the room, oozing into the spaces between the seven of us and settling in like a fog.

"I don't get it," I say. "He said something about . . . a memory? Or was he talking about family? I assume he wants us to remember, well, something about . . . a family?"

Nicholas holds the Pappy bottle in his left hand. He has more color in his cheeks than at any time all day, and I hope our soul-baring conversation and his commitment to the 100 More Initiative has invigorated him.

"It doesn't really matter what he's shouting. And if you're worried about them, I have a feeling the college isn't going to press charges against them. Maybe a slap on the wrist—"

"I heard it too," Natalia says.

"Heard what?" the captain asks.

"What the guy said as they were leading him away. I heard it clearly."

"Memory?" I ask. "Or did he say 'family'?"

"I didn't hear a damn thing," the captain says. "But my wife thinks my hearing's bad from all the time I spent on the gun range. She might be right."

"Not *memory*," Natalia says, one index finger raised. She speaks to me like I'm her elderly grandfather who has started seeing and hearing things that aren't there. "He said 'Emily.' *Emily*. You heard it too, Sydney, right?"

"I did."

"Now, wait a minute—" I say.

"That's such bullshit," Emily says. "He didn't say my name. You heard Mr. Gaines. He said the word 'memory.'"

"Or family," Nicholas says. "One or the other. I'm sure he's angry at my family. He can join the club."

"This is such bullshit, Natalia," Emily says. "You couldn't hear what that guy said. Nobody could. He's shouting outside through that thick glass. But you've never liked me. You're pissed because of the way you got picked on in the dorm freshman year. And you've always lumped me in with those girls who harassed you."

"Hold it," I say. "Hold it. We can't—"

Now Sydney steps forward. "This morning, you were out there with the protestors. Remember? Chief had to walk you in, and he said you showed up there by mistake. But how do we know it was, like, a mistake? You probably hated Milo because everyone thought he was a better writer than you. A better writer than anybody on campus. Especially since you're an English major."

"Are you kidding me?" Emily asks. "I don't care about that."

"You were talking about it in the other room. During tea. You and Natalia went off to the side and started talking. About sophomore seminar . . ."

"I wasn't in that seminar," Emily says. She points. "That was all Natalia saying that. I was making a different point. About someone else . . ."

Natalia seems small. Very small. But she thrusts her chin out again the way she did on the portico. "I don't want to speak ill of the dead. My family doesn't believe in doing that."

"Bullshit, Natalia," Emily says. "What did you tell me in there?"

Natalia waits a moment. I can't tell if she's choosing her words carefully or taking a dramatic pause. "Okay," Natalia says, her eyes widening even more. "He cheated. Milo cheated on all his papers. We had peer workshops, and I ran one of his through Google Scholar. He lifted whole passages. That's why it's not right that everyone thinks he's a great writer. He plagiarizes. I reported him in sophomore seminar and the professor ignored me. For all I know he cheated on his essay for that contest, and that's how he managed to win. I mean, come on, we all just want a level playing field of some kind."

"Is that why you're so obsessed with citing sources?" Duffy asks.

"I don't like any of this," Nicholas says.

He speaks in a normal voice, but somehow he carries an authority and an ability to redirect the students that even I don't.

Everyone stops talking, and they all turn to him.

"Remember," he says. "*Comportment.* We're just about to start the second half of the process, but my dad always told me to not forget about comportment. And all of this . . ."

I take my opening. "Look, I don't know what that guy said outside. I don't know if he said someone's name or not. And even if he did say the name of someone inside this house, what does that mean?"

"If she's in league with the protestors and she hated Milo—"

I cut Sydney off. "Enough. We can't speculate. This is a small campus. We all know a lot of people here. We can't just assume the worst about any of us. Or anybody else for that matter."

"Thank you," Emily says.

"You're welcome."

"I mean," Emily goes on, "okay, I do know Michael. I'll admit that. Hell, this place is so small that if I deny it, one of you will contradict me. I know him. But that doesn't mean anything. And I don't think he said my name. He said 'memory.' That's all. *Memory*. Like, *remember* what the fucking Hyde family has done to the planet. That's what he means."

"Easy, now," Nicholas says.

"Sir?" Captain Stephenson has his hand up. Again, like we're in class.

I really don't want to hear his opinions on the situation. But then again, I welcome the diversion.

"Yes, Captain?"

"I had an idea, sir. Something I was going to suggest earlier but didn't. And now it seems like the right moment. Something to bring us all back together. To unite us."

Does he mean sing? Trust falls? I'm not sure where he's going . . .

"What are you talking about, Captain?" I ask.

"With Mr. Hyde's permission, of course, and assuming we have time and can manage to try something a little off the course of those pesky bylaws. Well, I just thought it would be a nice gesture if we all got together and drank a toast to Milo. To honor him and to mark his passing."

It sounds great, but it's not my six-thousand-dollar bottle of bourbon to hand out.

Nicholas appears a little misty-eyed. He holds up the bottle.

"Captain," he says, "I think that's a fucking fantastic idea. Shall we all head into the dining room?"

31

BACK IN THE DINING room, we all stand around the table again. The plates and food debris from lunch still sit here. The students mostly managed to finish, but my plate is untouched. And I know Nicholas hasn't eaten anything since the morning. I'm not sure how much Pappy he swallowed while he sat alone upstairs.

The mood remains tense. Emily stands at the far end of the table where she originally sat, and she refuses to make eye contact or engage with anyone around her. I can't say I blame her. I don't think the guy outside said her name, and even if he did, what does it prove?

That she knew one of the protestors?

There's a pretty good chance every student in the room knows one of the protestors, maybe even one of them who threw a brick or a bottle at the house. Does that prove anything except that it's a small campus?

The empty glasses from the first shot of Pappy remain at everyone's places, and once we're gathered, Nicholas goes around the room, filling them up again. I wonder about the effect two shots of bourbon will have on the students as they prepare for the interview portion of the process. But then I look on the bright side—maybe it will loosen them up, help them relax. After all, most of them probably drink more than I do. And I anticipate the soothing properties of the bourbon. With everything going on, I barely felt the first one at all.

Nicholas returns to the head of the table and again smacks the cork into the mouth of the bottle of Pappy.

"Well, Captain," I say, "would you like to lead the way?"

"Thank you, sir." The captain bends down and picks up his glass of Pappy. "Look, it's been a difficult day so far. For all of us. It's stressful enough to have to come here and participate in this exam."

"Process," Nicholas says.

"This *process*. But we have agitators on the outside. And we lost one of our comrades on the inside. Thanks to the beneficence of Mr. Hyde, we have this wonderful bourbon to drink. And it only seems fitting that we would use it to make a toast to Milo, a young man cut down in his prime. I didn't know Milo. Not at all. We just met today. But from everything I've heard about him to-day, he was an intelligent young man. With a bright future. And I think we should honor his loss and his memory with some words we use in the army. 'The girl and boy are bound by a kiss. But there's never a bond, old friend, like this: We have drunk from the same canteen.'"

The captain raises his glass in the air, but before he takes a drink, he looks at me and then at the other students.

"Would anyone else like to say anything?" he asks. "After all, you all knew him better than I did. So it's only fitting you would speak about him as well."

For a moment, we all stand there. For some reason, I find Captain Stephenson's military toast oddly moving—and appropriate. People are always slow to speak up in these situations—just as they are in the classroom—so I let the silence play out.

Nicholas clears his throat next to me. "This is tough. I don't know Milo at all. We were talking about climbing in there." He nods toward the parlor. "He was entranced by the sport, as am I. And he was teaching me some things I didn't know." He clears his throat again. "I guess sentiment and such things aren't my strong suit. But . . . well, anyway, he seemed like a cool guy. Real salt of the earth. Real Hyde College material. Someone I'd like to hang out with. And climb with. And I'm sorry I won't get that chance now."

Everybody nods.

But Nicholas goes on. "Loss is hard. Very hard. I've known some lately . . . painful loss. It's crippling, to be honest. Just crippling."

Things grow awkward, and no one wants to look at Nicholas.

"Dude was smart," Duffy says, saving us. "That's what I know about him. Really smart. And he partied hard too. Sometimes too much. My roommate, Steve, kind of knew him. Told me Milo once downed a six-pack before a calc exam, and he aced the thing anyway. That's smart, man. Real smart."

A few people laugh.

Natalia says, "Well, I didn't know Milo that well. I mean, just from that one seminar. But I'm sorry this happened to him. I mean, I'm just sorry for anybody who dies. I'm going to pray for him. And I'm going to ask my grandmother to pray for him too, which is practically a direct line to God. That's how devout she is."

"That's great," the captain says.

I wait a moment in case either of the other students who haven't spoken—Sydney or Emily—wants to say something. And when they don't, I go for it.

"I didn't know Milo either, since I don't really get to know the students the way I used to. But everything you've all said is right. He seemed like a fine young man and an outstanding student. Maybe I'm thinking of myself as well, as a parent, but I'm thinking about his mother, who we heard mentioned earlier. When she finds out . . ."

My vision swims. In my mind's eye, I see my girls—all three of them. And Rachel. I'm not able to get any more words out.

Nicholas takes a step closer and pats me on the back. "You okay, man?"

"I'm good. I'm good." I clear my throat. "Yes, I just wanted to say that about Milo's family. And friends. You're right about loss being hard, Nicholas. I lost my mother five years ago. It's not the same as losing a child, but . . . 'crippling' is the right word."

It seems that perhaps the toasting and speechifying have run their course, that everyone who wants to say something has. But then Sydney lifts her glass into the air.

"Well, Milo," she says, "I guess this is how it ends."

She stares at the glass like it's the only object in the room. And rather than offering a tribute, she seems to be speaking directly to her deceased friend, just as she did when I walked into the music room earlier and she apologized for something.

"You once told me that karma is a bitch, which seemed like kind of a harsh way to look at things. But maybe you were right.

Maybe I should have listened to you. I guess everyone is right. You are—*were*—smarter than all of us."

Her words put an odd kind of punctuation on the toasting.

I, for one, am ready to throw back my drink. But I know Emily hasn't said anything. I want to make sure she has a chance to speak if she wants, but I also don't want to make her more uncomfortable.

I pause a moment. If she doesn't speak, we'll go on. But Captain Stephenson steps in.

"Emily, you haven't said anything. Would you like to?"

My grip tightens on my glass, wondering what she'll have to say. I can't be sure, but I think I notice a hint of a smile growing on her face.

"Drink up, everyone," she says, lifting her own glass and taking a big swallow. "Happy days."

32

EMILY'S TOAST—OR LACK of one—in honor of Milo adds to the tension.

Everyone sips from their glasses, but there's a muted, obligatory feeling to it.

I try to think of anything that might swing the mood in a positive direction. I sound like my grandmother, but it's the only thing that comes to mind.

"Who wants to go back for seconds?" I ask. "That food was delicious, wasn't it?"

Captain Stephenson nods at my untouched plate. "Did you even take a bite?"

"I didn't. Not yet this year. But I've had it before, and it's always good." I look over at Nicholas. "And I don't think you had anything. Why don't you go get a plate for yourself?"

"I'm fine," he says. "I don't eat much." He drains a decent amount of the bourbon from his glass. "In fact, maybe we should get on with the rest of the process. We have the interviews to carry out. That's the afternoon portion. And I need to . . ." His voice trails off. He turns one way and then the other. "Shit."

"What's the matter?" I ask. And I really don't want to know if anything else is the matter. I've had enough of that for one day. For one year, really.

"My briefcase," he says. "I don't . . . I must have left it upstairs when I was sitting up there. You came up to talk to me. . . ."

"I can go grab it, sir," Captain Stephenson says.

"No," Nicholas answers quickly. "That's okay. I can't let— I mean, I need to go get it. I appreciate your offer, Captain, but I'll go get it. I remember where I left it." He looks at me. "In the meantime, what do we do about . . . ?" He nods to the table, which is covered with dirty plates and silverware and water glasses.

"Oh," I say. "Well, in years past, we just carried our stuff out to the kitchen. The dining staff comes in when the process is over. We can do that while you get the briefcase."

"Excellent."

Nicholas leaves the room, drink in hand. We all start gathering up the mess.

"If you stack them," Duffy says, "I can carry them to the kitchen. Back home, I worked summers as a busboy at Bob Evans. I can stack dirty plates almost to the ceiling and carry them."

"Then we're going to take you up on that," Sydney says. "But no tips."

There's a lot of clanking and clattering of dishes and silver, but pretty soon Duffy has his hands full. I grab some remaining pieces of silverware and follow him out.

"Why don't you all chill out until we start the interviews?" I say.

Nobody responds. Even the captain holds on to his glass of bourbon like it's a life raft.

My leg bumps against something, and I freeze. Nicholas's briefcase is sitting on the floor against the table leg.

"Oh," I say.

"What's that, sir?"

"The briefcase. It's here, not upstairs. Maybe— Never mind. He'll be right back."

I follow Duffy out to the kitchen. He places his stack of dishes in the sink, and then I add what I'm carrying. He finds a towel and wipes his hands and passes it over to me.

"It's been kind of a crazy day, hasn't it, Mr. Gaines?"

"I don't think 'crazy' is an adequate word."

Duffy looks back toward the entrance to the kitchen, making sure no one else is around. I follow his eyes and see no one either.

"I'm kind of glad we're here like this," he says. "I wanted to tell you something."

"Sure," I say.

"It's about Sydney. I'm kind of worried about her."

"I see. You mean, because she and Milo are friends."

Duffy makes a disgusted noise deep in his throat. Kind of like a bone is stuck there.

He goes over to the kitchen entrance and sticks his head out into the hallway. Satisfied the coast is clear, he comes back and stands close to me.

"More than friends," he says, "at least as far as she was concerned. We talked about it outside on the . . . What did you call that porchico thing?"

"Portico."

"That's it. My roommate dated her roommate at one time. Well, 'dated' is kind of a loose term for what they did. You know how it is."

"I used to."

"It's not really my thing. I mean, I just don't have a lot of luck in that department. I go home a lot of weekends and work on the farm. Or at Bob Evans during the holidays. It's frustrating. . . . People think because I joke around and stuff that I'm easygoing, but I'm not. College has been a little lonely for me."

"The fellowship money will help your finances. And maybe you'll get more if you win the whole thing."

"I hope so. My mom sure does. But anyway, about Sydney. She and Milo did have a thing going on. That's what I heard from my roommate. Steve. Not really dating exactly. Casually dating. That's what Milo does a lot around campus. He was kind of known for it. A lot of girls liked him. You know, he's smart and good-looking and shit. I guess. And, you know, the student population is about sixty percent women. The odds are supposedly stacked in favor of the straight guys. Hasn't helped me much, but there you go. Maybe girls aren't interested in a farmer. I showed up here as a freshman with cow shit on my boots."

"It's more like fifty-seven percent women. But I see your point."

The floorboards above our heads creak again. And then there's the sound of water running. Nicholas is using the bathroom upstairs, which I assume means he'll be coming back down soon.

"Milo just stopped dealing with Sydney. Just cut her off. I guess that's also the way he does—did—business with the ladies. And Sydney was very upset about it." Duffy pats his pants. "See, if I had my phone or if anyone had a phone, I could show you. But apparently she posted some stuff on his Instagram. Harsh shit calling him out for being an asshole."

"Are you saying you think Sydney had a reason to hurt Milo?"

I remember Sydney standing over his body. And what she said before I walked in the room, those words I heard: *I'm sorry.*

"To be honest, Duffy, it's pretty clear you're having some feelings for Sydney yourself. So why tell me all this?"

"I'm trying to protect her from people saying that crazy stuff," he says. "When we get out of here, everybody's going to go wild, trying to assign blame for what happened. And they're going to dig into all kinds of motives. Well, Sydney has a pretty good one. She was tossed aside by Milo, and then she said all that stuff on social media. A lot of people saw it."

The kitchen faucet drips, a steady beat below our conversation. I reach out and twist the handle, hoping to shut it off.

"I appreciate you saying this to me, Duffy. I do. And I know Sydney's pretty upset about Milo. We all are. But they seem . . . they seem close. They walked up together this morning."

"He was probably coming out of another girl's room when he ran into her."

"It's hard to believe anyone's going to jump on blaming Sydney too much. It's one thing to have your heart broken. That happens to all of us along the way. But it's a big leap to go from there to killing someone. There's no reason to think Sydney would do anything violent."

Something crosses Duffy's face. A shadow that changes his expression. He taps his boot.

"What is it, Duffy?" I ask.

"You don't know about her getting suspended from the volleyball team last year?" he asks.

33

"WHAT ARE YOU TALKING about, Duffy?"

"I thought everybody knew. All the students heard about it."

"Well, the students hear about a lot of things that the administrators and faculty don't," I say. "And sometimes the athletic department likes to keep matters in-house."

"True enough. I was a student manager on the basketball team my freshman year. I thought about walking on. I played a little in high school, but I don't think I'm good enough. I like to watch and think about the game more than play it. You know, strategies and substitutions and stuff. I might want to coach someday, work with kids."

Footsteps rumble down the stairs. They sound expensive—like leather boots hitting one-hundred-fifty-year-old wood.

I raise my finger. "Hold on, Duffy."

I step out of the kitchen. Nicholas comes down the stairs. He reaches the bottom and turns toward the dining room, carrying a now-empty glass. His shirt is completely untucked, and I wonder if he was getting sick in the bathroom.

"Are you ready to get moving?" he asks.

"The briefcase," I say.

"What?"

"The briefcase. You went upstairs for it?"

"Oh, yeah." He looks back up the stairs. "I guess I . . . I mean . . ."

"It's down here. In the dining room."

"Right," he says. "That's what I thought. Great, let's get going."

"Yeah, just one second. If you go on in, we'll be there."

"But we're kind of in a hurry now," he says.

"Okay," I say. "I mean, to be frank, we picked up a little time. We have one less interview to do."

"Yeah, well, still . . ."

"Okay, I'll be right there."

Nicholas goes on into the dining room, and I head back to the kitchen, where Duffy waits for me.

"We should probably wrap this up," I say. "The boss man is getting impatient all of a sudden. Can you tell me about Sydney?"

"I should keep my mouth shut. Really, I just assumed you knew."

"I didn't know, but if it's relevant to what we're doing here, you should tell me. My knowing might help Sydney."

"Okay, real quick," Duffy says. "There was this freshman on the team last year. She came from a small town, never been away from home before. And some of the other players were giving her a bad time. Making fun of her accent, calling her a farmer and shit like that. I can relate, clearly."

"Okay."

"The men's and women's teams sometimes practice together since gym space is limited. And one of the male players picked up on this stuff, calling the freshman names too. Sydney told him to back off, and he wouldn't. He just kept riding the girl until she was almost in tears. So Sydney went up to the guy. She threw one punch. And I mean it was a direct hit. Right in the nose. The dude was bleeding all over the place. Apparently, Sydney has two older brothers in addition to the little sister she mentioned, so she knows how to throw a mean punch."

"She was protecting someone from bullying," I say. "Right?"

"Maybe. But some people say she and the dude she clocked were, you know, *involved* as well. And that she wasn't really trying to protect that freshman as much as she was trying to get back at that guy. See what I'm saying? If I know that, then all the students know it. And that's going to come out when we leave here and everybody finds out Milo is dead. And Sydney was in this house too."

"He was probably poisoned before he got here. *If* it was even poison. And wouldn't it make more sense to do something to him somewhere else on campus instead of here?"

"There are more suspects here. All of us closed in. Competing."

"Duffy, the anger of 'a woman scorned' thing isn't much of a theory anymore. Let's just keep this to ourselves. Okay? You need to concentrate on the interview that's coming up."

He nods. "Okay. I just wanted to get that off my chest."

"No worries."

"It's just—when you couple it with what she did in high school, it might make her look really bad. And I don't want to see that."

He starts to go, but I reach out and place my hand on his arm. "Hold up. What about high school?"

Duffy sighs. "I didn't want to mention it. I figured you might not know about that."

"About what? And you did mention it, so you must have wanted to."

Duffy sighs again. His eyes move around the room, inspecting everything but avoiding me. Finally, he says, "Okay, since you asked. Sydney went to juvie when she was in high school. Six months in the lockup."

"How do you know this?" Something prickles at the back of my neck. Little needle jabs.

"We have a lot of the same friends. People talk."

"Well, if it's just talk—"

"When she was in high school—junior year, I guess—they had a teacher who was giving some of the volleyball players a rough time. A math teacher. He was going to fail a few of them, and if they failed, they couldn't play. And if you can't play, then, you know, you can't really get recruited. Sydney's really good. She thought she was going to play Division One before this happened."

"Before what happened?"

"Well, she and some of the other volleyball players who were going to fail, they came up with a plan. I guess Sydney ran with a tough crowd in school. She grew up outside Chicago."

"What did they do to this teacher?" I ask although I don't really want to know.

But I have to. I have to know anything that can affect the day's events.

Or that might relate to Milo's death.

"They cooked up some plan to kidnap the guy," Duffy says. "You know, jump him in his car, drive him someplace remote. Then—I don't know—threaten him until he changed the grades. It all sounds pretty asinine out loud. Anyway, they tried to jump the guy, but it turns out he was a martial arts champion in college. One of Sydney's friends brought a knife, but this math teacher disarmed her and took care of things until the cops arrived."

"Shit."

"Yeah. Sydney got six months. You really didn't know this?"

"I didn't."

"That's why she really didn't get recruited by a better school. But she has that athlete's mindset. If something gets in her way, she just runs it over. You know? Never take no for an answer."

"Duffy . . . Okay, we need to get back." The needles in the back of my neck poke me with greater intensity. "I try not to make too much of what people do in high school. We're all stupid then."

"Sure, of course."

But I can't dismiss Duffy's story as easily as I would like. If true—and I don't know if it is—it means Sydney has a violent streak. A serious one.

And if she wanted Milo gone for some reason . . .

"Let's just keep this to ourselves, Duffy. Okay?"

"Sure. But it's possible everybody knows. They for sure know about the volleyball thing. They might know about her stint in juvie as well."

"We don't have to spread it. Okay?"

"Sure, boss."

"Hold on, though." I step closer and lower my voice even more. "Why are you telling me this if you're her friend?"

"Isn't it better to hear it from a friend?"

"When we were in the music room earlier—you know, moving Milo in there—you said something about hating the Hyde family. What were you talking about? Did you say your mom worked for them?"

Duffy's about to speak when Emily steps into the hallway from the dining room. "*Mr.* Hyde says he's ready to start, and he wants you both to come back. I guess we're all at his beck and call now."

"We're coming," I say.

Emily's eyebrows knit together behind her giant glasses. Then she shrugs and turns around.

When she's gone, I say, "Well? What is it?"

He starts to speak, stops. Then he shrugs as well. "I'm an ag major. I hate what they're doing to the environment as much as those freaks outside do. I just don't smash stuff up over it."

"That's it?" I ask.

"Sure. Isn't that enough?"

"Yeah, it is."

"Aren't you sick of babysitting him?" he asks, smiling.

I give him a friendly smack on the biceps. "Let's go back. The best revenge is winning their money."

34

WE'RE GATHERED AROUND THE dining room table. All five students in their places.

Nicholas stands at the head of the table and unlatches his briefcase.

His hands shake again as he does so, and I really wish he would have eaten something instead of just drinking who knows how much Pappy on an empty stomach.

But I'm not his mother, so I keep my mouth shut and let him go.

My eyes roam around the room, stopping for a moment on Sydney. My mind trails back to her arrival alongside Milo. Their close conversation, her vigil over his body.

Her propensity for violence.

Nicholas brings out his leather book of bylaws and opens to the correct page. He glances at it, then speaks quickly, like he thinks someone is going to come along and yank the book out of his hand.

"As you know, of course, the final portion of the process will begin now. And it consists of a personal interview to be conducted by the presiding officer"—he looks up—"and Vice President Gaines here." He points at me, then looks at the book again. "The personal interview will be a chance for you to demonstrate your oral communication skills and also allow us to have a better sense of who you are as an individual. We may ask you all the same questions. We may ask you all different questions. There are no set questions for this portion of the day. This is one place the bylaws allow for a little flexibility."

As he speaks, a slight ripple of panic spreads through me. I have no questions prepared. No idea of what to even ask.

Nicholas goes on. "We may look over your essays and use them as jumping-off points for our questions, so you may see this interview as a chance to expand on, explain, or clarify things you wrote in the essay. Then again, we may not bring the essay up at all. We'll just have to see." He slaps the book shut. "Any questions?"

I'm surprised. I know there's a letter from Major Hyde he's supposed to read—one that discusses the "manly virtues" of speech and oral communication. His father, Ted, read it each of the last four years. But Nicholas seems to be in a hurry, and do I really want to cause any additional distractions or trouble?

"Where will these interviews take place?" Captain Stephenson asks.

"In the—well—" Nicholas turns to me. "You said you thought the parlor would be best. Isn't that so?"

"I think we can use the parlor," I say. "We can even slide those pocket doors shut for privacy."

"And how long does the interview take?" Sydney asks.

"Each student has thirty minutes allotted," I say. "So no more than that. But it could be less."

Natalia might be about to lift her hand, but before she can get it all the way up, Nicholas says, "Great. If you don't mind, Vice President Gaines and I are going to go to the parlor and make sure everything is ready and set up the way we want it. When the time comes, we'll call the first student in. Oh, and we're going to go alphabetically. By last name. Vice President Gaines?"

I stand up, ready to get to work.

"And then they open the doors?" Natalia asks.

"What's that?" I ask.

"After the interviews, they open the doors?"

"That's right," I say. "Chief unlocks the doors at four o'clock. So we have to be finished with everything by then."

"Then let's get moving."

Nicholas puts the leather book inside the briefcase and starts walking out of the room. I follow along behind like his faithful valet.

It feels weird to leave the students alone without any instructions, so on my way out, I say, "You can talk amongst yourselves. Or eat more. Or just, you know, get focused. Whatever you want to do."

Five faces look at me blankly, so I leave.

35

IN THE PARLOR, NICHOLAS stands by the tea service.

His briefcase sits on the floor by his feet.

"We could move those two chairs together, and we can sit there." I point to another chair. "And we could drag that one over for the student to sit in."

"That's fine." He sounds tired.

"Do you want to get something to eat?" I ask. "The food's back there in the kitchen, and you didn't touch it. There're a few minutes."

"Maybe."

But he remains rooted in place, staring at the floor. I start to move the chairs around, making a sitting area where we can ask the students questions. I intend to let Nicholas lead the way since it's his show, and I'm just the second-in-command.

While I'm moving the chairs, I say, "I really appreciate what you said upstairs."

"Upstairs?"

"About the One Hundred More Initiative. I have to be honest. I was worried you'd forgotten all about it. I haven't heard from you since the fall, and I thought maybe you decided to take the money somewhere else."

As I slide one of the chairs next to another, it clips an end table and sends an empty vase toppling over. It just misses the area rug and lands on the hardwood, where it shatters.

"Shit."

Nicholas seems not to have heard or noticed.

I attempt a bad joke. "Glad nobody's ashes were in there."

He continues to ignore me.

I brush the glass shards out of the way with my foot and try to be more careful. The wood varnish of the chair arms is chipped and peeling, the fabric stained and worn. But isn't it better to spend the money on people and not things? Isn't that what I'm in my job for? Sure, it's nice to have buildings and statues and gardens, but if we can get money that actually helps people . . .

I walk across the room to move the other chair into place.

"I think this One Hundred More Initiative is really going to change the way people think about the Hyde family. It's a unique, powerful plan. A game changer."

Nicholas belches behind me. "You mean the protestors . . ."

"Not them. Maybe you can't make them happy. I mean the community. The town, the school. The larger world." I get behind the chair and start pushing it across the room, sliding it over the area rug. "We'll probably get some national press out of this. I'm not saying that's the only reason to do it, but it will help the college. I bet our number of applicants goes up overall, thanks to this."

"A rising tide . . ." Nicholas's voice trails off, like he's falling asleep standing up.

Is his night of partying catching up to him at last?

I pick the chair up to try to keep it under better control. And that works. But when I put the chair down, it makes a loud thump against the carpet.

"Whew," I say.

A nice place to have a conversation, in front of the fireplace under the watchful eyes of Major Hyde. There's no fire, because the chimney was deemed unsafe in an inspection about a decade ago, but you can't have everything.

"Lifts all boats," I say, finishing the thought. "Would you like to sit? I can go bring in the first student if you're ready."

Nicholas looks peaked and pale. He pulls a limp tissue out of his pocket and pats his forehead. A piece of the tissue breaks off and sticks to his skin just above his right eye.

"Milo," he says.

"Milo? What about him?"

"I meant what I said . . . about helping his family. . . ."

"I'm sure you did."

"His mother . . . A mother shouldn't . . ."

"I'll do anything I can to help."

"A good kid . . ."

"Did you know him before—"

Nicholas wobbles a little. He puts his hand out against the marble-topped table, steadying himself.

"Nicholas? Would you like to sit? Or can I get you some water?"

He doesn't answer. Like a felled tree, he pitches forward, face-down onto the carpet, with a sickening thump.

"Holy fuck."

I rush to him, turn his body so he's on his side. His nose is smashed and bleeding like a faucet. His body starts to convulse. His limbs twitch. His torso thrashes in my arms.

A gurgling sound comes from deep in his throat. His eyes bug out as giant as cue balls.

He looks like he's dying. . . .

He looks . . . exactly like Milo did.

"Captain? Hey! Everybody? Help!"

36

THE ROOM FILLS.

I'm surrounded by feet and legs as I still kneel on the floor.

The captain is down next to me, and he takes over. Mercifully. Thankfully.

He sticks his fingers into Nicholas's mouth and works them around. He lifts his torso up and slaps him on the back a few times, trying to make sure his airway is clear.

Then the captain eases Nicholas back to the floor and begins chest compressions. Just as he did with Milo a few hours ago.

"What the fuck is going on here?" Sydney asks.

No one answers, but she speaks for all of us.

The captain continues with his work, pressing against Nicholas's chest over and over. But his eyes have rolled back in his head, the color draining from his face like a tide receding. His nostrils are covered with blood, a smear across his cheeks. His body moves with each compression, but that's it. He's stopped convulsing. He's limp. Lifeless. The tiny speck of tissue remains on his forehead like a surrender flag.

Empty.

I stand up, my knees creaking. The students are bunched tight, all staring down. Only the captain remains on the floor. He keeps pushing and pushing.

"Come on, damn it. Come on. Not this bullshit again. Not this."

"Captain?" I say.

"No, sir. Not another one. Not on my watch."

I reach down, place my hand on his arm. I apply gentle pressure. "It's okay. You tried. You really tried."

"Sir . . ." He doesn't say anything else. He leans back, putting his weight on his heels. He's sweating again. His forehead and cheeks are soaked. He's breathing hard. "Sir, I tried. . . ."

"I know you did. I know."

The captain exhales long and loud. It's the only sound in the room before someone sniffles.

"What happened to him?" Natalia says. "It's not the same thing, is it? He's not really foaming and seizing the way Milo was."

No one else says anything. The room is strangely quiet. Uncomfortably so.

"Captain, what do you think? Was he poisoned?" I ask.

"It could be, sir. He was seizing some. But the blood . . . not much foaming. Different people can have different reactions depending on the amount ingested."

"Holy shit," Sydney says. "Was it the food?"

"He didn't eat," I say. "I know that. He went upstairs, remember? And when he came down, I tried to get him to eat something because he looked weak, but he wouldn't."

"What else happened in here?" Duffy asks. "You came in here with him alone."

All eyes are on me. "We came in here and looked at the layout of the room. I suggested we move the chairs so we could do the interviews. He seemed to be okay with it, so I started pushing the chairs around. Like they are right there." I point. "I talked while I did it. I told Nicholas—we had talked upstairs in the bedroom about another donation he's making to the school, something I've been working on for a while. He finally agreed to do it. Before the toast to Milo."

"You were alone with him upstairs and then down here?" Duffy asks.

"Yes."

"What was he doing upstairs?" Emily asks.

"Nothing. He got pissed earlier, remember? And stormed out. Then he went back up to look for his briefcase. When we talked, he was sitting in one of the bedrooms upstairs. In fact, I think it's the room that Major Hyde's oldest son, Leander, lived in when he was growing up."

"Leander?" Emily asks. "Like Hero and Leander?"

"Yes. Leander went out west, joined the cavalry. He died out there. Somewhere. Utah maybe. California."

"How did he die?" the captain asks.

"Nobody knows," I say. "And it doesn't really matter now. Probably one of those awful diseases that killed everybody a hundred years ago. But I talked to Nicholas upstairs. He had the bottle of Pappy in his hand. He agreed to fund this initiative I'm trying to get off the ground to give scholarships to underrepresented students. He said he'd do it, and he promised a lot of money for it. Then he came back down. You all saw that."

"And nothing else happened in here?" Duffy asks.

"No. We talked. I thanked him for the money, told him how much it mattered." I snap my fingers. "He mentioned Milo. Said he meant it when he said his family would help pay for Milo's funeral. He told me to see to that. And I said I'd do anything he wanted."

"And then . . . ?" the captain asks.

"He collapsed. He looked like shit. Pale and weak. I offered to get him food and water. But he said no. Then he went down like he'd been struck by lightning. Right onto the floor."

"He and Milo were talking this morning," Duffy says, "about climbing."

"Did they know each other before today? Do any of you know?" I ask.

"Not me," Emily says.

"Milo liked to climb," Sydney says. "He loved to, really. Maybe they met at a climbing gym or something? Or in a park? Milo liked to go to Red River Gorge. Maybe Mr. Hyde went there."

"Is that how Mr. Hyde's nose got smashed?" the captain asks. "When he collapsed?"

"Yes, of course."

Everyone kind of shifts their feet.

"What?" I ask.

Emily says, "We heard all that . . . noise. Like something slamming around."

"The furniture," I say.

"It kind of sounded like a fight. That's what some of us thought. And then . . ."

"It wasn't a fight," I say. "Why would we fight? He's a donor."

"Well, Mr. Gaines," Sydney says, "you two seemed to disagree about leaving or staying. You were pretty certain back there that we should go. And *he*"—she points at Nicholas on the floor—"really wanted everyone to stay. So, like . . ."

"Did you talk about leaving when you were alone?" Duffy asks.

"We talked about it upstairs."

"Okay, sir. I guess you didn't reach any accommodation then. I can imagine you don't want the scholarship money to go away. Even if Mr. Hyde is a challenge to deal with."

"He was poisoned. Like Milo. That has to be it. I'm the one who wanted to leave. Remember?"

Again a silence descends.

It's Emily who breaks it. "I thought we weren't sure Milo was poisoned. And if he was, you said it happened before he came in here. Right?"

"Then what the hell's going on?" Natalia asks. "What is all of this?"

"Isn't it obvious?" Sydney says. "We're totally getting picked off one by one."

37

"WHAT DO WE DO now?" Natalia asks. "Sydney's right. They're picking us off one by one."

"*If* it's poison . . ." the captain says.

"*If* it's poison? We have tea in the morning—somebody dies. We have lunch at noon—somebody else dies. What exactly does that tell you?"

"Okay, but Mr. Hyde didn't eat lunch," the captain says.

"But he drank." Sydney stands with her hands clenched into fists, ready to run.

"We all did," the captain says. "The same stuff. The same bottle. We all had two shots. And Milo probably had a heart condition."

"*Maybe* he did," Sydney says.

"So are we all about to . . . ?" Emily looks more curious than scared.

"Anybody sick?" I ask. "Symptoms? Anything unusual at all?"

"Does being terrified count?" Duffy asks.

"Any indigestion?" the captain asks. "Headaches? Nausea? Anything?"

I'm not sure what we expect. Somebody's head to explode? An alien to emerge from somebody's chest? We wait, each of our bodies a ticking time bomb.

But there's nothing.

Yet.

"You all feel okay?" I ask. "Besides being terrified?"

They nod, looking more and more like scared children. And I ask myself a question I've asked myself many times, both as a parent and as an employee with an important job: How did I end up being the adult in charge of things? Is it really me who has to figure things out?

Then the track in my mind skips to another thought: They're not children. Not really. One of them is quite likely a murderer. And I'm stuck in the house with them.

"None of this makes any sense."

I rub my forehead and pace a little, moving back and forth in the parlor. Each step creaks on the floorboard. I feel cold and shiver like a fever is coming over me.

"Why would anyone kill Nicholas?"

"Why would anyone kill Milo?" Sydney asks.

Someone clears their throat behind me. I'm not sure, but I think it's one of the women.

"What does that mean?" Sydney asks.

"I'm not sure, but I think it means let's not go down that road again," the captain says.

"What road?" Sydney asks.

"Let's stay focused," I say. "I think we all know what we need to—"

"No, really. What road?"

Sydney's height gives her an intimidating edge, her athletic body relaxed and prepared for battle at the same time. She cuts a warriorlike figure with all eyes on her, and my mind flashes back to a volleyball game I attended the year before. Sydney transformed into someone else on the court—she screamed at her opponents and her teammates. She preened and flexed after every winning point. She enjoyed destroying—and winning. And if what Duffy said about her formative years is true, she wasn't afraid to use violence to solve her problems.

"You mean you all think I killed Milo? Is that it? You all think we had a thing, so I killed him?"

"You did have a thing with him, right?" Emily is making a statement more than asking a question.

"How do you know that?"

"It's a small campus. And besides, it might be easier to count the women Milo didn't have a thing with. I'm one, but I'm not really that into dudes."

"I'm definitely two," Natalia says.

I expect Sydney to push back at them, to continue her fierce defense against her peers. But she turns to me. Her eyes aren't sad. They're angry. Her brown irises look like hot coals.

"Did you tell them about this? I thought what we talked about in the other room was private. Jesus. You're a professor here. That's like . . . doctor-patient confidentiality or whatever. You can't just go and tell everybody while I'm going through the buffet line. And you totally misunderstood."

"Sydney, I didn't say anything to anybody. And maybe you need to cool off. Would you like to—"

"Cool off? I'm not going to cool off when someone attacks me. I fight."

"We know," Emily says.

"Why would I kill the guy giving out the scholarship?" Sydney asks.

"I'd want to kill him if he creeped on me the way he did to you," Emily says. "It was gross."

"So maybe *you* killed him," Sydney says.

"What did you two talk about?" the captain asks. "If it's relevant to the case, we all need to know. We're all stuck in here together. And one of us might be a murderer."

Sydney turns away from me and points at the captain. "Duffy was right. *You* knew all about the poison. You were all over that. Right? You wanted everybody to leave when Milo died. And you were the one who pointed out right away that Milo was the best student."

"We're all aware of that," Natalia says. "*Allegedly*, he's the best student."

Sydney keeps going at the captain. "You wanted him gone. You wanted us all out of the way."

"Sydney," the captain says, his voice strikingly calm, "you should be careful with your accusations."

"What else was it? Do you not like his politics? You're a military guy. You probably hate his liberal views."

"Sydney, he was wearing a Black Lives Matter T-shirt," the captain says. "I'm one of the few Black men at a predominantly white college, and I'm going to murder the guy in a BLM shirt? Let's be real, okay?"

"You hated the way he talked about the protestors when he said it was free speech. When you disagreed about the brick. You were, like, pissed. I saw it. It probably felt good to get rid of him."

"Sydney," I say, "I know you're upset. I know you cared about

Milo a great deal. After you went to visit his body and talk to him . . ."

"Visit and talk to him?" Emily asks. "What does *that* mean? He's dead." She shivers. "Ugh, this is getting really bizarre."

"You said something to Milo?" Duffy asks. "In the music room?"

Sydney's face flushes the color of blood. She's back to staring at me, her eyes locked on mine like she's hoping she can get me to catch on fire with the intensity of her glare. "Are there no god-damn secrets on this campus? It's like living in a phone booth."

"What did you say to Milo?" Natalia asks. "We all just want to know what's going on and how these two people ended up dead. We're all in danger, and someone in here is a murderer, so if you know something that could help us, I think you need to share it."

Sydney's fierce glare hits everyone. "No. I'm not. Some things are going to be private. I'm keeping my mouth shut."

"It's better to just get all this out, Sydney," the captain says. "I think if you know something, you should say it. You've accused *me*, but I have nothing to hide. Are *you* hiding something?"

"Maybe *she's* hiding something." Sydney spins and points at Natalia. "You hated Milo. Fine, you weren't a girl he slept with. Lucky you. At least I've lived a life. But you sure as hell hated the fact that he beat you in class. You're hung up on him being a cheater, but isn't that just what people say when they lose and want to discredit their opponent?"

"Wow, words of profound wisdom from the volleyball court. I'll tell you something—Milo *was* a cheater. All the time. In class and out, as I'm sure you know."

"That's bullshit, Natalia."

"Maybe so, Sydney. Do you want to prove your point by punch-ing *me* in the nose?"

Sydney's mouth drops open like a trapdoor falling. "Are you for real? You're going to throw in my face that I punched a bully?"

"And we all know you tried to murder one of your high school teachers and went to jail," Emily says.

"She what?" the captain says.

Sydney's face turns the color of a setting sun. "Oh, that's so low. That's so fucking wrong to say." She moves toward Emily.

"We're not going to do this," I say, stepping between them. "We're not going to lose our minds." My hands shake, and I hope they don't notice. "Okay? We don't need to be saying things we're going to regret. There's one thing that has to stay true here. We're all in this together. And we need to think about what we want to do next—and I say we focus on getting the hell out of here."

38

I WANT TO LEAVE the room.

The tension is thick, a fog blinding each of us. We're irrational, desperate, growing capable of doing anything.

Nicholas's head is tilted back slightly, the sightless eyes staring at the ceiling. A trickle of foam runs down his pale cheek. His long fingers—dirty nails and all—clutch at nothing.

"Let's get out of here," I say. "Back to the dining room."

"Are we going to leave him like this?" Emily asks. "He's kind of a jerk and everything, but he is a human being."

"Maybe it's more important than ever not to disturb the crime scene," Natalia says. "I've watched *Law and Order* too. It's a nice break from studying."

"I think you're right," Emily says. "We agreed to move Milo, but this is really getting crazy."

But even if we leave the room, I can't bear the thought of those sightless eyes staring at the ceiling. We put Milo on a couch and covered him up. Somehow it felt more dignified, more respectful. To just leave Nicholas on the floor . . .

I crouch down next to him, reach out with my fingers, and press on his eyelids. They close, and that helps a little.

"Here, sir."

The captain takes his suit coat off and drapes it over the upper half of Nicholas's body, covering him from the top of the head to the waist. We can't see the gray skin, the smashed nose. The foam trickling from the mouth.

"I think that's better," he says.

"It is. Much. Even though I can't forget what's underneath."

"As I get older," the captain says, "I guess I just feel like that's all we do. Cover up our fear of death."

"I want everyone in the dining room," I say. "We'll make an exit strategy there. But nobody eat or drink anything else, okay? No more food. No snacks. No tea or Pappy. Okay? There's buttermilk pie in the kitchen, but we're just going to have to forget it. In fact . . ."

While the students file into the dining room, I walk to the back of the house to the kitchen. The buffet remains, and plenty of food is left. I open the refrigerator that sits in an alcove in the kitchen. It's almost empty except for the two pies. I take them out, pull the Saran Wrap off the top, and sniff.

Nothing. Except they both smell so good they make my mouth water. I know the pies aren't baked on campus. For purposes of the process, the campus dining services use a bakery in town—one that's been in existence almost as long as the college. And they claim to use the same recipe Major Hyde's mother, Clydette Hyde, used back in the nineteenth century. It sounds like bullshit, to be honest. But a lot of things are starting to sound like bullshit to my ears.

I throw both pies in the trash can. Then I lean close to each of the serving dishes on the counter. I smell the food. The tangy sauce for the rabbit. The freshness of the beans. The buttery grits. Nothing odd or out of place. The only discordant note in the bouquet comes from the Sterno flames underneath, the ones keeping the food hot.

Could there have been an accidental poisoning? Something from the Sterno?

Did some of the toxic lighter fluid make its way into the food?

But how could that affect only two people and not all of us?

Especially since Milo and Nicholas are the two people who didn't partake of the buffet. The rest of us did. So if they were poisoned—and we don't know that for sure—the poison came from something besides this food.

I bend down and blow out the Sterno flames. The burned wicks smell like birthday candles, which reminds me that Rebecca, my oldest, turned sixteen two weeks earlier. Sixteen? How is it even possible? She's going to start to drive, so insurance will cost more. And our worries will increase. Robyn turns fourteen this summer, and she'll be driving soon as well. Do we buy another car for them to share? Does Rachel transition from part-time to full-time at work? And that's not getting into Rita's braces.

All of these decisions—and more—wait for me outside of this house.

I walk over to the wooden back door—one that leads to a small patio and an old firepit that rarely gets used and then the woods. I tug on the knob.

Locked.

Even though it's locked—and I know it's locked—I tug and tug like a manic idiot. But I know the door won't open.

It's a two-way lock, one that requires a key to open from either side. A dead bolt.

There's no key in sight.

I leave the kitchen and walk toward the front of the house. I know I'm on a hopeless mission—it all feels hopeless—but I decide to try. Just to set my own mind at ease. Just to . . . just to try to find a fast solution.

As I pass the dining room, someone steps into the hallway.

"Sir? If I may—"

"Just wait, Captain."

"Do you need help checking the perimeter?"

"Just stay with the group. I'll be right back."

I go to the front door, the one I heard Chief lock after he stepped outside. It's the same as the back door. Dead bolt. Two-sided. I tug to no avail.

I remember what Chief told me that morning. He made sure all the doors and windows were locked after he let the dining staff in.

And he locked the front door when he left.

I go back to the dining room, where the students are gathered around the table.

Sydney and Duffy sit on one side, Natalia and Emily on the other.

The captain stands at the head, holding Nicholas's magic book of bylaws. But he's not reading it.

They look up when I enter. Faces ashen, eyes haunted. Like they've emerged from the aftermath of a bombing or shooting.

Terrified. Fear hangs over the room like a toxic cloud, a smothering presence.

"Maybe I'm a fool for trying, but I wanted to make sure the doors were really locked. But they are. So it's time for us to find another way to get out."

39

"THESE WINDOWS . . ." I'm thinking out loud. "So many things are falling apart in this house. . . . How secure can the locks on the windows be?"

"What are you saying?" Duffy asks.

Hope quickly rises in my chest. I see a path forward, a way to keep everyone safe.

"My house here in Bluefield is about fifty years old. It still has the original windows, which isn't much fun when it gets cold in the winter. But the windows aren't that secure. The locks are flimsy or don't work at all. They're pretty easy to get through. So I'm wondering if the locks are the same here."

"About that, sir," the captain says. "The locks. And getting out of here."

"What about it?" I ask.

"I understand this is a distressing situation," he says. "That's why I want to make sure we're intentional about what we do."

"'Intentional'?"

I look around, wondering if anyone else in the group will say anything. No one speaks up. Sydney sits with her arms folded across her chest, her face still flushed. Duffy taps his finger against the chair arm. On the other side, Emily starts to clean her glasses with a ragged-looking tissue. She squints as she does so. And Natalia shifts in her chair like she's uncomfortable.

"Two people are dead, Captain," I say. "*Two*. And we don't know why. It's possible—and I'm not accusing anyone—but it's possible, maybe even likely, that someone in this room is a killer. I think we need to leave the house and let the authorities take control of the situation. It's beyond what any of us can handle."

"Okay, sir, I hear you. And I respect your authority and position, and I don't mean to question it. And even though I don't show it all the time, I'm upset by this loss of life. I am. But I do want to know something before we leave here."

"What's that?"

"We all heard what Mr. Hyde said several times during the day. He kept reminding us that if anybody left, they were disqualified. And if we *all* left and the scholarship wasn't given today, then the money went away forever. So if we decide to leave now, all of us, what happens to the scholarship? I can only speak for myself, but I still want to have a chance to win it. This scholarship is the ticket to a better life for me and my family."

"Are you all wondering about this?" I ask.

"Not me," Sydney says. "I want to go. This is, like, crazy now. And I'm tired of the shit people are talking."

"Duffy?" I ask.

"I've got to be honest, boss. I'm a little scared. I mean, shit. Do we still get the five-thousand-dollar fellowship if we leave now? I know we all get five just for getting selected to come here today. To be honest, I never expected to win, so that five would really help me."

I turn to the left. "Natalia? Emily?"

"I really *need* the scholarship," Natalia says. "Desperately. The whole thing. I'm under a lot of pressure to graduate and get into medical school. I just don't know. . . ."

"I'm staying to the end," Emily says. "But the captain brought up a good point while you were out of the room."

"What's that?" I ask, looking over at the captain, who is still holding the bylaws.

The captain taps the book with his index finger. He seems like a guy who should always be wearing a suit, not just the tie and a nice shirt.

"The question I have is, what happens to the money now? I did a little reconnaissance when I was selected for this opportunity. I learned in the military that you always want to know your enemy well. Sun Tzu."

"Your *enemy*?" Sydney asks. "Are we your enemies? And you think *I* killed somebody."

"Yeah, Captain," Duffy says. "I don't like the way you're talking about us."

"Fair enough. 'Opponent' might be a better word," the captain says. "Okay? But I looked into Mr. Hyde and his company as well. There's a lot of information out there. But the key thing that applies to this situation right now is that Nicholas Hyde is the sole surviving heir to the Hyde family fortune. He's it. And I mean he's *really* it. Over the years, the Hyde family hasn't been that fruitful or good at multiplying. For the last few generations, each family has had only one child. So there aren't any cousins or anything.

Distant relations, sure. But pretty much everything belongs to Nicholas Hyde. It all rests on him."

"It's like a Dickens novel," Emily says.

"Or *Downton Abbey*," Duffy says.

"What's your point, Captain?" I ask. "And how does it relate to the danger we're in?"

"My point, sir, is that we have to figure out what becomes of the money if Nicholas Hyde is dead. Is there even a scholarship to compete for if he's deceased?"

I scratch my head. I hate to say it, but I've been thinking the same thing. It's terrible to think this way when two people are dead. And instead of thinking only about them, I'm thinking about how their deaths—specifically Nicholas's death—affect my job. If he is the only heir to the Hyde fortune, and he's dead, what happens to it all? What happens to the college?

"These things are very complicated, as I'm sure you all can imagine. When people have this much money, their estates and wills are like reading ancient Sanskrit. It doesn't make any sense to regular people. But I believe the Hyde family would have all of this spelled out and locked down. They've been giving money to the college for more than a century. They're not going to forget about us now."

I inject my voice with confidence and certainty. The same way I always tried to sound in the classroom, even in those moments when I wasn't exactly sure what I was talking about. I always believed that people listened and went along if I sounded like I knew what I was saying. Even if I didn't.

But I'm not sure. Before today, I worried if Nicholas would continue to honor his family's commitment to the college. And now that he's gone, I'm just not sure who will make the decisions.

The captain is correct—there isn't anyone else in line to the Hyde fortune.

"So you think the scholarship will be there?" Duffy asks. "That's what it sounds like you're saying. If we all stay and finish, someone will get the grand prize?"

"I believe so. But I think we have bigger problems than—"

It's Natalia who speaks up this time. "Okay, then here's another question. If we stay and finish, who decides who wins the scholarship? Doesn't it have to be you?"

40

I'M SHAKING MY HEAD.

"It's not going to be me," I say. "And that's because we're *not* going to be in here. I know some of you might want to risk staying and you want to try to get the big prize, but it's not safe. We need to find a way out."

"But what about—"

I cut Emily off. I hate to interrupt a student or play the authority card, but I have to.

"I'll do everything in my power to see that *someone* wins this scholarship based on the essays you have already written. And maybe we'll do the interviews, or maybe someone else representing the Hyde family or their board of directors can step in and help. I just don't know. But I want to find a way out of here. I suggest we all go around and check these windows. See if one of them can be opened. If so, one of us can go out and get Chief. If not, we smash a window."

"Smash one now," Sydney says.

"I'd like to not destroy the house if I don't have to."

"The school probably can't afford to fix a broken window," Emily says.

"I think it sounds safer to go out an open window rather than a broken one," I say. "But if we have to break one, we will."

The captain drops the book of bylaws onto the dining table, where it makes a loud splat. He comes around the side of the table, walking behind the chairs occupied by Emily and Natalia, and walks up to me. "Sir, if I may—"

"What, Captain?"

"Sir, what about *democracy?* We voted before. So let's vote again." He points at Natalia and Emily. "The three of *us* want to stay and finish if we can. The two of *them* want to leave. That's three to two in favor of staying."

"*I* voted last time too," I say.

"I'm talking about the students voting."

"You must be a Republican," Sydney says. "You only want to count the votes you know are on your side."

"I'm a registered Independent, for what it's worth," the captain says. "Sir, I don't think you've thought this all the way through. If we could stay after Milo's death, as disturbing as it was, then we can stay after this one. The doors will open at sixteen hundred. That's less than three hours from now. If we don't eat or drink anything and keep a close watch on one another, we can gut it out."

"Captain, it's very likely there's a killer in here. And I can't allow us to stay in here under those conditions. And you're awfully damn insistent on keeping us in here."

The captain throws his shoulders back. Affronted.

"Are you saying you think it's me?" he says.

"No, I'm not saying that."

"Sir, I've been hearing that kind of stuff my whole life. I thought you were better than that."

"Oh, come on," Duffy says. "Are you really going to call *him* a racist?"

It's out. And once that kind of thing is out, it's hard to put back.

Everyone tenses more than at any other time during the day. My own face flushes with shame. I respond by saying the stupidest and most hollow words I could find in such a moment.

"I'm not a racist," I say.

"Everyone's a racist," Emily says. "Besides, you *are* a middle-aged white dude."

But the captain ignores me. He points at Duffy. "You know, *you* started it. Way back when Milo died. *You* accused me of killing him. Pointing out that I knew a lot about poison. Saying I did CPR to cover up the crime. I know all about that, Mr. Whitley County."

Duffy's mouth falls open like somebody cut the strings holding it in place. "Oh, bullshit."

"It's a sundown town," the captain says, gesturing to the room. "I know."

"It's a what?" Sydney asks.

"It's a sundown town," the captain says, letting his words hang in the air.

"I don't know what that is," Sydney says.

The captain remains silent.

Emily clears her throat. "I know what it is. We learned about it in Kentucky history with Dr. Porter. But I don't think it's my place to talk about it. . . ."

"Go ahead," the captain says. "I don't mind if you explain it."

"Okay, well, a sundown town is a town where all the people of color, usually Black people, have to be out by sundown. Or else."

"Or else what?" Sydney asks.

"They get killed," Emily says. "Lynched. I'm sorry, Captain."

"It's okay," he says. "I'm glad you know. Everybody should know."

"Oh, shit." Sydney shudders. "I can't even . . ."

Duffy's jaw is set hard, like the prow of a ship. Waves could smash against it and get turned away, evaporating into foam. "That's so wrong. My papaw hired Black men to work on his farm when nobody else would."

"Hired," the captain says. "Hired. Oh, wow. Thanks for hiring us to pick the crops."

"A farm?" Natalia says. "Hmmm."

"What are you talking about?" Duffy directs his question to Natalia.

"Just thinking of something. About farms and stuff."

"What about farms?" Duffy asks.

"Well, the captain said the poison could be an herb or something. So you live on a farm. You said you like to grow things."

"So *I* killed them?" Duffy asks. "Because I live on a farm?"

"Is this sundown thing true, Duffy?" Sydney asks.

"There was a horrific race riot in Corbin in 1919," Natalia says. "Dr. Porter told us all about it. Isn't Corbin located in Whitley County?"

"That's right," the captain says. "I'm glad you know about that. I'm glad they're teaching it."

"You said Porter only pushed his own agenda," Emily says. "Now you like him?"

"Well, he got the part about Whitley County right."

"Nineteen nineteen, Captain?" Duffy says. "So eighty years before I was born, and you're holding me to account for it?"

"Now, everybody, stop," I say. "No one is calling anyone a racist. And no one is calling anyone a murderer. Okay?"

"I think I was kind of accused," Sydney says. "Right?"

"Join the club," the captain says.

"I'm going to go check these windows," I say. "This room and then the rest of the first floor and upstairs if needed. After we've checked all the windows, we can decide who's going to go out. Does anybody want to help me?"

Nobody moves. Except the captain, who returns to his spot at the head of the table, where he picks up the book of bylaws and plops into a chair.

"I just want to get some answers before we leave, okay? If you all want to go without knowing the consequences of that decision, be my guest. It's possible I can win this thing by default. Maybe I'll win by sitting right here. I'm willing to do whatever it takes."

Whatever it takes . . .

The phrase stands out, but I don't comment on it. No need to stir the pot any more.

"Nobody wants to help me?" I ask. "Sydney? You're taller than any of us. You can reach the windows easily."

She stares straight head, ignoring me. And ignoring Duffy.

He stares at her profile, then shrugs his shoulders. "I'll help you, boss. It looks like the temperature's a little too cold in here for me anyway."

"Okay, thanks." I point to the three windows that line the wall of the dining room. "Let's do this. We'll be out of here in a second."

"Sir—"

"We'll be out of here," I say. "And safe."

41

THE THREE WINDOWS LOOK out on the side of the house.

The trees grow close, their branches still filling with leaves after the winter. The windows are rectangular in shape, the glass slightly cloudy. The wooden grilles are painted dark brown to match the furniture in the room. Each window has two sashes, an upper and a lower. A lock, which is meant to keep intruders out, sits on top of the lower sash. But it should be easy enough to turn the lock open on one and lift the lower sash.

"Duffy, can you reach that?" I ask. "It's a little high for me."

"Sure." He stretches his body to its full height, extending his arm as far as it can go. He manages to reach the lock and gives it a twist. He lets out a held breath and comes down off the toes of his boots. "That should do it, boss."

Before I grab the lift to raise the lower sash, Emily says, "I'm thinking of staying too. Like the captain is. If you all want to go, that's fine, but we don't know what happens if we leave. You can read both of our essays and decide whose is best."

"You're assuming it's going to be you because you're an English major," Natalia says.

"Not necessarily."

"You were ready to leave this morning because you found out Major Hyde was involved in a massacre during the Civil War," Sydney says. "Now you totally want his money. What gives?"

"I don't want *his* money. He's long, long dead, so he can't have money anymore. But I want what his family is offering."

"Even though it comes from fossil fuels?" Sydney asks. "And the Civil War?"

"It might be kind of sweet to take that dirty money and finish school with it," Emily says.

"And work for the Hyde Corporation?" Sydney asks. "Remember, the job is part of it."

Emily laughs. "Well, I'm *not* going to take the job. What do you think? I don't want to go to work for a company like that. They can give me the other stuff and keep that."

My hands are on the window lift, and when I yank, it doesn't move.

"What is the job they give you, Mr. Gaines?" Duffy asks.

"It's usually an entry-level position, but they try to cater it to your interests. So if you're an English major, they might find something for you to do that involves writing. We had an art major win once, and she went to work in the advertising department. Or they'll move you around so you can see all aspects of the business."

"What about an ag major?" Duffy asks.

"Maybe they'll let you mow the grass," the captain says.

"I don't mind that kind of work, Captain," Duffy says, unruffled. "My hands have been dirty before. They will be again."

"I'd love to have a job when I graduate," Sydney says. "I

wouldn't care what field it was in so long as I had benefits and a salary. I could help my family."

"Amen to that," Natalia says.

"That's fine for all of you," Emily says. "They can keep the job if I win. Maybe they can give the job to one of you. Split the award. Can they do that, Mr. Gaines?"

"No, they can't."

"They can give the job to somebody, though," Emily says. "I mean, if I'm not taking it, then somebody else can get hired. They don't really want me working at their company, with my tattoos and everything else."

I tug on the window a few more times, getting nowhere. "Duffy? Can you try to move this?"

"I think it's painted shut," he says. "Or busted. But I'll try."

"I'm sure I'm not Hyde Corporation material," Emily says.

"That's not exactly how it works, Emily."

"What do you mean?"

"It's a whole package. All or nothing. It's in the bylaws. If you don't take the job and work for the Hyde Corporation for an entire year, then you don't get the rest of the money. The tuition or the loan forgiveness."

"How does *that* work?" Natalia asks. "They pay your tuition, and you don't keep the job . . . then what? You're gone already, right? What are they going to do to you?"

The captain has opened the book of bylaws at the head of the table. He's licking his fingers and turning the pages rapidly. "Hold on a minute. . . ."

"They require you to sign a contract if you win," I say. "You have to agree to those terms if you want all of that. If you don't fulfill the contract, then they can compel you to pay back the other benefits."

"Are you fucking serious?" Emily asks.

"I am. This all gets explained to the winner after they've been chosen. I used to argue with Theodore Hyde, Nicholas's father, that we should make this clearer up front, but he liked doing it this way. The Hyde family wanted to know a student was *really* committed once they won the scholarship. It was like a final test."

"We don't even know how we got picked," Natalia says. "How much does the Hyde family or corporation or whatever know about each of us?"

"Wait, wait, wait," the captain says. "Here it is." He taps the page with his finger. "'The student selected the winner of the Hyde Scholarship will agree to carry out the terms of the Hyde Scholarship contract. Failure to do so will result in forfeiture of the award and expose the scholarship recipient to potential legal action.' Hmm. And they only tell us after we win?"

Emily stands up. "Yeah, who knew? Why didn't anyone tell us that?"

"I heard about it," Duffy says. "That friend of Milo's who did it last year. What's his name?" His brow wrinkles. "Andrew . . . Andrew Pratt. He heard about this provision. If you don't do it all, they might sue you." Duffy shrugs. "I didn't care. I mean, work for a year, get the money. What's the big deal?"

"Seems reasonable," the captain says. "It's their money. They can attach whatever provisions they want. And if you fail to follow through, they can ask for it back."

"I saw it on a Reddit thread," Natalia says.

"I don't always have reliable access to the Internet," Emily says.

"Maybe we need to have more transparency in the future," I say. "But I'd like to get back to the windows—"

"But to work for *that* company?" Emily asks. She makes a face like someone stuffed a dirty sock in her mouth.

"Are you rethinking it?" the captain asks. "Maybe you *do* want to leave. Duffy's about to open that window. You can crawl right on out."

Emily doesn't look happy. "I can't believe this. . . . I can't . . . This is really—this is so different from what I thought. It's . . . pathological. . . ."

But the captain is right—Duffy is working on the window. He's yanking on the lift, trying to get the sash to go up.

"Is it painted shut?" I ask.

Duffy is bent down, his face pressed against the glass.

"Mr. Gaines, you'd better come over here and check this out."

42

I LEAN DOWN NEXT to Duffy.

He's tapping the glass with his index finger, calling my attention to something outside. I wonder if he's trying to get me to notice a bug or something crawling around on the ledge.

"See that?" he asks.

I look down, through the pane of glass and outside where his finger directs me. It takes another moment, but then I see it.

See *them*.

Nails. Driven through the sashes and into the window frames. Nailing the windows shut from the outside.

"Shit," I say.

"Those have been there a few years at least," Duffy says. "You can see how weathered and old they are. They're starting to rust."

"Is this what the chief meant by the windows being locked from the outside?" I ask, knowing no one can provide me with an answer. "Did he nail them shut sometime in the past?"

"What are you talking about?" Emily asks from behind us.

"Check the other ones," I say.

Duffy moves to his right, to the next window and the next. He leans down at each of them, pressing his face to the glass. He shakes his head at both of them.

"No go, boss. They're all nailed shut."

"What are you saying?" Sydney asks.

"The windows are nailed shut in here," I say. "We can't open them."

The captain stands up, tossing the bylaws onto the table again. "How can they do that? You can't nail windows shut in a building. Not on a college campus. It's a fire hazard."

"Somebody did it," Duffy says.

"But why?" the captain asks. He looks at me like I'll know.

"It's weird. There've been some break-ins on campus over the past few years. About five years ago, somebody got into the dean's office and stole a bunch of computers."

"Oh, yeah," Duffy says. "And there was that cafeteria thing last year. That couple from town broke in and took all that meat."

"They were hungry, Duffy," Emily says. "They had children and needed food. Do you know what it's like to be hungry?"

"I'm not saying anything negative," Duffy says. "I just don't like stealing."

"And a few years ago, somebody broke into the Robert Frost house in New England and trashed the place," Emily says. "That's disgusting too. This is all disgusting."

"There's a lack of respect," the captain says. "It's pervasive. But doesn't anyone inspect here?"

"The dorms get inspected," I say. "The fire marshal from Bluefield comes every year and checks them out with the chief. But nobody lives here. It's not really used for classes or anything. . . ."

"It's still a fire hazard," the captain says.

"Inspectors can be bought off," Natalia says. "It's a small town. Who knows what goes down? I mean, the college covers up a lot of unpleasant events they don't want getting out. My freshman year, a girl in my dorm died from alcohol poisoning."

"Who?" Sydney asks.

"Katie Gunn."

"Oh, yeah," Sydney says. "But I thought . . ."

"They *said* she died of natural causes," Natalia says. "They *said* she had undiagnosed seizures no one knew about. But she drank a fifth of Wild Turkey the night she died. And vomited all over her room while she slept. I knew her roommate. They covered it up because it looks bad. It doesn't fit the whole Hyde College image."

"What happened to Katie was a tragedy," I say. "The college doesn't like to cause panic. But we have our own issues to deal with right now."

"Are you going to smash the window, then?" Sydney asks. "I'm all for that."

"We can do that when—"

"Sir?"

"—we have to—"

"Sir? I think you—"

"Oh, shit," Sydney says. "Emily?"

I turn.

Emily stands, both hands pressed against her stomach. She's white as milk. Wobbly.

"Emily?" I say.

"Fuck me," she says. "I feel sick. So fucking sick . . ."

43

EMILY'S BODY FOLDS IN half. Her cheeks puff, and her eyes squeeze shut.

We all rush toward her.

No no no no no.

"Fuck, she's dying," Sydney says.

"Emily." I place my hand on her back, try to think of something that might help. "Emily?"

"I'm sick. So fucking sick . . ." She drops back into the chair. "Ooooof . . ."

"Get her some water," the captain says. "Give her air."

I step back along with everyone else. Natalia leaves the room, heading toward the kitchen.

"Emily? Do you want to lie down?" I ask.

Duffy comes over with a trash can and places it on the floor in front of Emily. "You can puke in there. It might be better if you puke. You know, get the poison out. Stick your fingers down your throat if you have to."

"She might not be poisoned."

"She ate the food, Captain," I say. "All of us in here did."

"Where did Natalia go?" Sydney asks. "She's not here."

Natalia comes back in, holding a glass of water. "I'm trying to help, Sydney. Chill, for God's sake."

"Well . . ." Sydney lifts her arms in a hopeless gesture. "Fuck, I don't know what to do."

I take the glass from Natalia and offer it to Emily. "Would you like to sip this?"

"I might . . . if I do . . ." Her eyes remain squeezed shut. "I might puke."

I hand the glass back to Natalia. "Would you like to lie down, Emily?"

"There's that couch in the other room," Duffy says. "The one Milo is on."

"You want to move Milo's body so Emily can lie down?" Natalia asks.

"Yes, I would," Duffy says. "Life is for the living."

"I don't want to move," she says. "It hurts. It hurts so bad."

"This is it, sir. Proof the food is poisoned too. Milo and Mr. Hyde didn't eat it, but Emily did."

"We're all fucked," Sydney says.

"But you only ate the sides, right, Emily?" I ask. "You're a vegetarian."

She rocks back and forth, midsection clutched. "Well . . . I did eat a little rabbit. That god-awful rabbit . . ."

"How much of it did you eat?" the captain asks.

"A few bites. Just a few."

"Could be a smaller dose, sir. Less of an effect than on the ones who died."

"But they didn't eat," Duffy says. "She did."

"But what about us?" Sydney asks. "We all ate it, so we're fucked. I think I feel sick now."

"Sydney?" Duffy asks, stepping toward her.

"I just . . ." She fans her face with her hand. "It's the stress . . . the craziness here maybe. . . ."

"Okay, go check the other windows," I say. "Now. Duffy and Sydney. Just go."

They move, but Natalia's voice stops them. "Wait."

"What?" Duffy asks.

"Sydney, do you want me to go with you?"

"What?" Sydney asks. "No. I'm okay. I don't think I'm really sick. . . . I'm just . . . scared."

"I know. Do you want me to come along?" Natalia asks again.

"We've got it," Duffy says. "I'll keep an eye on Sydney. You help Emily."

They leave the room, Duffy leading the way. I bend back down. "Emily?"

"It still hurts. . . ." Her breath comes in short huffs and puffs. Like she just ran a marathon. "It's a steady pain. . . ."

"Okay, okay," I say. "Try to take some deep breaths. We're here for you, okay? We're with you. We'll get out one of these windows."

"Mr. Gaines?"

"What, Natalia?"

"Can I tell you something?"

"Sure. What is it?"

"Well," she says. "It's . . . Okay, I'll just say it. And it's about Sydney and Duffy, okay?"

44

"WHAT IS IT, NATALIA?" I ask. "Are *you* sick?"

"No. I don't think so." Natalia looks toward the door of the dining room, making sure no one is there. Then she looks at the still-doubled-over Emily. "Do you mind if I tell him, Emily?"

"Oh," Emily says, more of a word than a grunt of pain. "You're getting into that?"

"I think it's time," Natalia says. "I mean, what about Sydney? He's clearly into her."

"What are you two talking about?" the captain asks.

"Yes, what?" I ask.

"Go ahead," Emily says. "I think . . . maybe I'm . . . I don't want to talk. . . ."

"Sure," the captain says. "Keep breathing deep. We're with you."

"Okay, okay." Natalia looks at all of us. "So here goes. Let me know if I get anything wrong, Emily."

"I'm trying not to vom right now, but I'm listening. . . ."

"Okay, Mr. Gaines, so I guess freshman year Duffy was crushing on a girl who lived in Emily's dorm. Right? Her name was Sarah Drury. And they talked and hung out and all that, but then Sarah was kind of not interested in Duffy anymore. He wasn't her type, and she met another guy. And *they* started dating."

"Not Milo," the captain says.

"No," Emily says, wincing. "This isn't a Jane Austen novel."

"Okay," Natalia says. "But Duffy kept coming around . . . you know, showing up at her room. Showing up at parties and stuff wherever she went. Even, like, standing out in the hallway when her classes were over. Totally creepy."

"Lots of students show up at the same parties. And outside classrooms. It's a small campus," I say.

"Yeah, but these would be parties where he didn't know anyone, where he wasn't supposed to be. He was really freaking this girl out."

"It's true, Mr. Gaines," Emily says, gasping. "I was there for this. I knew Sarah."

"Well, you can tell he's into Sydney, and Sydney was hooking up with Milo. And now . . ." Natalia gestures toward the front of the house, where Milo lies. "And then Mr. Hyde said that about Sydney during tea, and he's . . . you know, gone. Do you see what I'm saying? Duffy's very . . . You know, he's hovering over Sydney. And now he's off with her."

"He did get very angry when that brick hit the tire of his truck," the captain says.

"Did you see what he looked like when Mr. Hyde was being all flirty with Sydney?" Emily says, her voice a little stronger. "Duffy looked like he wanted to kill him."

"Okay," I say, "I don't like these accusations."

But Duffy said he hated the Hyde family. And he sounded like he *really* meant it.

"Will you just go check on them?" Natalia asks. "Or I'll go do it if nobody else will."

I look at the dining room door. All of Duffy's jokes and aw-shucks charm start to feel . . . discordant. Off. Misplaced.

"Emily, are you feeling any better?"

"I'm not any worse." She sniffles. "I'm still alive."

"Captain, can you keep an eye on her? And if anything happens, can you call me right away?"

"I will, sir."

"Okay, I'll go see what's going on with Duffy and Sydney."

My body feels light, empty, as I walk to the hallway, almost like I'm floating. Or disconnected from myself. Nothing feels real.

I step into the hallway and listen. Voices reach me.

"It's the kitchen," Natalia says from right behind me.

"What are you doing?" I ask.

"I'm coming with you. There should be a woman along. So Sydney feels safe."

When we reach the entrance to the kitchen, we hear the conversation more clearly.

"Not now, Duffy, okay?"

"Just once . . ."

"Duffy—"

Sydney backs away from Duffy when they see us at the kitchen entrance. Her face flushes. "Oh," Sydney says, "you're here."

"Everything okay?" I ask.

"Peachy," Duffy says. "We were just— I mean, the window here. We were just about to check it. . . ."

Sydney stands with her hands folded. She looks flustered.

There's one window in the kitchen, and it's large. It sits above the sink and reveals trees and more trees. Looking out that window, I can see just how far away from any form of help we are.

Duffy swings his body so he's sitting on the counter.

"Are you okay, Sydney?" Natalia asks. "Are you safe?"

"I'm fine," Sydney says, but she doesn't sound entirely certain. "It's okay. We were just . . . talking."

It doesn't take Duffy long to check the window. "No soap, boss. Nailed shut."

"Figures," I say.

"Are you sure, Sydney?" Natalia asks.

"She said she's okay," Duffy says. "Give it a rest."

"I'm talking to *her*, not *you*," Natalia says.

"And she says she's fine. Are you trying to imply something about me, Natalia?"

"I want to make sure Sydney feels safe," she says. "Unlike Sarah Drury."

"Sydney can take care of herself."

"Can I just say something, then?" Sydney asks. "Since you're both kind of talking about me as though I'm not here."

"I'm trying to help," Natalia says. "Duffy has a reputation—"

"Okay," I say. "Sydney, what is it?"

"Thank you," she says. "I really don't feel safe in here, but not because of Duffy. It's starting to feel like the walls are closing in on me. I really need to get out."

"We're going to figure that out," I say. "I promise."

"I really want the scholarship. And I thought I might win it, even with Milo here. I'm a pretty good writer. Always have been. But I don't think this is really worth it."

"We're going to get out, Sydney," Duffy says. "Mr. Gaines is right. And I'm going to be true to my word—if you want to leave, I'll go with you. Okay?"

Sydney looks unsettled. She takes a deep breath. "You don't have to do anything for me."

"Are you pissed about the sundown thing still?" he asks. "Look, my papaw was a pretty enlightened guy. He put a big Obama sign out on his property. Somebody came by and riddled it with shotgun pellets. It looked like Swiss cheese. But he did put it out and try."

"It's not just the sundown thing," Sydney says. "I knew Sarah Drury too. I don't know everything that happened, but . . ."

"Oh, great. You too."

"Did you two check the parlor?" I ask.

"All the windows there are locked as well," Sydney says. "And Mr. Hyde is still . . . you know . . . on the floor."

"Let's look upstairs," Natalia says. "Maybe Duffy can stay down here?"

"I'll go wherever I want—"

"I was wondering something," Sydney says. "Duffy, did your mom start to work for the Hyde Corporation when you had to sell the family farm?"

"What do you mean?"

"You said earlier your mom worked for a subsidiary of the Hyde Corporation. And that they were really hardcore. I guess I just assumed she went to work there when you had to sell the farm."

"Why do you think we had to sell the farm?" he asks.

Sydney shrugs. "I'm from Illinois. A lot of people sold off their family farms. It was just too hard to make it."

"We didn't sell it all, just a large chunk. We still have a tiny piece left."

"So . . . did you happen to sell it to the Hyde family?" I ask, trying to sound casual.

He looks at Natalia and me like he's forgotten we were in the room. "What? No, we didn't. But they contributed to us having to sell it. They're involved in a lot of stuff, own a lot of companies. As my papaw used to say, they have their fingers in a lot of pies. And one of them was poultry. They put up a poultry-processing plant in my hometown. Sounds good, right? I mean, they need feed for all those chickens. But they wouldn't buy grain from any of the local farmers. We stopped raising cattle at some point and started trying to grow things. But they trucked it in from far away. They'd rather do that than buy from us to save a few pennies. It really hurt things with the farm. . . ."

"I'm sorry."

"My mom did go to work for them. In the poultry plant."

"That's tough work," Sydney says. "There's one in the town where my aunt lives."

"It's not *tough* work. It's *shit* work. Bad ventilation. Low pay. That's why they mostly hire . . . well, people who are . . ."

Natalia sighs. "You can go ahead and say it. They hire people who look like me to do that work."

"That's right," Duffy says. "Sorry. They think they can get away with treating them any way they want. I don't like the way those workers get treated."

"Most sane people don't," Natalia says.

"My mom and some of the other women who worked there tried to get the workers organized. Band together for better pay and conditions. All that." He reaches up, fiddles with the string tie around his neck. "The bigwigs at the plant got wind of it, and my mom and the other women got fired. Then the Hyde Corporation blackballed them around town. Said they were troublemakers, tried to keep them from being able to get other jobs."

"That's terrible," I say.

"I was already in school here. But I wanted to quit and go home. I knew the same people who bankrolled this school made those decisions about my mom's job. But she wanted me to stay and finish my education. Any way I could. So I did. Can't argue with Mom. She has visions of me getting a degree and saving the farm. Not sure about that . . ."

"Wow," Sydney says.

"We just don't have the money, unless I win this. My mom . . . she hurt her back working in that plant. All they do is prescribe her pills. Lots and lots of pills. I'd like to get her to stop that, but I don't know. And my dad, he took a job in Michigan, working in a plant up there. We don't see him much. Not that we saw him much before he left."

"That's shitty, Duffy," Sydney says.

Duffy cocks his head to the side, indicating the parlor. "People get what they deserve. The world works those things out, doesn't it?"

His words are cold, and I shiver.

"Maybe we should check upstairs," Natalia says. "Real quick."

"Did you check the door?" Sydney asks.

"I did. Earlier. It's locked."

"Not that one," she says, pointing. "That one."

"That door? That goes down to the basement," I say. "I guess more properly to the cellar. It has a dirt floor and a low ceiling. They stored vegetables and other food down there way back in the old days. I got a peek down there once. It was full of old junk. Boxes and crates. Old lawn equipment the college stored there. Mowers and rakes. They just threw anything there they didn't know what to do with. Oh, and it's full of spiders and mice. You can't even walk around."

"Is there a way out down there?" Sydney asks, shivering.

"There's an exit into the yard through a set of bulkhead doors, but I assume they're locked from the outside."

"You assume?"

"They'd have to be if Chief was thorough. And he is."

"The chief has a key to everything, right?" Sydney asks.

"Everything on campus."

"Including this house," she says. "And he was here before you were, right?"

"What are you saying?" Natalia asks.

"We're talking about the caterers messing with the food and our fellow students poisoning us. But Chief has access to everything. Anytime he wants."

"Sydney," I say, "I've known Chief a long time."

"He is a cop," Duffy says. "Some cops go rogue. Dude has a lot of power and access on this campus. Maybe he has a beef with Mr. Hyde. He didn't seem too fond of Milo."

"Or maybe he just hates his job," Natalia says. "Instead of being one of those people who goes in and shoots the place up, he just poisoned us."

Just that morning, Chief told me: *A lot of people aren't happy about the way things are going.*

"No," I say. "No. That cellar is a minefield of garbage. I think we'll find a better way than that. And accusing or suspecting Chief doesn't help. Come on."

45

AS WE MOVE TOWARD the front of the house, we stop at the dining room door so I can check on Emily.

She sits at the table, sipping from the glass of water. The captain stands next to her.

"Are you feeling better?" I ask.

"She's holding steady," the captain says.

"Emily?"

"I'm okay. I—I think I'm okay. I haven't puked or anything. Not yet."

"We're going to check the second floor," I say.

The four of us trudge up the stairs. There are four bedrooms, so it's easy enough for each of us to take one and check it.

I enter the room where I was with Nicholas less than an hour earlier. I wish I could go back and change whatever occurred in the intervening time. I replay our conversation—the talk about fathers and legacies. And his promise to fund the 100 More Initiative. What becomes of that now? What becomes of any of it?

Again I push the thought away. I'm now responsible for five students whose lives are in danger. I can *only* think about that.

I go to the windows and check. Before I lean down, a wave of hope crests in my heart. Who on earth would nail shut windows on the second floor? And if they're not nailed shut, we can easily open the ones that face the police, start waving or jumping up and down or hang a bedsheet out the window and be seen. Salvation is that close.

Except the windows in Leander's room are nailed shut as well. Someone went to a lot of trouble to make sure no one could get out of this house if they didn't want them to.

I return to the hallway and meet my three associates.

"All nailed shut?" I ask.

They nod in unison.

"Every damn one," Sydney says. "But we can see the cops from the ones that face the front. All we have to do is wave, and Chief will see us."

"I don't think waving will do it," Duffy says. "Maybe a sign. I don't know. We're pretty far. And the cops only seem to get close when somebody makes a break for it."

"The truth is," I say, "the college takes this whole thing pretty seriously. And they give the Hyde family free rein to do as they please. They don't want anyone disturbing the process. That means the cops too. Chief always stays far away after he locks the doors."

"Why does he stay so far away?" Sydney asks. "Is he happy to let us—"

"Sydney, not that."

"What about the basement?" Duffy asks. "You said there's a door, but more important—" Duffy makes shooing gestures at us. He wants us to go into Leander's bedroom. "Can we?"

"Duffy—"

"Come on, come on," he says.

Pretty quickly, all four of us are moving into the room, and once we're in, Duffy closes the door, locks it, and turns to face us.

46

DUFFY SPEAKS IN A lower voice than normal.

"I didn't really come up here because I thought we'd discover an unlocked window," he says. "I figured once one was nailed shut, they all would be. I came up here because I wanted to talk about something."

The three of us stand across from him, waiting. Sydney shifts one step to her left, moving farther away from Duffy.

"I don't really care that much about the exam," he says. "Like I said, I didn't expect to win. Now, to be honest, I'm just worried about not dying."

"Do any of you feel sick?" I ask. "Stomach pain? Nausea? Anything?"

Sydney and Natalia shake their heads.

"See, that's just it, boss," Duffy says. "None of *us* are sick."

"Not yet," Natalia says. "Just wait."

"So why is Emily sick?" Duffy asks.

"Because it's hitting her first, that's why," Sydney says. "Duffy, you and I went through the line last, so Emily and the captain and Natalia ate before us. This is getting really insane. I feel more trapped. Mr. Gaines, let's get out of here. They can pump our stomachs or whatever. Okay? Just let's get out of here."

Sydney moves for the door, but Duffy steps into her way. "Wait a minute—"

"Duffy—"

"Let her go," Natalia says.

"What if Emily's *not* sick?" he asks.

"You mean what if she's not poisoned?" Natalia asks.

"I mean she's faking it," Duffy says.

"Duffy," I say, "I don't feel comfortable getting into accusations like this. We just need to work together and—"

"No, seriously, just hear me out for a second. The captain knew all about the poison, like I said. He jumped right on it. As soon as Milo died, he said it was poison. He had training in it. And Emily clearly hates the Hyde family and all they stand for. That's why that protestor said her name when they came running to the house."

"We don't know that they said her name," I say.

"They did," Natalia says. "It was clear as day."

"I agree with Natalia about that," Sydney says.

I decline to point out that Natalia and Sydney were ready to come to blows in the wake of Nicholas's death. Now they seem to be joining Duffy in an accusation against the captain and Emily. Strange bedfellows.

"Why would the captain want to kill Milo or Nicholas?" I ask.

"The captain researched everything," Sydney says. "He would

have known Milo was the best student. And you have to admit, the captain is pretty desperate to win."

"Okay," I say, "you've made a case for why each one of them would possibly want to kill one of the two victims downstairs. But you haven't come close to convincing me that one of them killed both. Hell, Natalia brought up the war-criminal thing against Major Hyde."

Natalia appears taken aback for a moment, like she can't formulate an answer to my very logical point. Then she says, "I only brought up the war-criminal thing because I was curious. Genuinely curious. I was a history major when I started school here. I wish I still was, but my parents told me I needed to do something more practical if I was going to stay at Hyde, so I switched to biology. But the history of this region interests me, so I asked about the war."

"And Milo," Sydney says. Her voice cracks a little when she says his name. "You hate him, Natalia. And you were talking to Mr. Hyde before the exam. You seemed kind of pissed. What was that all about?"

Natalia tucks her chin to her chest and takes a step back. "Well . . . nothing. We were just— It was nothing. I just explained something to him. Clarified something from earlier."

"I think they're working together," Duffy says. "Like Sydney pointed out, the captain said he did reconnaissance on everyone before he came here today. He could have gotten in touch with Emily and worked something out. A plan. They each get rid of someone they want to get rid of."

"But if they got caught . . ." I say. "Is it worth it?"

"For a hundred thousand dollars in loan forgiveness *and* tuition *and* a job?" Sydney asks. "That could be worth it."

"If you kill Mr. Hyde, you might not get anything," I say.

"Emily doesn't care about all that," Duffy says. "You heard her say she doesn't want the job. So she pretends to be sick to make us think she's not guilty. Who knows what she and the captain are down there planning right now?"

I step forward, trying to stop Duffy from going any further. "Okay, I don't like the way this is going. We need to get back downstairs, which is what we said we were going to do, and we need to regroup. And everything needs to be about the safety of all of us. The police will figure out what happened in here today once we're out."

"But listen—"

"No, I won't." I start for the door.

Duffy remains in front of it. I don't doubt his willingness to block me. "Just hear me out. They're killers, okay? Do you know the danger we're in here? That's why I came upstairs."

"Duffy, please."

"Can we hear what I have to say, Mr. Gaines?" Duffy asks. "We're in deep shit from those two."

Someone pounds against the closed bedroom door.

And I mean pounds. Three thudding knocks that make everybody jump—including me.

Duffy moves away from the door and gets behind me, making me the person closest to whoever is on the other side. And I obviously know who it is.

He knocks again three more times.

"Sir?"

"Come in," I say.

The knob rattles, but the door doesn't open.

"I locked it," Duffy says. "I knew someone would try to get in."

"Sir? What's going on in there?"

"Just a minute." I go over and turn the lock. Before I can open the door, it swings inward, pushed by the captain. It brushes past my face, just missing me, and reminds me of the brick that almost smacked me earlier in the morning.

The captain stands there, one hand on his hip, the other holding the book, his body filling the doorway like a superhero. And Emily stands behind him, her eyebrows pushed together behind her glasses in confusion and concern. She rests one hand on her stomach, but some color has returned to her face. She's up and looking better.

The captain runs his eyes over each of us. "I don't understand why you all are up here with the door locked. Did you find out if any of the windows open?"

"They're all nailed shut, Captain," I say.

"Then why are you all in here?" Emily asks. "Locked in?"

"We were just talking," Sydney says.

"Oh, just talking?"

"We were trying to figure a way out of the house," I say. "All the windows are nailed shut on both floors. And both doors are locked from the outside. So that's where we stand."

"I could have told you that before you came up here," the captain says. "I think you knew it too, sir. Which doesn't answer the question of why the four of you were inside this room upstairs with the door locked. Talking about something that apparently you didn't want Emily and me to know about."

"That's not it, Captain," I say. "The two of you said you wanted to finish the exam. No matter what. And we were trying to figure out how to get out of the house. That's all."

The captain is nodding, a smile growing across his face. "Well, we've been standing out here longer than you realized. And what we heard is a discussion about how all of you are in deep shit because of the two of us. Does that ring any bells?"

47

THE ROOM SHRINKS.

Small and close.

And of course, our way out of it is blocked. The captain cuts an imposing figure.

"You were spying on us?" Natalia says, her voice rising.

"No," Emily says. "We came up to see what was taking so long. You were trying to find a window that opened so someone could leave. It shouldn't take as long as it did, since we're all in trouble here. When you didn't come back down, we decided to come up and see what was happening."

"These doors don't suppress much sound," the captain says. He raps the knuckles of his free hand against the wood.

"Are you feeling better, Emily?" I ask, Duffy's theory stuck in my brain.

"I feel a little better," she says. "Yes."

"You *look* better," Natalia says. "So . . . maybe you weren't poisoned?"

"Sir, there's something I think we need to make clear right now. I've been going through these bylaws while you all were up here. They're extensive, and they cover pretty much everything that could possibly happen."

"Murder?" Duffy asks. "Do they cover murder?"

"Well, not in so many words. But there is some interesting information in here." The captain opens the book, the spine resting in the palm of his left hand. "The Hyde family was prepared for a lot of things. I admire them for that. Maybe being forged by the Civil War made them aware of how quickly things could go wrong. But I noticed something earlier, sir. When Mr. Hyde asked you to sit in on the interviews, you acted surprised. Like you'd never heard of such a thing."

"I never did it in the previous years," I say. "Mr. Hyde's father was in charge then, and he really ran the show efficiently. And the person in this job before me never did it either."

"That may be so," the captain says. "But there is a provision in here that relates. At some point, they must have imagined today's events playing out in some way. Not necessarily murder, but the presiding member of the Hyde family becoming incapacitated. Right?"

I can tell where he's going. "They had to have some kind of backup plan."

"Exactly. In fact, it's interesting. It looks like that provision of the bylaws was added in 1921. Which is right after a pandemic."

"The Spanish flu," Duffy says.

"Not *Spanish* flu," Natalia says. "Please."

"Well, what was it, then?"

"Just flu," she says. *"Influenza."*

"Anyway," the captain says, "look here. They added a provision that says that if the presiding member of the Hyde family becomes incapacitated for any reason, then the college's liaison has the full force and authority that would have been invested in the member of the family. That means, sir, that you can decide who wins the scholarship. You can do the interviews and read the exams and decide."

The captain's words make me feel a lot better. He and Emily still block the doorway, which seems strange, and the air in the room gets stuffier, like we're in a steam room.

"Okay, then," I say. "That helps a lot, Captain. I'm glad you dug into all that. If that's the case and I have the full authority of the presiding member of the Hyde family, I'm going to use that authority. I say we go, and later on we can sort out what to do about the scholarship. And like I said, I'll do everything in my power to make sure one of the five of you gets it."

Sydney's face brightens. She raises her hand like we're in class. "Wait a minute. I just thought of something."

"What's that?"

"What if we just did this?" she says. "It seems like the fairest solution. What if we leave and then we split the scholarship five ways? Each of us gets twenty percent of our senior tuition. Each of us gets twenty thousand dollars of loan forgiveness. And then the job . . . Well, someone could take it. It doesn't have to be me. I don't care."

Duffy snaps his fingers. "That's a great idea. I could go along with that. Then everybody gets something."

No one else responds. The captain is staring at the book of bylaws. Emily stands behind him, taking an interest in a faded painting on the wall that appears to show a fox hunt.

Duffy turns. "Natalia, what about you? Would you split it five ways?"

"I don't know," she says. "I was kind of hoping to get the whole thing. That's what we showed up to do. And I think I have a good shot at it."

"I agree," Emily says from the hallway, looking away from the fox hunt. "One person should win. I don't want to share. I earned my way in here, and I want to win."

"*Earned* your way in?" Sydney asks. "How did you do that? I thought it was, like, based on need."

"It is based on need," I say. "They take students who have a certain amount of need and academic achievement, and then, as far as I know, they randomly select you. So it could have been six other students in here competing just as easily as it was the six of you."

"So it's random," Sydney says. "Just like Hyde down there was born rich and we weren't. So why not undermine that? Say the hell with it. Split the money among all of us and screw the Hydes."

"We don't know if that can happen," I say. "No one can promise that."

"And I understand what you're saying, Sydney," the captain says. "I really do. I probably would have thought the same thing when I was twenty-one. I was pretty crazy back then before I went into the army. Partying. Drinking. I didn't own a damn thing. But I wised up. Got straightened out. And now . . . I have a family. And a lot to live for. That's why I need all that prize money if I can get it."

"So just because you've struggled and been through it, you think the rest of us have to suffer too?" Sydney asks.

"I'm not close to being through the struggle. We never are."

I want to head off the conversation and steer it back in the direction it needs to go. "We're going to leave. That's it."

"Not so fast, sir." The captain has his index finger in the air. "I found something else in the bylaws that relates directly to your role in all of this. And it casts everything in a new light."

48

THE CAPTAIN HAS MANAGED to seize everyone's attention. He's ready to make a pronouncement like Moses coming down from the mount.

"What is this all about, Captain?" I ask.

The captain flips through some pages in the book until he finds the one he wants. He stabs the book again with his index finger. "This additional information is about your role here, sir," he says, "as the presiding officer. See, it says if the presiding officer leaves the house before four o'clock, then the entire scholarship process is null and void. Forever. Just like Mr. Hyde said that if the scholarship isn't awarded during a given year, it's forfeited forever. It really comes down to you. Emily and I thought we'd stay and then one of us would get the scholarship no matter what. But apparently that isn't the case. It all comes down to you. *You* have to stay."

While I'm happy to be the good soldier as much as I can—especially on behalf of the college and its students—I don't like feeling like I have no choice. And people's lives are being put in danger.

A trickle of sweat runs down my back. My armpits grow slick.

"Captain, we're not safe here. And that's what matters. Let's go downstairs and break a window. That's it."

Emily puts her hand on the captain's arm and gently moves him out of her way as she steps forward. Her glasses reflect the light from the fixture over our heads, making it tough to see her eyes.

"Mr. Gaines, we all know the shape the school is in. The captain researched it, but he doesn't live on campus." She points past me to the three traditional students. "Those of us who live here know. This place is falling apart. The dorms never have hot water. Not enough heat in the winter, blazing hot in the spring and fall. Three times since I've been in school, a pipe has burst in one of the dorms and flooded everything. My friend had her laptop ruined, and it took three months for the school to pay to replace it. And that's not even getting into the mold and the bugs and the dirt we have to live with." She looks past me. "Am I right?"

I turn to the other three. No one offers an argument. They nod along to Emily's words.

I can't argue with her either. The school is struggling financially. And I know the facilities are in disrepair. The entire campus needs electrical upgrades and better Wi-Fi. Almost every building needs a new roof.

"We're not a rich school," I say. "A lot of small private schools like Hyde aren't. We offer something more than the fancy amenities other schools can offer. It's something about the place and the people. You all know this."

"A few weeks back I visited my friend at UK," Duffy says.

247

"You should see how sweet those dorms are. Granite counters. Their own bathrooms."

"My friend plays volleyball at Davidson," Sydney says. "Now, *that's* a private school, and they're living high on the hog. They have so many food options you wouldn't believe it."

"That's a private school with *a lot* of money," I say. "Besides, do you think that stuff is the most important thing about a school? Bathrooms and . . . and food options?"

Even as I say it, I know the students aren't going to be convinced. It happens all the time—one school gets something, and the rest have to follow. One student tells a friend at another school about their amenities, and the friend feels like their school is lesser if they don't have it. For years, Hyde has been getting by on being a special place with special people. It's been selling its spirit and its magic.

But when the hot water doesn't work in the morning, how magical can the place be?

Emily goes on. "You were kissing up to Mr. Hyde all morning. That was obvious. Clearly the college needs the Hyde money if they want to stay afloat."

"It's my job to kiss up to anybody who wants to give money to the school. I've kissed up to people donating one hundred dollars just as hard as I kiss up to Mr. Hyde. I have to do that. But for now, let's go downstairs and get the hell out by breaking a window."

"*But* if you walk out this door before four, then the whole thing goes away," Emily says. "They might pull all the money from everything at the school if this is the first time this award isn't given. That could be the end of Hyde College. Certainly it's the end of this process."

I know Emily's probably right.

She's not saying anything I haven't been thinking on my own.

But I don't want to be pushed to do anything. Or be backed into a corner.

Like I told the captain just moments ago—the safety of the people in the house is more important than any amount of money. And I think I know what I can do if they insist on staying.

But before I can act, Natalia surprises me by speaking up.

"Okay, okay," she says. "I think I know an easy way out of this that doesn't involve breaking or climbing out a window. You all just have to promise to be chill and not lose your minds when I tell you what it is."

49

NATALIA SEEMS TO BE hiding inside her oversized sweater.

"You can't look at me," she says.

"I thought you wanted us to," I say.

"I have a solution, but you can't *look* at me while I take care of it. And you have to promise not to be mad."

"What are you talking about?" Emily looks at me. "She's not making any sense, is she?"

"Natalia, if you know something that can help us—"

She cuts me off by raising her hands, holding them up to the group palms out. Like she wants to push us all away. "Just don't look. Okay? Everybody, turn your backs to me. For just a minute or two. Okay? That's all you have to do."

"Sir, this is highly unusual. We've already had two people die, and she wants us to turn our backs to her."

"Natalia," I say, "I want to respect your wishes and give you a chance to say whatever you want to say. But can't you just tell us what your plan is so we can all know what we're getting into? The captain is right. We're in some trouble here, so we need to be open with one another."

"No more locked doors, then," Emily says.

"*I* locked the door," Duffy says. "Not him. Not anybody else. Okay? That was me. So what gives, Natalia?"

The giant eyes scan the line of us. Down one way and then back up the other. Natalia looks like she's deciding something right in front of us.

"Okay, fine," she says. "I guess when you're locked in a house with a group of people all day, privacy kind of goes out the window."

She uses her right hand and reaches for her back. The hand slides under the sweater and appears to be digging around, trying to get ahold of something in her jeans.

"Are *you* getting a weapon of some kind?" the captain asks. "Sir, how do we know she doesn't have something in there?"

Natalia sighs at the comment but doesn't say anything. She continues to move her hand around for another twenty seconds. She scrunches her face with the effort. Then her arm stops, and the tension eases from her face, indicating she has in her hand what she set out to get.

"Okay," she says. "Here we go."

She brings her arm out and holds the object up in the air in front of all of us.

It's red and oblong. Sleek, it catches the light.

Sydney says it first. "It's a fucking phone. A flip phone, but a phone."

"Where did that come from?" I ask.

Natalia keeps her fingers wrapped around the phone. "I'd heard we all had to give up our phones when we got here. And I did. You took mine along with everybody else's. But my friend had this old flip phone, and they said I should bring it. Just in case. I mean, I didn't think anybody would get murdered, but it seemed strange to go somewhere without any way to call for help."

"Then we're set," I say. "We can call the police."

"Sir, this is highly irregular. You just heard what happens if—"

"No, no," I say. "We're calling for help."

Natalia opens the phone and starts to dial but stops.

"Wait. . . ."

"There's no service, I bet," Duffy says. "I've tried to make a call out here in these trees before, and it didn't work."

My heart sinks like a stone. But I know he's right. Cell service is spotty away from campus. I've had my own share of calls drop as I drove away from my office and through the woods that lead out to the main road.

Natalia presses buttons with her thumb. Over and over.

"Shit. No service."

"A phone that old—"

"Even newer phones struggle out here."

"Damn it," Natalia says. "Shit."

"Do you want me to—"

"Here, I can—"

"Okay, okay," Natalia says. "There's a signal. One bar. Shit. Hurry. It's not working— Oh, it is. Should I call campus police or nine-one-one?"

"Just call nine-one-one," I say. "Here. Let me."

I reach out. As I do, another hand comes over mine. I recognize the arm, the tattoos.

Emily snatches the phone out of Natalia's hand. Without hesitating for a moment, she takes each half of the phone in one of her hands and bends it back in a way it's not supposed to go, the muscles in her arms tensing like wires. With a sickening plastic crack, she breaks the phone in half, rendering it useless.

50

THERE'S A COLLECTIVE GASP.

Everyone makes a noise in the aftermath of the crack. Even the captain does, and he wants to stay in the house and keep me here as well.

"Emily, are you fucking crazy?" Natalia says.

Emily takes the two halves of the phone and tosses them out into the hall, where they rattle against the wood floors like large tumbling dice. "You can't call that way. Not when we don't all agree. Not when so much is at stake."

"That was our way out," Sydney says.

"We get out at four o'clock," Emily says. "That's it. The stupid phone wasn't going to work out here anyway. We all know the service is for shit on this part of campus."

"So you just break it?" Duffy asks. "Are you the killer? Do you want us all to stay in here and not talk to the cops because you're guilty?"

"I want the fucking scholarship, okay? That's what I want."

"We all wanted the damn thing. This morning." Sydney points at Emily, looms above her. "But everything is different now. There are more important things going on. People are dying."

Emily folds her hands like she's praying. She brings them up to cover her nose and mouth. She closes her eyes, like she's deep in thought. And like the rest of us aren't here. "I don't just want it. I need it."

"We all need it too," Duffy says. "None of us are rich."

"No . . ." Emily takes a deep, shuddering breath. "Sydney, you talked about my poem. And my parents. And how I've changed. My parents cut me off. Completely. Like nothing. They don't understand who I am or how I'm changing. So I'm just here alone. And my friends want something else. They act like it's so easy, but most of them have families who are paying their way. Do you know how easy that sounds? To have someone just mailing checks to the school whenever you need it? Buying you a computer or a car or clothes . . . on a whim." She sniffles and runs her hand under her nostrils. But no tears spill from her eyes. "I need the money. I *have* to stay. I don't want to. I don't want to grovel for some millionaire's handouts. But what else can I do?"

"Not break other people's shit," Sydney says. "Right?"

"I understand what you're saying, Emily." Duffy's voice is calm, a soothing presence in the heated moment.

Sydney looks at him like she doesn't know who he is. Like she's been betrayed. But he ignores the glance and keeps talking.

"I know rich kids. There's a dude in my dorm who came here with two cars—an SUV and a Mercedes. One for going out and having fun. One for driving around town. Whatever that means." He shakes his head. "Goddamn, I'd like to have that money. I'd like to not worry for just one day. I'd like to go into town and eat at McDonald's—McDonald's, for fuck's sake—and not feel bad because maybe I could be spending that money on something else. A book or clothes . . . or maybe send it home to my parents so they could relax a little. People like the Hydes . . . or *any* rich people . . . look, they have us at one another's throats like we're animals in a cage. In history class we learned about the Roman circuses. You know, stick people in an arena and tell them they have to fight a lion or something. Give them a broom or a feather as a weapon to defend themselves with. Things don't change."

Natalia is giving Emily a death stare. "I have to buy my friend a new damn phone."

"Stay and win the scholarship and you can afford it," the captain says.

"That's not helpful," Natalia says, moving the death stare toward the captain for a moment.

But Emily's admission and Duffy's empathy lower the temperature for most of us. Only Natalia seems unfazed. She swings her head toward Duffy.

"You seem pretty unhappy with the wealthy," she says.

"Aren't we all?"

"You seem particularly unhappy," she says. "All those things you were saying earlier about your mom and the chicken-processing plant."

"What about a chicken-processing plant?" the captain asks.

"It's nothing—" Duffy says.

"The Hyde family put a big dent in Duffy's family farm because they put in a chicken-processing plant. And wouldn't buy feed from Duffy's family. Then his mom went to work in the plant, and the Hyde family fired her because she tried to organize her fellow workers. Is that about right, Duffy?" Natalia asks.

The captain whistles.

"You're coming after me?" Duffy asks. "She just broke your phone."

"But you're the one who hates the Hydes. And Mr. Hyde is dead."

"I didn't hate Milo."

"Really?" Emily says.

Even I can't help it. I look at Sydney and then look away.

But Duffy has caught it. "Oh, come on."

Natalia turns to the rest of the group. "He was coming on to her in the kitchen. Pawing all over her. We saw them. Duffy didn't waste any time. Milo is barely cold and he's moving in. He must have wanted Milo out of the way. I don't think Sydney wanted anything to do with him. I was worried about her."

"That's sick as fuck," Duffy says.

The cross talk starts. Voices rise in volume and pitch.

Fingers point.

I'm in the cross fire. And I'm sick of it. They're too loud, too immature.

Too crazy.

I'm not staying in the house a moment longer.

I don't say anything. I just start out of the room, brushing past Emily and coming face-to-face with the captain. When everyone notices my movement, they stop talking and watch.

"Sir?" the captain says. He still holds the bylaws, cradles the book to his chest like a baby. "Is something wrong?"

"We're leaving. And I know how we're getting out now."

I start to go, and the captain puts his big hand on my arm. "Sir?"

I look down where his hand has my arm. "Captain, let go."

He releases his grip. I lift my left hand and gently but firmly guide the captain out of my way.

I start down the hall, the group following along behind like I'm the Pied Piper.

51

I GO INTO ONE of the bedrooms that faces the front of the house.

The two large windows face the yard—and in the distance the cops and the protestors stand at the barricade. Duffy's right—a sign pressed against the glass wouldn't work. At best, someone looking at the house and seeing a sign in the window would be confused. They'd need binoculars in order to read any text in the window.

And I doubt we even have anything to make a very large sign.

And I'm past the sign stage anyway. I'm ready to do something more.

I've been told the bedroom I enter was used as the nursery by the Hyde family. The Hyde children slept in here as babies, and a wooden cradle, something that no one in their right mind would stick an infant in today, sits in one corner of the room. At some point, someone refurbished it, because the finish is buffed to a high gloss.

There's a dresser and a wooden rocking chair. It's easy to

imagine Mary Hyde sitting in that rocker, holding a baby. Perhaps holding one of their children as they battled against the deadly illnesses that ultimately took three of them away. A very different time with very different stakes.

But here we are—fighting for our lives and survival.

If a sign won't do to get the attention of the police, we have to go bigger. And there's only one thing I can think of.

The students come through the doorway and enter the room. They fan out near the entrance, watching me. Maybe it's the way they might watch one of their parents who has flown into a rage.

Or maybe it's the way my students used to watch me in the classroom when I admitted some vulnerability. When my mother died, I spoke frankly to my students about it, going so far as to choke up in front of them. The students didn't know what to do. It's so strange to them when an authority figure loses their cool.

"Sir?"

"We're leaving," I say, bending down to pick up the cradle. "I'm going to alert the cops. And they can open the door."

"Sir, is that wise?"

I lift the cradle, which is surprisingly heavy. Made of mahogany. About three feet long. The muscles in my arms and back strain. They burn, and they'll burn more tomorrow.

"Is it wise, Captain? Is it wise to stay in here with a killer? Is it wise to put money above everything else in life?"

"I'm not sure this is the best approach," Sydney says.

"I don't put money above important things, sir. But I need money for my family," the captain says.

"I thought about it," I say, breathing heavily. "I could smash a downstairs window, but that might be less likely to get their attention. You see . . ." I adjust my grip on the cradle by placing it on my knee and getting a firmer hold. "You see, if I throw this out the window here, then it spends more time in the air, falling to the ground. That way, the cops and the protestors are more likely to see it. Even the protestors won't be able to keep their mouths shut if they see this cradle flying through the air. Right, Emily?"

"That's shitty," Emily says.

"Maybe it's you," I say, sorry I singled one of them out. "It could be any one of you. Or maybe it's me. You think I fought with Nicholas Hyde in the parlor. Or maybe I poisoned his bourbon. Why? Hell, I don't know. Maybe I thought I could get more money from his family if he's dead. But the cops will come in now and sort it all out. And nobody else will get hurt. That's my job—to keep you all from getting hurt. And I already failed. Just like I failed to keep the other two people alive. I'll pay for the window and the cradle out of my lofty salary."

I take two halting steps toward the window.

I position my feet like someone getting ready to throw a javelin. I use my left hand as a guide and shift my weight to my right side, placing that hand on the end, and prepare to launch.

"Somebody's going to get hurt," Duffy says.

"Two people already are," I say.

"Sir, I don't think that's the best solution."

I take a deep breath. Bend my knees.

And then I heave.

I send the cradle flying toward the giant window, my mind anticipating—almost joyfully—the enormous splintering smash of the glass, the cradle breaking out and into the air in front of the house. The wooden object floating through space like an object freed of its bonds—

Until it comes down in the yard in a rain of broken glass, the wood smashing into bits.

And the police and the protestors seeing it all. Running toward us—releasing us—

Except . . .

The cradle hits the window and bounces directly back.

It hits me in the lower body, the heavy weight of the wood smacking into my thighs and knees, knocking me backward while my legs start to sting.

"What the . . . ?" Natalia says.

"Sir . . . ?"

I pick the cradle up again. More voices speak behind me, but I don't hear them. I can't. I have a mission, a goal.

I take the cradle, and this time, instead of throwing it against the window, I keep my hand on the back and drive it against the pane. Like a battering ram. A driven spike.

The cradle meets the pane and there is instant resistance.

It sends a jolting wave of pain up my arm and into my shoulder and chest. The force of the resistance knocks my body backward, and both the cradle and I fall to the floor with loud thuds.

Then the room descends into an intense silence.

The entire right side of my body hurts. Arm, shoulder, back.

I breathe heavily, not sure if I can stand. Or move at all.

I want to stay still. Very still on the floor. Maybe it will all go away. Maybe it's a dream.

Maybe the cops heard the thud against the window and are coming to pull us out now.

But I know that's wishful thinking.

The five students gather around, their faces looking down at me with pity and concern.

"Are you okay, Mr. Gaines?" Sydney asks.

I don't answer. I nod, which hurts the right side of my neck.

"Sir?"

The captain shows genuine concern.

"Sir, if I may. Part of my reconnaissance was reading up on this house a little. I believe there once was a stained glass window below us. Rather an impressive piece. But some hellions occupied the house during Vietnam. They smashed that window and wanted to set fire to the premises. Did you know that?"

I work up some saliva in my mouth. "Yes, I do."

"I'm guessing all the windows were replaced with shatterproof glass. To deter the protestors."

Duffy wanders over to the window. He steps around the cradle. "But you can still shatter shatterproof glass. If you hit it enough. With the right object."

"Possibly, with a great deal of effort," the captain says. "But given how hard Mr. Gaines hit that, and with such a heavy object . . . it's got to be more than shatterproof glass. It has to be something like . . ."

"Polycarbonate," I say.

"What's that?" Emily asks.

"Polycarbonate," I say again.

"Oh, yeah," the captain says. "Polycarbonate. That's two hundred fifty times more shatter resistant than shatterproof safety glass, sir. They must have been serious about keeping people out of here."

"Yes," I say. "They were."

And now they've made sure none of us can get out.

At all.

PART 3
AFTERNOON

52

I'M HELPED OFF THE floor.

My legs wobble a little. They're rubbery and loose.

It takes a moment, but I regain my equilibrium. I rub my chest, my arm. I shake my head to clear the cobwebs.

Across from me the offending cradle sits on its side on the floor. Unscathed apparently.

"Duffy, did the cops hear me?"

Duffy presses his face against the glass. He cups his hands around his face to cut down on glare. "Doesn't look like it, boss. They all seem kind of . . ."

"Kind of what?" Emily asks. "Pissed? They're cops, so they're always pissed."

"Indifferent," Duffy says. "About half the protestors have left. Even the cops look bored."

"Sir, if I may—"

"You may not." A chill has run through my body, perhaps an aftereffect of charging against the unforgiving polycarbonate window. I rub my hands together. "Okay, here's what we're going to do. If we're all trapped in here, as it appears we are, then we're going to finish the process as spelled out in the magic bylaws."

A smile spreads across the captain's face.

"Unless," I say, "some other way out of this house is presented to us. I guarantee you if the police officers come close again, for whatever reason, I will do everything in my power to notify them of our situation." I check my watch. "But it's almost two o'clock now, which means we're in here for two more hours. If I'm now the presiding officer of these proceedings—"

"You are," the captain says. "You most definitely are."

"—then I'm going to carry out my duties to the best of my ability. And I'm going to interview each and every one of you."

"I see what you're doing," Natalia says.

"Oh, you do. And what exactly am I doing?"

"You're investigating the murders," she says. "You say you're doing the interviews, but you're going to utilize them as a way to figure out who you think killed Milo and Mr. Hyde."

"What about our rights?" Emily says.

"We've already had our rights violated by the Hyde family," Natalia says. "Digging into our backgrounds the way they did."

"Rights?" I say.

I pace around the room, walking close to each of them as I speak. The floorboards squeak underneath me, and I resist the urge to give the cradle a good kick. Likely, I would only end up breaking my foot against its solid American craftsmanship.

"I'm in charge. I'm the presiding officer. But"—I raise my index finger into the air—"if anyone feels their rights are being violated, they can choose not to participate in the interview. After all, we still have a certain degree of freedom here, don't we? Naturally, should one opt not to sit for the interview, that will be duly noted when it comes time for *me* to decide who wins the scholarship."

They're all looking at me like they've found themselves in a cage with a wounded or rabid cougar.

But then I notice something.

The absence of *someone.*

"Where's Sydney?" I ask.

Everyone looks around as though the tallest person in the group could disappear under a piece of furniture.

"She *was* here," Emily says. "When we came in and you threw that thing against the window. She was here then."

"But then?" I ask.

"I bet she went to the bathroom," Duffy says.

"That's weird," the captain says.

"Going to the bathroom?" Duffy asks.

"Not saying anything when you leave the room."

"Okay, we'll find her downstairs," I say.

Natalia raises her hand. Tentatively. Like someone might bite it off. "There're five of us and two hours left. So is each interview going to last the same amount of time?"

"Why are you always so worried about the rules?" Duffy asks.

"I'm not *worried* about them," Natalia says. "It's my nature to want to know what's going on so I can plan. Besides, a person of color kind of *has* to know what the rules are—and follow them more carefully."

"Captain, is there anything in the bylaws about how long each interview should last?"

Pages rustle. His brow furrows. "I don't see anything. . . ."

"There's your answer," I say. "From the holy book itself."

"And the questions are going to be about the exam?" Emily asks.

"Captain?"

"It says here that while the interview questions can refer to the written portion of the process, the examiner is not bound by the written portion alone. They may ask about anything—including any and all events that have transpired during the course of the process."

I hold my hands out palms up. *There you go.*

"Here's what I suggest we do," I say. "In fact, I insist. I say we all go down to the dining room, and everyone can sit around the table while they wait. Don't eat anything. Don't drink anything. Don't bicker or fight or argue. There's a murderer in this house. Just wait until I call you each into the parlor for your interview."

"But what if Sydney is up to something?" Emily says.

"I will be as fair as possible when it comes to everyone getting equal time. But if for some reason one person ends up getting more time than another, there's nothing I can do about that."

"It's like one person being born rich and another not," Duffy says.

"Pretty much. It's just the way it is." I point to the doorway of the bedroom and the staircase beyond. "Shall we?"

There's a moment of hesitation.

It is like being in the classroom again—maybe I have them behind me. And maybe I don't.

I can't know until someone responds. Someone acts.

It takes a few heartbeats. Mine echoes loudly in my ear.

But then the captain slaps the book shut and turns to go. Emily shrugs and follows him. Soon enough, all four are leaving the room and walking down the stairs, single file. Like obedient children.

For the moment anyway, I've managed to seize control of the situation.

53

THE GROUP HEADS FOR the dining room, with me at the rear.

But we all stop in the hallway.

Sydney emerges not from the bathroom but from the kitchen.

"What were you doing in there?" Duffy asks.

Sydney's dress is smeared with a stain on the right side. A stain I feel certain wasn't there before.

"Were you eating something?" I ask.

Sydney looks over her shoulder. Like someone might be behind her. "No way."

"Then what were you doing in the kitchen?" Emily asks. "You have a stain on your dress. Did you spill food on yourself?"

"No, I . . ." She looks over her shoulder again. "I was just in the kitchen."

I move through the students until I'm closest to Sydney. "Doing what? If you weren't eating, then what?"

She lets out a frustrated groan. "Okay, it's the food. I was . . . I threw it all away. Dumped out those platters and stuff. That's how

I got the stain on my dress. I couldn't stand the thought of it sitting there if it might be poisoned. So I threw it in the trash so no one else would eat it."

Emily is next to me. "That's evidence, Sydney. And you pitched it?"

"It's still there . . . in the trash," she says.

"Emily is right," the captain says. "You just can't throw that away or tamper with it."

"Well, you all moved Milo's body," Sydney says.

"That's different," I say. "And you're right. Maybe that was a mistake. We wanted to treat his body with respect and not leave it there while you all took the exam. We didn't move Nicholas's body. That food . . . the police need to examine it."

"I don't like this," Emily says. "I think we need to do something, Mr. Gaines." Emily speaks in a low, hollow voice. "If someone wanted to cover up their crimes, that's what they'd do. They'd try to toss the evidence."

"No, I'm protecting people," Sydney says. "I'm nervous about that food . . . if it's poisoned."

"Sir, this seems highly irregular. We can't have someone destroying evidence. Not only does it make me nervous about Sydney, but it will make us all look suspicious when the police come in."

"Okay," I say, "we were all headed for the dining room. Why don't we go in there—"

"No," Emily says. She's shaking her head next to me, like a terrier with a chew toy. "No. I have my problems, lots of them. But Sydney is screwing around with the food."

"Emily, you're crazy—"

"Hold it, Duffy. What did I say about not accusing one another?"

Emily backs up, hands out. "I'm not sitting in a room with them. That's all."

Sydney stands alone in the hallway outside the kitchen. The five of us, including Duffy, remain grouped together, even as Emily and Natalia both now back up. Even the captain looks uncertain, not sure if he should retreat or hold his ground.

"You should all be able to—"

"There's a simple solution," Emily says. "If Sydney liked the kitchen so much, she can sit in there while the rest of us go into the dining room. Then we're all safe."

Sydney's jaw drops. Her hands jumble together in a tangle of nervous fingers. "I don't want to sit in the kitchen *alone*. Like I'm being punished. Why should I be sent in there alone?"

"You don't have to—"

"You have to because we don't trust you," Emily says. "You're acting weird."

"You broke off from the group when we were supposed to be together," the captain says. "We need everyone to fly in formation."

"Are you serious?" Sydney asks. "Me?"

"I'll sit in the kitchen with you," Duffy says.

"That's perfect," Emily says. "For all I know they're planning to take us all out together. Starting with Milo."

"That's so nasty, Emily," Sydney says.

Duffy steps forward and places his hand on Sydney's arm, gently guiding her toward the kitchen. Sydney pulls away but walks with him.

"We'll sit in here," Duffy says. "People like Emily are mad at everybody for everything. They don't even know why they're mad."

They go into the kitchen, and I herd the other three students into the dining room again.

They settle around the table, Emily on one side, Natalia on the other. The captain is at the far end. Natalia fidgets. I let my gaze roam over them. How do I spot a murderer?

Or are the murderers in the kitchen?

"Captain?" I say.

"Sir?"

"The book." I point.

He looks down at the black book of bylaws that sits on the table in front of him. His right hands rests on it like he thinks someone is about to snatch it away. Which I kind of am.

"What about it?" he asks.

"I'd like it."

"Sir—"

"If I'm the presiding officer here, I should have the bylaws in my possession, right? I mean, who knows what else might be in there that can help me do my job and keep everyone safe?"

The captain hands me the book. As he does, he whispers so no one else can hear, "Check the last page."

"What?"

His voice booms again. "Sir, should we check inside Mr. Hyde's briefcase? It's right there."

"Check for what?"

"Anything. Maybe he has a phone."

"He tossed the phone in the trunk of his car. I saw him do it. And he kept locking the briefcase." But I walk over and bend down to examine it. I try the clasps, but they don't budge. "See? Locked."

"Why would he have to keep it locked?" Emily asks.

"He's a businessman," the captain says. "He'd have to keep certain things private and protected. Documents, reports."

"He's hardly a businessman," Emily says. "He's a brat who was born into the right family and fell into a pile of money. Then randomly exercises his power and privilege as he sees fit."

"Forget the briefcase, then." I scan the faces at the table. "Why don't we start the interviews with . . ."

They all avert their gazes. Who wants to be first?

"Natalia," I say. "How about you?"

"Me?" She plants her index finger against her chest, burying it in the giant sweater. "Why me?"

"Somebody has to go first," I say.

"He thinks you're guilty," Emily says. "Of course he's going to interview the person he thinks is guilty first."

"What?" Natalia says. "That's so wrong."

"I don't think anyone is guilty," I say. "I'm assuming you're all guilty right now." I point to the doorway that leads out of the dining room and into the hallway. "Shall we?"

Natalia stands up. "It's unfair."

"Remember," I say, "comportment is part of the decision, so maybe less bickering." I carry the bylaws with me, and I look back. "Are you two okay?"

"Yes, sir," the captain says, and Emily nods.

"Keep an eye on each other. And be safe."

Natalia and I walk to the parlor. Only when we go inside do I remember that Nicholas Hyde's body remains on the floor, covered by the captain's jacket.

"Oh, shit," I say.

"I told you, dead people don't concern me," Natalia says. She takes a seat in one of the parlor chairs. "Maybe that makes me appear guilty, that I'm not bothered by death. It's a natural phenomenon that comes for all of us."

"Okay, no assumptions here," I say as I sit across from Natalia. I have the bylaws in my lap, but I don't think I need them. "Why did you have a phone the whole time and not let us know about it? When Milo died and then Nicholas . . . you let all of that happen without telling anyone about the phone. Why?"

She sighs, her eyes trailing over Nicholas's inert form on the floor.

"You didn't seem to like Milo very much. You called him a cheater. And I guess a biology major might know something about how poisons work. You were talking about herbs."

Her head whips back. "Oh, that's it. You do think I'm guilty."

"Just tell me about the phone."

"Isn't it obvious?" she asks.

"You want to win the scholarship, so you didn't want the process to stop?"

She stares at me for a beat. "You're too polite to say it, so I will. I'm undocumented. I can't get mixed up with the police."

"So if you called them to report Milo's death . . ."

"They'd start hassling me. Asking questions. It's hard enough to come to school this way. I'm lucky Hyde is in such financial trouble. They don't mind if you're undocumented. They just want students, and they were able to put together some aid for me. Not federal, of course, but from the school. But I'm always looking over my shoulder. . . . My older brother got pulled over for running a stop sign about six months ago. They've been trying to deport him, and he's—*we're*—trying to fight it. But it's expensive. My parents are helping, but they have to stay hidden at the same time, so everyone's scared and tense."

"Okay, I understand. And I'm sorry. Truly." I know we have undocumented students on campus, but I've never talked to one as far as I know. "So you were protecting yourself more than anything else?"

"And I'm already here at a murder scene. How is that going to look? I'm going to have to talk to the cops when I leave this place, right?" She shakes her head. "It makes me sick to think about."

"We're all going to have to answer to the police at four o'clock. But you shouldn't worry about your status. You're right that Hyde College accepts undocumented students. We'll do everything we can to make sure you're treated fairly."

"And God bless us, everyone."

"Why did you take the phone out when you did?"

She rubs her eyes with her right hand. She rubs like she wants to jam her eyeballs farther back into her head. "I just got sick of the arguing. Nothing was being accomplished. We were going to be split against one another no matter what. And we're in danger, so I just decided to do something. Kind of like you throwing that cradle against the window. Weren't you just sick of not getting anywhere?"

"I hear you."

"Is this all we're going to talk about?" she asks. "It's really not fair if I get brought in here for my interview and you only ask me about murder. You get to decide about the scholarship, so you should interview me."

She's right. I nod my head. "Okay." I realize I don't have the essays before me. And I haven't read them. So I punt. "Why don't you tell me why you deserve the Hyde Scholarship?"

She answers. Quickly. "Did you know that no student of color has ever won the Hyde Scholarship?"

"No, I didn't."

"Don't you think it's time?"

"Of course. Obviously."

"And I'm not saying that's the only reason I should get it. Okay? You can read my essay. Written in my *second* language. And you can read about what my family has been through as they came to America from Mexico."

Someone knocks on the pocket doors. The sound makes me jump. I fear every sound is going to be making me jump for a while.

"I don't know why they'd interrupt. . . ."

"You'd better answer," Natalia says. "Who knows what's going on?"

"Good point."

I go to the door and slide it open.

The other four students stand out there looking at me with grave concern on their faces.

54

I'M RELIEVED ALL FOUR of them appear before me. Standing up.

Apparently unharmed.

If they'd knocked on the door to tell me that someone else had dropped dead in the dining room, I'm not sure how I'd have responded.

But I can tell from their faces something is wrong. So I ask what the problem is.

The students shift their weight from one foot to another. Even the captain looks reluctant to speak.

"Well?" I say. "Is somebody else hurt? Or sick? I thought all of you were staying away from one another."

"No," Duffy says. "Not exactly."

"Then why are you interrupting this interview? Come on—tell me."

Behind me, Natalia rises to her feet. She walks over and stands next to me, leaning toward the open pocket doors in order to see and hear what is being discussed.

"Well?" I ask. "Spit it out."

Emily says, "Maybe you should come out here, Mr. Gaines, and then we can talk to you."

"You mean out of *my* presence?" Natalia asks.

"Yes," the captain says.

"You can't just talk about someone in the house and not tell them what's going—" Natalia stops herself. "I guess it doesn't matter what I say right now. You all have something in mind, some theory you want to play out. What is it?"

"I'm not sure what's going on," I say. "Are you all accusing Natalia of something? She's been sitting in here with me. You all know that."

"Look, here goes." Duffy is standing with one hand hooked in his belt, the other behind his back like he's hiding something. He brings the hidden hand out and extends it toward me. "Check this out. Emily found it on Natalia's chair after she left the room with you."

I try to process what it is. Plastic and wrinkled.

I lean closer, then reach out and take it in my own hand. It's a sandwich bag crumpled from being stuffed into someone's pocket. I hold it between my thumb and index finger. At the bottom of the bag is a powdery white residue.

"What's this?" I ask.

"It's mine," Natalia says.

She pats her pants pockets and then makes a grab for the bag, but I pull it out of her reach.

"Come on."

"Hold on," I say. "What is this?"

"It was sitting on Natalia's chair," Duffy says. "After she got up to go off with you for her interview, that was sitting on her chair like it had fallen out of her pocket."

"It *did* fall out of my pocket."

"How did you all get together on this?" I ask.

Duffy sighs. "Okay, I went back into the dining room to tell them off for exiling Sydney."

"I didn't ask him to do that," Sydney says.

"When I went in there, Emily had found the bag of powder. So we all tried to figure out what it was."

"And then we came here," Sydney says. "Together."

I turn to Natalia. "Okay, what is it?" I ask.

"It's my ADHD meds. You heard me mention them before. I need them."

"Why are they all crushed into powder like this?" I ask.

"That's the way I like to take them," she says. "I don't like swallowing pills, so I crush mine up. I always have. It's common to crush pills this way."

I look over at the group of four, who stand arrayed against Natalia. "That seems reasonable."

"Sir," the captain says, "we have two people dead. Apparently the victims of some kind of poisoning. To crush up pills like that . . ."

"We don't know it's poisoning for sure," I say.

"But it's certainly in play. That's why you told us not to eat or drink. That's why you're questioning everyone. And now we've found one of us with a bag of powder that could easily be placed into a drink. Or food."

"Do you know this is poison and not ADHD medication?" I ask.

"Well, I sniffed it," the captain says. "I couldn't really tell."

"Can any of you tell by looking? Or sniffing?"

"A lot of ADHD meds are capsules," Sydney says. "The ones that aren't are pretty small. They're not hard to swallow."

"How do you know what's hard for me to swallow or not?" Natalia asks.

"You hated Milo," Sydney says. "That's obvious. And when we were all pouring our tea, you were right next to him. You easily could have sprinkled something into his drink."

"Are you nuts?"

"He was talking to Mr. Hyde. A lot. I guess that's kind of Milo's approach to life. Was his approach." Duffy scratches his head. "Kiss as much ass as possible. But maybe the poison went into his cup."

"Maybe it got Mr. Hyde too," the captain says. "Collateral damage."

"I guess you'd know all about that," Natalia says.

"Are you impugning my service—"

I'm still holding the bag as I wave my arms in the air like an umpire signaling someone safe. "I'm going to hold on to this. It's evidence. The only people who can really sort this out are the police. Okay?"

"So I don't get my medication back?"

"Do you need to take more of it?" I bring the bag closer to my face. "This doesn't even look like enough to be one dose."

Natalia looks away. "Ugh."

"In the meantime, no one is accusing anyone of anything. Okay?"

"She was talking to Mr. Hyde right before the exam started," Sydney says. "Remember, Duffy? She was up there, and it was like they were arguing? Right?"

"He was pissed at me because I called the major a war criminal."

"You shouldn't have done that," the captain says. "A person's military service deserves respect."

"My favorite uncle served in the marines," Natalia says. "My godfather. Okay?"

"Really?"

"Yes, really. He . . . well, he couldn't be an officer, but he served."

"Oh."

"She said she didn't like to drink," Emily says. "Nobody else said that. Maybe she planned on poisoning the bourbon so the rest of us would die."

"I drank it."

"Did you?" Emily says. "Maybe you just did that thing we've all done at parties or while playing drinking games. Just pretend to drink. Or throw it over your shoulder."

"I've never done that," Duffy says.

"Then why aren't all of you deceased?" Natalia asks. "Milo didn't drink the bourbon."

"I'm going to hold on to this." I slide the bag into the inside pocket of my jacket. "I'll hand it over to Chief when he lets us out."

Natalia's face is flushed. She stares at me like I'm the lowest form of life on earth. She speaks to me through gritted teeth. "After what we just talked about in there?" She storms off, heading for the music room. "Nobody knows that about me."

"What did you talk about in there?" the captain asks. "What does nobody know? Sir, if this is relevant to the investigation—"

"I can't discuss other people's interviews with the group. Sorry."

"But, sir—"

"I can't."

"She's going to the music room," the captain says. "That's where Milo is."

283 •

Natalia hears him and comes back. "What do you think I'm going to do? Kill him again?"

"There's evidence," the captain says. "You could tamper."

"Do you think I'll mutilate his corpse?"

"That's disrespectful," Sydney says. "And gross."

"I think the captain is right," I say. "You should all stay in the same place. That way you can keep an eye on one another. You don't have to like one another, but you can watch one another. Safety in numbers. Why don't you all return to the dining room now. Except Emily. You can be the next interview. Okay?"

Her mouth pops open. "Me?"

"Yes, you."

"Is this because I broke her damn phone? And that makes me look guilty?"

"If the phone fits," I say, pointing to the parlor.

55

EMILY STANDS IN THE middle of the parlor. Her hand is pressed against her face.

"This is so offensive," she says.

"I'm sorry, but this is the only room that offers privacy."

"What about those bedrooms upstairs?"

"It's not right for me to go upstairs with a student alone. And go into a bedroom with the door closed."

"Some professors around here do it," she says. "People talk."

"I'm happily married and intend to stay that way." I point to the two chairs. "Why don't we sit?"

She does, smoothing her dress over her thighs, but she doesn't stop complaining. "I don't think it's right I have to come in here to talk. With a stiff in the room."

"Do you want to do the interview or not?"

Emily seems to accept the conditions. She grips the arms of the parlor chair tight, her nails painted a dark color. "So which thing do you want to hassle me about? The protestors or the phone?"

"Breaking the phone was pretty shitty. We all could have gotten out of here."

"*If* the phone worked. *If* there was service. Did you see her struggling to get it going? That old-ass flip phone was never going to work out here. People with brand-new phones sometimes struggle to get reception on this part of campus."

"So you broke it? How did that help?"

She sighs and rolls her eyes. "I guess I fail at comportment. That's always been the thing I get in trouble for—not playing well with the other kids. 'Well, Mrs. Paine, your daughter is quite intelligent and gifted. It's just that she's so surly with the other children.' *Surly.* That's me."

"You broke the phone because you didn't want to leave. Because you wanted to win the scholarship."

"Seems at cross purposes, doesn't it? Bust the phone in order to stay, but breaking the phone means I lose comportment points. Catch-22." She shrugs. "I guess I get the five thousand. Every little bit helps. My dad got laid off last year. My mom . . . she works in a school cafeteria. She drives Uber some weekends. It's kind of embarrassing when people I knew in high school message me and say my mom was their Uber driver. My dad's been so depressed. . . ."

"I'm sorry. Are you feeling better? You seem like you're doing okay."

"Better." She rubs her stomach. "It's weird with parents, you know? I mean, I can't stand them. We have nothing in common. But . . ." Her eyes fill with tears behind the big glasses.

"But you love them."

"I do." Her chin quivers. "They're such assholes. If you saw who they voted for. But I feel sorry for them . . . and I don't want them to be unhappy. And they are. I mean, really unhappy. Things really got bad between us this last year. . . ." She sniffles, wipes her nose. "I'm not what they want me to be."

"They don't care what you major in or what your politics are. They're parents. They want you to be happy. That's how it works."

"You think so?"

"I do."

"Okay, but you're going to think I'm just telling you this for sympathy."

"I won't think that."

She shakes her head. "They cut me off. Financially. What little help they could give, they cut it off. I don't have anything, Dr. Gaines."

"I'm sorry to hear that."

"No, I don't have *anything*. I've been . . . Different sets of friends have let me stay with them for a while. Off campus. One couch to the other, you know? And the food . . . there's a food pantry in town. I'm not the only student who goes there, but it's . . . I know I shouldn't be embarrassed by it. . . ."

"You shouldn't."

"Well, I have to eat. And I really don't give a fuck if it has gluten in it or not. I say that, but I can't be that picky. That crappy food out there tasted like a feast."

"Maybe you ate too much and felt sick?"

"I don't know. But let me tell you—I hate what Mr. Hyde's kind of wealth has done to all of us. The gross inequality of it."

"Do you have a place to stay now?" I ask. "I can call the housing office—"

"A friend of mine has given me a steady place for the last few weeks," she says. "I think I can finish the year there. But the scholarship, you know? It would . . . it would be huge, but I don't think

I can stomach it." She gets her sniffling under control. "Did you say you have kids?"

"Three."

"What do they think of you?"

"Hmmm. A lot of the time they think I'm the stupidest man to ever live. But that's par for the course. They're teenagers. I know they love me."

"Do you love them?"

"Yes, I do."

She nods, relief on her face. "That's good. Really, it is."

"Do you want to tell me anything else about why you think you should win the scholarship?"

She adjusts her glasses. Then she sticks one finger underneath them and wipes at her left eye. She has one leg crossed over the other, and her heavy Doc Martens boot swings freely, as if it's looking for something to kick.

"I wanted to explain something," she says.

"Okay."

"About the protestors . . ."

I wait. And she doesn't go on. But I don't want to push.

She opens her mouth—

Someone knocks on the door to the parlor.

"What the . . . ?"

"Who is that?" I ask.

"Do you think there's more trouble?" she asks.

I can't tell if she's relieved or scared. "Hold on."

They knock again. Louder.

I go over and slide the door open. But no one is there.

"What?" I stick my head out. "Hello?"

Maybe I'm hearing things.

"Emily?" I ask. "Did you hear someone knock?"

"I did. Maybe the cops are breaking down the door."

"Why would they do that?"

It remains quiet. I don't even hear students talking in the dining room.

I turn back into the parlor and start to slide the pocket door shut. But Emily is up on her feet and acting like she's going to leave.

"Emily, I'm sorry for the interruption."

"It's okay. I've taken enough time."

"No, you were going to tell me something. Why you deserve the scholarship— No, you mentioned the protestors. Is that what you wanted to talk about? Do your politics inform your academics?"

She looks distant, removed.

"Is that what you wrote about in the essay?"

"No. Yes. I guess so." She reaches up, rubs her forehead. "I want to stay, though—"

Running footsteps come down the hallway. Thumping and thumping.

"Mr. Gaines?" Sydney's face is in the opening of the pocket doors. "Mr. Gaines? You need to get out here. Quick."

56

SYDNEY STANDS IN THE hallway.

Pointing toward the back of the house. Once and then twice.

"What's the matter?"

"It's Duffy."

"God. Is he sick?"

"No." Her head shakes, her eyes wide and full of fear. "He's trying to get out of the house."

"Where? In the kitchen?"

"No. He went down into the basement."

"Oh, crap."

I run to the back of the house. I enter the kitchen, catch sight of the emptied buffet. An odor of simmered onions hovers over the room.

In the corner the basement door hangs wide open, revealing darkness beyond. I stop at the top of the stairs, my shoe on the edge of where the kitchen floor drops off. Cool air wafts past me. And a musty odor of a long-closed room rises to greet me.

My hand fumbles on the wall. My fingers grip the switch and flick it up. Then down. Up and down. *Click click click click.*

"No light," I say, mastering the obvious.

Sydney appears next to me. "He said he wanted to get out of here."

"Duffy?" I call. Rather than echoing, my voice disappears into the darkness, absorbed by the thick foundation walls and the gloom. "He could get hurt down there. It's full of crap. Sharp edges and old wood."

"Duffy?" Sydney calls.

More steps into the kitchen. The linoleum squeaks. Past Sydney, Natalia looks curious. Emily, angry.

"Where's the captain?" I ask.

Sydney points, her finger moving into the gloom of the stairway. "He went after Duffy. He thinks Duffy's trying to get out of the house because he might be guilty. The captain wants to stop him."

"Both of those idiots are down there? In the dark?"

I tilt my head, strain to hear anything. Silence rolls up with the dank air.

Something clangs down there. Metal against metal. And a voice, low and faint, swears.

"Duffy? Is anybody hurt?"

My hand scrabbles at my rear pants pocket. Nothing.

"Shit. My phone has a flashlight."

"All of ours do, I'm sure," Sydney says.

"Duffy? Captain? Get out of there and back upstairs."

The metallic clanging happens again. Sharper. Like someone is forging a blade in the dark. I take one step down, the wooden stair squeaking under my weight.

I turn back and point. "You three, look around. Find a flashlight or a candle. Anything."

Sydney jumps into life. She's at the cabinets in the kitchen, ripping them open, standing on her tiptoes to examine the top shelves. She moves objects around, sends some tumbling out onto the counters.

Natalia and Emily watch.

"You two, go look. Check the dining room. The parlor. Upstairs. Go."

They disperse.

"There's nothing," Sydney says. "No fucking flashlight. Not even, like, a candle. What kind of creepy old nineteenth-century house is this if it doesn't have fucking candles?"

Two soft thumps from the cellar bring my head back around to the darkness.

I take another step down.

"Captain?" I wait. Listen. "Duffy?"

Sydney crosses the room back to me. She presses her hands to either side of her face, scrunches her eyes shut. "This is a nightmare. And it's my fault."

"Why?"

"When we got exiled to the kitchen and were sitting in there alone, I told Duffy how much I wanted to leave. I mean, I said I was going crazy, like the walls were closing in on me. And I just wanted to leave and go back to my room. And sleep for a week. I was just sick of everything going on in here."

"That doesn't mean it's your fault. He's an adult. And look, I'm sure he's— They're both—"

"It is my fault. I know how he feels about me. How he's all, you know, chivalrous and shit. Maybe he did do something . . . to Milo . . . and to Mr. Hyde. . . ."

Natalia comes back into the kitchen, something clutched in her hand. "There's a flashlight, but no batteries."

"That helps."

"Hey, I tried."

Emily comes back right after. She holds a box of matches. "I found these in the music room. In a drawer right by Milo's head."

"Okay." The matches rattle inside the worn box. It's decorated with a fleur-de-lis and looks like it's been in the house since Major Hyde first moved in. I slide it open. "Shit. Two matches. Was this the only box?"

"It was."

"And nothing else? Anywhere?"

Natalia shakes her head, swishing her curls from one side to the other.

Another thump from below. Like a body falling. Slumping to the ground.

My head spins that way. "Hello? Duffy? Captain?"

Another thump. Louder. Another body on the floor? Then shuffling. Tentative steps coming toward the bottom of the stairs, which I can't see.

"Sir?"

The captain's voice sounds distant, cold. Faint, like he's speaking through a filter.

"Are you okay?" I ask. "Are you with Duffy?"

"Sir? I think you need to come down here."

"Why? Is someone hurt?"

"Sir, I think if you just come down, you'll understand everything. I'd rather talk down here."

Sydney shakes her head. She waves her hands like she's erasing a chalkboard. She speaks to me in a sharp whisper. "No. It's a trap. What if the captain wants to hurt you?"

"Why would he hurt me?"

"You heard those noises down there," Sydney says. "Something's wrong."

Natalia slides over. "Close the door." She's whispering as well. "Get out of there and lock it. They can remain down there."

"Duffy's down there."

"Maybe he got out," Natalia says. "Maybe he's fine."

"Maybe the captain's the one picking us all off," Sydney says. "The poison first. He said he was in the Special Forces. That's badass shit, like James Bond. He's going to finish you too and then come for the rest of us."

"Maybe Duffy's picking us all off," Emily says. "Maybe he killed the two guys who were after Sydney."

"Emily," Sydney says. "Just stop—"

"Mr. Hyde was acting kind of creepy with you," Natalia says.

"But the captain—" Sydney says.

"Sir? I can hear what's being said. And I don't like it."

Sydney grimaces.

"Hold on, Captain. Can you just tell me if Duffy is okay? Is he right there with you?"

"I'm not sure I can answer that question so simply, sir."

"Why don't you come up and we'll talk about it?"

"Sir, with all due respect, you need to come down here. Okay? And can you bring some sort of light so we can see?"

"Natalia, grab me one of those Sterno cans. I'll use it as a light. It's the best we can do."

While she does that, Sydney leans in closer to me so the captain can't hear. "I'm coming with you. To help you."

Natalia hands me the little can, which is still slightly warm. And I know it's not going to be easy to hold once it's lit.

"No," I say to Sydney. "You all stay up here, okay? Go sit in the dining room. And . . ."

"And what?" Emily asks.

"If you hear trouble downstairs, lock this door. And wait. For four o'clock. I'm not sure what's going on down there. But I'm going to see."

I hand the matches to Sydney and nod. She strikes the match for me while I hold the can. The sulfur smell stings my nose, but the wick ignites, sending a faint glow up against all of our faces.

Sydney hands the matches back. "You only have one more."

"I'll make it count. Remember what I said?"

"Don't worry," Natalia said. "I'm not trying to be a hero."

I turn and take the first cautious step farther down the squeaking wooden stairs.

57

THE STERNO FLAME WARMS my face. And the fingers of my left hand, which holds the Sterno, are singed by its flame.

The cellar chill grips the rest of my body.

The stairs lack a bannister or railing, so my right hand trails along the stone wall, touching the damp cold there.

"Captain?"

Squeak. Squeak.

Can these stairs, which are as old as the house, even hold me? Have the years and the damp cold taken a toll on them? Weakened them?

"Captain?"

"I'm over here, sir."

The dirt floor comes into view, illuminated by the cone of light cast by the flame. When I step off the stairs, it's like traveling from the present day to far in the past. A time lit only by candles. But I do it anyway, my heart working like someone has wrapped my chest in tight bands.

The captain's voice came from the left, so I turn that way, lifting the Sterno flame ahead of me. The glowing light does just enough to pick out dark shapes and heavy shadows. A narrow path through the junk stretches ahead.

"Captain, can you tell me what's going on down here? And where's Duffy?"

"He's over here, sir."

I get a read on the captain's location based on his voice. I angle that way, navigating through the cleared path between all the debris. As I go, shadows resolve into actual objects. The stacks of wooden crates I remember from my one other time down here. On my right, an old push mower, aqua blue, the blade rusted, one wheel missing. On my left, an ancient coal shovel, the handle broken off. And just beyond that, an old bicycle resting against a cracked mirror. Mice droppings dot the ground.

"Where?" I ask.

"Keep coming," the captain says. "There's kind of a path through this shit."

"Where's Duffy? Why isn't he saying anything?"

"He's hurt, sir."

I freeze in place. "Hurt?"

"He is, sir."

"What happened to him?"

"That's hard to explain, sir."

The temperature of the Sterno can rises. The skin on the fingers of my left hand starts to sear. I shift it to my right hand, wave the left in the air like I'm shaking out a match.

"Why is it hard to explain?" I ask. "What's wrong with him?"

"Well, sir—"

The door at the top of the stairs opens with a whoosh. "Mr. Gaines?"

"What is it, Sydney?"

"Are you okay? Is Duffy okay?"

"Close the door," I say. "Do what I told you. We're fine."

"Can you just get Duffy to tell me he's okay?" she asks, her voice thin and distant.

"I'm figuring this out now. Will you shut the door? Please?"

A different voice calls down. Emily. "Are you all planning something? It's not right that the men are all down there and we're up here. We don't know *what* you're doing."

"Would you like to switch places?" I ask. "Just wait up there for us. We'll be up soon."

"Shut the door, Sydney. And lock it. Don't be daft," Emily says.

The door slaps shut. And I feel more alone than I have all day. Maybe ever. Something scurries below me. I jump, jerking the flame in my hand. A mouse runs along the edge of illumination, its gray body disappearing between two wooden crates.

"Are you okay, sir?"

My knees shake like a child's. "It's a mouse."

"Ah, yes. There are a few of them down here."

"I know they're harmless."

"They are, sir. A nuisance more than anything. But actually, seeing them here might be a bit of good news for those who want to get out of the house."

"What do you mean?"

"I think there's a little opening in these bulkhead doors, one that might be made larger with some effort. An opening that might allow for mice and other varmints to come in and out of the house. I think that's what Duffy was working on when he got hurt. The doors are wooden and old. Probably pretty worn down by the elements."

My mind jumps in two directions. An opening that might be a way out . . .

Duffy got hurt—

"You still haven't told me what happened to Duffy," I say.

There's a pause. The basement grows colder.

"I said I'm not sure, sir. But I'm glad you're here. You have the light, so if you just come over here and use it, we can tell what's wrong with him. Just follow my voice and you'll get here. Okay?"

Am I walking toward a murderer? One with military training and the advantage of being better adjusted to the dark?

Could he have found a weapon in the basement?

Something he's ready to use?

No, I think. *No.* I know the captain. I've spent time with him. I can't let these suspicions rule me. I need to trust myself. My own judgment of a person.

Right?

"Okay," I say. "I'm coming over."

58

I CONTINUE FORWARD.

The Sterno can grows hotter in my right hand now, but I keep it there, not risking a switch while I'm moving.

I keep my eyes on the dirt floor, trying to see the path ahead, using the light as my guide. Even as I'm doing so, my right knee bangs against something, causing a knifelike pain.

"Shit."

"Sir?"

A pipe of some kind extends from the junk and into the path, about eighteen inches off the floor. Direct contact—metal on knee-cap. My eyes water from the pain.

"Sir? There's a metal rod over there."

"Thanks. I found it."

"Sorry, sir."

I resume my slow, shuffling progress, my shoes scratching over the dirt. "Is Duffy unconscious?"

"He appears to be."

"Is he alive?"

"He appears to be breathing, sir. But it's shallow."

The bands around my chest tighten. Nausea chokes me. Another person hurt during this craptastic day.

The flame flickers, shrinks. I'm tempted to turn and leave the cellar. Wait upstairs for help to arrive at four o'clock.

But Duffy . . . he'd be left behind. Hurt and with the captain. And the captain might be the cause of his injuries. Sydney's right—the knowledge of poisons, the military training. His absolute determination to stay in the house no matter what.

He chased Duffy down into the basement to keep him from getting out—

But Duffy . . .

His anger at the Hyde family. His resentment of Milo.

His pursuit of Sydney. Has it all led Duffy to exact revenge?

Did Duffy attack the captain and get injured?

I stop my thoughts again. It's *not* really possible, is it?

Is anything I've experienced this day *possible*?

"I can see you pretty clearly now, sir. The candle lights up your face, and my eyes are well adjusted to the dark. By the way, where did you find that?"

"It's Sterno. From the buffet."

"Very industrious, sir."

"It's hot. And now I wish I'd grabbed more than one."

"True enough. It won't last forever. But nothing does."

As if it possesses a mind of its own, the flame gutters and hisses. With one last shuddering flicker, it goes out. I read in a book once that it's so much darker when a light goes out than if it had never been lit at all.

I get it. Profoundly.

The can still retains its heat, but my heart turns cold.

"That's okay, sir. You're almost here. Just keep coming."

"I have a match—"

"Save it. When you get over here, we can reignite it. Sometimes if you shake those cans a little, you can get them going again. I have a part-time job here in town working for a caterer. We use them all the time."

Without a light, going back is out of the question.

I'm closer to the captain—and Duffy—than the stairs.

"Straight ahead, sir."

I move the Sterno can to my left hand again, bringing some relief to my right. Then I continue shuffling ahead in the dark.

After a few more steps, I catch a shadowy movement. Tall and slender, ten feet ahead. Beyond the figure, something glows faintly. Is it the opening in the bulkhead doors the captain mentioned?

As I move forward, the shadow becomes more distinct. Man shaped. The outline of a person. A white shirt.

"Almost there, sir."

A few more steps, then the captain says, "Okay, halt."

I freeze. The captain is five feet away. I catch the outline of his face, his rigid posture.

"Duffy's right at your feet," he says. "Can you get those—that—match out?"

"If we use it now and the can goes out . . ."

"Sir, it's more important to light that can now. If it's possible. We won't know Duffy's condition unless we light that bad boy. Do you need my help?"

"I do."

"Hand me the can, sir. I'll hold it while you light the match and bring it to the wick."

"It's hot," I say.

"Roger that."

I extend the can toward the shape, and he reaches out and takes it. My hand shakes as it slides into my pocket. For a moment, my heart locks up. I don't feel the match.

The other pocket—

I dig in the opposite pocket, working my fingers past the keys until they make contact with the cardboard of the matchbox. I draw it out, my fingers still shaky.

"Don't drop it, sir. We might not ever find it in here."

"Are you trying to make me edgier than I am?"

"Sorry, sir. It's part of my training to reiterate commands."

"Never mind."

I shift the matchbox to my left hand and slide it open with my right. I manage to dip my thumb and index finger inside and clasp the lone remaining match. I turn the matchbook so the strike plate is pointed the right way and slide the match head across it.

It sparks but fails to ignite. I try again with the same result.

"Take a deep breath, sir."

I do. The third time proves to be a charm as the match flares in the darkness, illuminating the captain's face as well as mine. His brown eyes reflect the light as he extends the Sterno can toward me.

"I gave it a shake," he says, "so let's see if we're in business."

I touch the match to the wick. I hold it there for countless seconds—seconds that seem to stretch for minutes. But the wick flares and ignites, and the captain is revealed even more clearly.

"Well done," he says.

Dirt stains one side of his white shirt, and his tie sits askew for the first time all day. I can't be sure, but it looks like his left cheek bears a scratch, one I feel certain wasn't there before.

I shake the precious match out and drop it, the sulfur after-burn stinging my nose.

"Okay, sir, let's look at our boy."

The captain holds the Sterno can like a holy relic as he crouches. I bend my knees, and as we lower ourselves, the light from the can shows me Duffy.

He's on the floor, his body resting slightly on its right side. His shirt is dirty as well, the bolo tie hanging loose, his hat gone. His eyes are closed like he's deeply asleep, and he breathes through his slightly parted lips. Even in the glow from the Sterno can, his skin looks gray-white, like marble.

"Duffy?" I say.

"I've called his name but nothing."

I put my hand on his right arm, feel for a pulse. It's there. Faint but there.

"Duffy?"

"I wasn't able to examine him, sir, but if I hold this, can you . . . ?"

I'm ahead of him. I lean forward, moving up Duffy's body as the captain moves the light accordingly. At the back of Duffy's head there is something dark. Wet and tacky.

I touch it gently and bring my hand back.

"Oh, crap."

The captain manages to state the obvious. "Blood, sir. That's a decent amount of blood coming from the back of his head."

59

I WIPE MY HAND on my pant leg.

"What happened to him, Captain? How did he get hurt this bad?'

"Apparently, he was trying to get out by hacking on that bulkhead door. Like I told you, and as I'm sure you can see for yourself, there's an opening there where the door isn't completely flush with the doorframe. Since it's old wood, someone could work on that with a crowbar or screwdriver—"

"*How* did Duffy get hurt? What do you know?"

The captain remains silent. In the flickering Sterno can light, he stares at me, his face a rigid mask revealing little.

"Are you suggesting something, sir?"

"Do you know what happened to him—"

"Sir, I don't like the way—"

"You came down here to stop him, didn't you?"

His eyes slide away from mine. "In a manner of speaking, sir."

"And this is what happened? Did you drag him away from that door? Did you hit him over the head to stop him?"

"Sir, I feel like whatever I say will fall on deaf ears. Certain assumptions are being made about me and others in the house. What if I put forth a theory that you killed Mr. Hyde? Some people upstairs think the two of you fought, that you did him in. You were alone with him when he died. There was noise. He was clearly pushing your buttons."

"That's crazy."

"So you'll believe me when I say I worried Duffy'd hurt himself in this mess? Besides, he may very well be guilty of these crimes. And if he's guilty, he'd be better off just telling the truth now. I would have advised him to do that."

"Okay, okay. We can sort this out later."

As I straighten up, my knees and back register their unhappiness about how I crouched down. The captain stands up too.

"We just need to get him upstairs. Stop the bleeding, keep him warm."

"I agree, sir. This is no place for an injured man."

"When we get up there, we're going to discuss this more."

"There is a lot to discuss, sir."

"I'll take his feet and walk backward. You take his shoulders."

Again, a silence as the light flickers across the captain's face. Something scratches across the room. No doubt another mouse—or something bigger.

"Is there something else?" I ask.

"In order to move him, sir, I have to blow the flame out. We can't carry him and the flame at the same time."

The chill in the air intensifies. It seeps inside me, burrowing into my skin. "Is there another way—"

The captain blows, a quick puff, and the flame goes out, plunging us into stygian darkness. The captain and Duffy disappear.

I sense them, presences in the dark. The only comfort I feel is the knowledge I'll be walking backward. Facing the captain, even if I can't actually see him.

"Are you ready, sir?"

He shifts his position in the dark, his shoes scraping against the dirt.

I take a half step back.

"Sir?"

"What are you doing?"

"I put the can down. And now I'm going to get ahold of Duffy's shoulders and lift. You're going to do the same thing, right? With his feet?"

My throat feels cracked and dry. My words come out with a croak. "I am."

"Then let's do it, okay? This man needs our help."

He moves again in the dark. And so do I, bending down and, after some fumbling, getting hold of Duffy's lower legs. The captain counts, and we lift together. I start walking backward. Slowly. Carefully. Like I'm going through a minefield.

Duffy is heavy. My biceps and back strain with the weight, and my body still hurts from throwing the cradle and having it bounce against me. I grunt like an old man, and our shoes scrape over the dirt floor, another set of scurrying feet in the dark space.

"Are you okay, sir?" The captain sounds like he's out for a stroll in the park. No stress or effort in his voice.

"I'm good," I say.

"If we need to pause and put him down—"

"We can at the stairs—"

"Sir, there's a—"

The back of my right knee hits the pipe. It doesn't hurt, since it's not metal-on-bone contact. But I lose my balance and start to go over backward like a stumbling circus performer.

"Sir?"

I regain my equilibrium. My weight shifts forward, and I stay upright.

Duffy makes a noise in our arms. He's trying to form words.

"What did he say?" I ask.

"He just moaned."

"No, he's saying something."

Duffy's face remains hidden in the dark. But his low murmuring reaches my ears.

"Be . . ."

He feels heavier, like a load of stones. I bend a little, shift his weight in my hands, and straighten back up, hoping to relieve some of the strain on my arms and back. I know I'll feel this tomorrow.

If there is a tomorrow . . .

"Let's get moving, sir. You're getting tired, I can tell."

Duffy makes more noises. I lean forward in the dark. "Duffy?"

"Behind me . . . be . . ."

"Something was behind him," I say. "Or someone."

"Sir, this speculation is unproductive. We need to stick to the facts we know."

"You've been pretty vocal about not wanting the process to end."

"I need the scholarship, sir. That's true. I have a family. You know what that's like."

"I do. . . ."

"Sir, did you look in the back of the bylaws like I asked?"

"No. I have bigger problems than those idiotic bylaws."

"I think you should—"

At the top of the stairs, the door makes a popping sound as someone pulls it open.

"Mr. Gaines? Is he okay?"

I call out as loud as I can, fighting against the feeling that my words will die in this space. "We're bringing Duffy up, Sydney."

"Bringing him up? Holy shit. Did the captain try to kill him?"

60

GETTING DUFFY UP THE stairs feels like moving a piano.

We grunt and struggle and—despite the cool—sweat as we carry him up.

Sydney steps onto the stairs, and she gasps at the blood on Duffy's head. She sounds like her heart has been punctured.

"Let's put him on the kitchen table," I say.

Natalia shows up. She uses both hands to sweep some loose napkins and silverware onto the floor. It all clatters and clangs against the linoleum, but the space is cleared for Duffy.

We heave him onto the table. He moans again, low and painful sounding. But he forms no coherent words.

Emily stands in the doorway, her hand to her mouth.

"There are some towels in the bathroom down the hall," I say. "Some clean ones. Emily, can you go get them? And any bandages if you see them."

She goes, moving like a shot, boots pounding against the floor.

Sydney rushes to the table and stands over Duffy. "Who did this to him?"

"He's bleeding," I say. "Natalia, can you grab some blankets?"

"I can see that. *Why* is he bleeding?"

"I don't know yet. Why don't you go find a pillow or something we can put under his head when it's bandaged?"

But Sydney turns to the captain, ignoring me. "You did this to him. You went after him like you wanted to hurt him. What did you do, hit him over the head?"

"Sir, these accusations are getting—"

"Go get a pillow, okay? The captain's going to check him out."

"Him?"

"He knows first aid."

"Just like he did CPR after he poisoned Milo. He hits Duffy and does first aid."

"Go, please."

My voice cuts through the kitchen like a cleaver. Sydney looks stung, but she turns on her heel and goes. I turn to the captain.

"What should we do? Get pressure on this?"

"Yes. Head wounds bleed a lot. They look worse than they are." The captain leans down and lifts Duffy's eyelids with his thumb. "His pupils react to light. That's good. They're not dilated. Also good."

Emily comes back in with an armful of towels. The captain takes them from her and hands one to me.

"Get that wet so we can clean this."

I do as he says. Sydney comes back in with an embroidered pillow clutched to her chest. I hand the wet towel to the captain, who starts dabbing at the back of Duffy's head.

Duffy moans.

"Easy," the captain says.

"He's trying to say something," Sydney says.

"He's delirious."

The captain grabs one of the dry towels and gently presses it against Duffy's injury, which has now leaked a small pool of dark blood on the butcher-block farm table. It looks like spilled wine.

"He'll need stitches when we get out, I think. And an X-ray, just to make sure."

Duffy moans. "Captain . . ."

"Shhh," the captain says. "Easy. Shhh."

He sounds like a father calming a child.

"Don't shush him," Sydney says. "He's trying to talk."

"He's out of his head."

Duffy's words spoken in the cellar come back to me: *Behind me . . .* I'm not sure how out of his head he is.

Sydney moves to the table, the pillow still clutched to her chest. She's on the opposite side of the table from the captain, and she leans down, her face close to Duffy's. "What is it, Duffy?"

"Captain . . . behind me . . ." His face contorts as if hit with a wave of pain. "Captain . . . behind me . . . *fell* . . ."

Sydney stiffens. Her spine goes rigid as the steel pipe I banged into twice in the cellar.

"Did you hear that?" she asks the room. "Get away from him."

"Sir, can you tell Sydney he's delirious? And she might be too."

In the harsh kitchen light, Duffy looks waxen and pale. The captain stands over him in a predatory fashion, his hands stained with blood.

"Captain, under the circumstances, maybe you should step away from the table. We need to keep everybody as calm as possible."

The captain turns to me. "Are you serious, sir?"

"I am." My temperature and heart rate rise. Adrenaline shoots through every cell in my body, making me quiver. I hope it doesn't show. "Just step into the other room, please. Thanks for your help with Duffy."

"Help?" Sydney says.

The captain straightens up, his grip on the bloody towel tightening. "You're accusing me? Really?" He tosses the towel to the floor, where it splats.

"Why don't you go into the parlor?" I say, trying to save things. "We can talk there in a minute."

"The talk has gotten ugly in here," he says, maintaining his authoritative calm. "They have the secrets."

He walks—almost marches—out of the room, his footfalls heavy and thudding.

"Sydney, why don't you . . . ?"

But she's already placing the pillow gently under Duffy's head, trying not to come into contact with his injury.

Natalia leaves the room as well, following along in the captain's wake. Her stride is determined, her body leaning forward. Her shoes clonk rapidly.

"Sydney, will you . . . ?"

"I'll stay with him."

"Emily, can you help if—"

"I'm here," she says.

"Are you still feeling better?" I ask.

"I think so."

I go into the hallway. Natalia stands at the end of the hallway outside the pocket doors that lead to the parlor. She's fiddling with the recessed handle.

"Natalia?"

"Check this out, Mr. Gaines."

When I get there, Natalia wears a beaming look of pride. "What?"

She points to the door. "The captain went in there and closed the door behind himself."

"I asked him to go in there and wait for me."

"Well, guess what. I locked him inside the parlor."

61

YEARS OF USE HAVE worn the finish on the pocket door. The lock Natalia turned also looks worn and tarnished.

"Isn't there a lock on the other side as well?" I ask. "Can't he just . . . ?"

Natalia shakes her head. "No, I checked it when I was in there with you. I tried it—it's broken. You can only engage it from this side."

"Why were you so curious about the lock?"

"Well, I . . . Just that. Curiosity."

I press my ear to the door, the wood cool against my face. Nothing.

But the captain must have heard the lock turn and click. He's too alert, too tuned in to everything

"Sir? I don't like this, sir."

The inch-thick wood muffles the voice. But it's unmistakable.

Emily comes down the hallway toward us, taking silent, tentative steps. She wears a puzzled expression, like she's not sure if there's a demon locked inside the parlor trying to get out.

The door rattles in its frame as the captain tugs at the other side. The rattling stops.

"He's not happy," Emily says.

"Can you blame him?"

"Sir? This is highly irregular."

"Okay, Captain, just hold on a minute."

"I'm not going to hold on a minute." His voice retains its calm authority. "And I'm not going to be locked up like a criminal."

"Can you just tell me what happened to Duffy? I need to know in order to make sure everyone's safe."

"I'm not going to talk through the door, sir. I refuse."

Natalia shakes her head, her hand to her chest. "You can't release him." She speaks so low I can barely make out the words. Like we're whispering in a church.

"How would you feel if someone locked you in a room?" I ask.

"I didn't try to kill Duffy."

"She's right, Mr. Gaines," Emily says. "You have to protect all of us by leaving him in there until the cops let us out."

I step back from the door and wave Natalia and Emily closer. Down the hall, Sydney stands by Duffy's side in the kitchen. She appears to be whispering something to him. Duffy's lips move as though he's speaking. Then Sydney whispers again, shaking her head.

"I don't like him being locked in there," I say. "It seems wrong somehow."

Emily starts to object, and I raise my index finger.

"We don't know what happened in the basement with Duffy.

That's true. But everyone is entitled to due process. You know, before I went into the basement, Sydney raised some questions about Duffy."

They both turn toward the kitchen.

"She did?" Natalia says.

"Yes, she did. You both did too. Remember? About the herbs and his anger toward Milo and Nicholas. What happened to that?"

"She's awfully cozy with him now," Emily says. "Maybe they're in it together. Some women like creepy guys like Duffy. I'm not sure why, but the weird, smothering attention doesn't bother them."

"All I'm saying is we don't know what's going on. So I'm going to talk to the captain. Person-to-person—"

"Man-to-man, you mean." Emily shakes her head and lowers her voice the way all women do when they imitate men. "'So, dude, why did you beat up the other dude, bro?'"

"Can I get a little more credit than that?" I wait—and she finally nods. "He hasn't had his interview yet. Both of you have. Okay. If you and Natalia want to wait in the kitchen with Sydney and Duffy, that's fine. I'll talk to the captain and see what I can figure out."

Natalia takes a step closer. "That's great. I like that idea."

"Thank you."

"Yeah, that's cool," Emily says.

They stand mute, expectant.

"Okay, I'm going to go in and talk to him. If you want to go—"

They start down the hallway, moving slowly toward the kitchen. Past them, Sydney looks our way, still standing over the wounded Duffy.

I lean close to the pocket door and knock.

"What?" The voice is right there on the other side like the captain has been waiting for my summons.

"Captain? It's Troy again."

"Are you going to let me out?"

"Captain, I'm going to come in. So we can do our interview. Like I promised. I just want to know that if I open the door, you're going to stay in there and not rush out. So we can talk."

"I have to promise something to *you?* I'm the one locked in."

"Just give me your word, Captain. I'm trying to come in and talk to you."

A long silence stretches. Blood pumps in my ears, the only sound. I think the captain has withdrawn, given up on any further talk, but then he says, "Okay. You have my word. I don't know why, but you do."

"Great."

Down the hall, Emily and Natalia stand side by side, arms folded. Watching me.

"It's all good," I say, trying to sound more confident than I feel.

My right hand quivers as I take hold of the lock with my thumb and index finger. I twist it to the left. I grip the handle and the door whooshes as it slides to the left. I open it just wide enough for my body to squeeze through, which I do, moving with what feels like a surprising amount of grace.

The captain stands back in the middle of the room. Parade rest.

I slide the door shut again and face him, pointing at the chairs. "Okay, a civilized interview. All part of the process."

One step forward and the lock clicks behind me.

I spin so fast I make myself dizzy. I grab at the handle, tugging on the door. But it remains flush in the frame.

I beat the door with my fist. "Hey! What the fuck?"

I pound some more, which I know only makes me seem crazy. So I stop.

"Open the damn door. Come on."

"Mr. Gaines?" Natalia's muffled voice sounds calm. "I do apologize for this. But we were talking while you were in the cellar. We think it's safer if both of you are in there. We don't feel entirely safe since someone here is a killer. And we don't know what happened downstairs."

"What do you mean, you don't know?"

"You and the captain went down, and then you came up and Duffy was bleeding. Can't you just stay in there until it's four?"

"No, we can't."

"And then there was the thing with you and Mr. Hyde," Emily says. "That fight. You clearly didn't like him."

"We didn't fight—"

"You were alone with him when he died. You were here *before* all of us. If anyone had access to everything, it's you. And the chief, who is a total fascist. He's always creeping around campus, spying on the students. Look, maybe it's better if the men are locked away in there. Duffy is the other man, and he's incapacitated. We'll all feel safer."

The captain's low voice interrupts me. "It looks like the shoe's on the other foot, isn't it, sir? Now *you're* being falsely accused of something. At least I think it's false. I don't know why you would want to harm a student like Milo, but I could see that you might want to get the spoiled, entitled heir of the college's largest donor family out of the way in the hopes you could deal with someone more reliable. Like an estate lawyer or a board of directors."

I turn away from the door in his direction, and he's pointing at the chairs, inviting me to sit.

"I think it's time for our interview," he says.

62

THE CAPTAIN DETOURS ON his way to the chair.

He crouches next to Nicholas, his tie dangling over the body like a pendulum. "It doesn't add up, sir."

"What doesn't?"

"These two deaths." He points at Nicholas's chest, which is covered by the captain's suit jacket. "Who would kill these two people, who seemingly don't have anything in common? We don't know if Milo and Mr. Hyde knew each other before today. Sydney mentioned that they might have gone climbing together. Or they could have met at a climbing site, even if Mr. Hyde wasn't living in Bluefield. There are climbing clubs and things like that around the state to bring people with common interests together. Both of them also seemed to have some kind of attraction to Sydney. Past or present. I'm not sure Mr. Hyde knew any of the other students."

"He only knew me. As far as we know."

"Sure. There might have been a preexisting relationship between people in the house—one that was concealed well enough that none of us knew about it." The captain straightens. "But let's assume there wasn't. That would mean some college kid goes out and gets poison and brings it to the most important exam of their life. And kills the guy who hands out the money?"

"They killed the guy most likely to win the prize. That makes a sick sort of sense. And maybe Mr. Hyde was coll—a mistake."

"You can say 'collateral damage' if you're not saying it in a way that denigrates the service of millions of men and women in uniform."

"Right."

The aches in my body ease when I settle into the chair. The captain follows suit. It's the first time we've both sat since we carried Duffy up the stairs.

"What happened in the basement?"

The captain rolls his eyes. "Do you really think I just went down there and beat Duffy over the head?"

"You didn't want anyone to leave. And you were the only one down there with him."

His eyes refuse to settle on mine. They point toward some far corner of the room. "Do you know why I want this scholarship so bad?"

"Same reasons as everyone else. It's a lot of money. And school is expensive. And then you get a job, your foot in the door with a major corporation."

The captain nods along to my words like I'm laying down a steady beat. "There's that, sure. And you know I'm older than the average student. I have a wife and kids. Like you."

"That's damn expensive."

"How many children do you have?"

"Three girls."

He nods. "I have two daughters. My older daughter, Vanessa, is seventeen. My younger daughter, Tanya, she's my baby. Fourteen years old." He closes his eyes now. "Daughters, they get you, don't they?" He pokes the center of his chest with his index finger. "Here."

"They do."

"And your girls . . . are they all healthy?"

An odd question, but I answer. "They are. By the grace of whatever controls the universe. We've only dealt with a couple of broken bones, some stitches, one chipped tooth."

He opens his eyes and stares right at me. "Tanya has spina bifida. And I don't care how much Uncle Sam tries to help. It's damn expensive when your child has special needs. Prescriptions, doctors' visits . . . It kills." He pokes his chest again. "There's a surgery, spinal fusion. It's not a cure, but it can help ease her discomfort. But it's expensive. Very expensive. We moved back here to Bluefield because my mother-in-law is dying, and someone had to care for her. She has ALS. You know, Lou Gehrig's disease? It's slow. And gut-wrenching. My wife, Kimberly, she's caring for a lot of people while I go to school and work. . . . It's a lot . . . and it stabs me right here. All of it. That's why I need this—to relieve Tanya's pain. To ease the burden on my wife. I don't like feeling desperate, but I do."

"I'm sorry, Captain."

"I'm not asking for any special treatment here. Just a fair shot. Like everybody else. I'm tempted to say I need the money more than anyone, but I know everybody has their problems and challenges they've faced in life. Speaking of challenges people face in their lives, did you read the bylaws like I asked?"

"You know I haven't had time. Why do you keep asking?"

The captain is out of his chair like he's been ejected. "They must be here somewhere."

"What are you trying to prove?"

"The bylaws. I want you to see—" He stops at the side table where the tea was poured. It feels like five thousand years ago. "Here they are."

He brings the book over to the chairs, flipping the pages to the back as he walks. He finds what he's looking for and then rotates the book as he hands it over to me.

"Feast your eyes on that. Right there."

Scrawled across the last page of the book is a note. The handwriting is sloppy and modern. It's not something written in the nineteenth century.

And it says: *No undocumented immigrant is eligible for the Hyde Scholarship.*

Underneath it is the messy signature of Nicholas Hyde.

63

I POINT AT THE book, my index finger hitting the handwritten note. "How do we even know Nicholas wrote this? Anyone could have done this to make him look like a bastard."

"I thought of that, sir. Remember when Mr. Hyde first pulled up outside of the house? And he came walking up and took the book of bylaws out of his briefcase?"

"I remember. . . ."

"He signed the book. He told us it's tradition that each new presiding member of the Hyde family signs their name at the front of the bylaws. You can flip back and see the signatures there."

The pages are thin and worn, the binding loose. I scroll back to the front of the book and find a page marked PRESIDING FAMILY MEMBERS. Seven scrawled signatures, from Major Hyde in 1872 to Nicholas's name and today's date. It's easy enough to switch from one to the other and see the signatures match.

"Why in the hell would he write such a hateful note, Captain? It doesn't make any sense. Hyde College admits undocumented students. Not every college or university does, but we do. In fact . . ."

The captain backs up and sits on the edge of his chair. He rests his elbows on his knees and wears an eager look on his face. "I think I know what you were about to say. But let's return to that subject in a minute. First things first: Would Nicholas Hyde know that the college admits undocumented students? He's not involved in that decision, is he?"

"No, President Chan and the board decided that. Anyone would know if they paid attention to news from the school."

"Mr. Hyde doesn't exactly seem like the type to do that, does he?"

"Not at all."

"So then he must have just learned about it today. Why else would he write that note into the bylaws with today's date?"

I stare down at the note. The shaky handwriting looks like an elderly person's. Fitting, considering the condition Nicholas was in all day. "Why would he think he could just make a statement like that? One person can't just amend the bylaws that way."

The captain's index finger points to the ceiling. "Not so fast, sir. I've spent a lot of time studying that book today. There's an exigent-circumstances clause in there."

"Exigent circumstances?"

"It means—"

"I know what 'exigent circumstances' mean. I just don't know why there'd be such a clause in here."

The captain speaks without hesitating. He's obviously thought all this through. "Clearly they wanted to give the presiding member of the family a certain amount of latitude in terms of controlling the day's events. And you never know what's going to come up during an eight-hour day of writing and interviews. Say you find out . . . say you find out that someone cheated. Or someone assaults another student in the house."

"Or someone dies."

"Exactly. Wouldn't you want to be able to deal with it?"

"If there's an assault, just deny the perpetrator the scholarship. Easy. You're the judge, jury, and executioner." I wince at my choice of metaphor. *Executioner.*

"But what if it's something you don't ever want to happen again? Not just a onetime thing like somebody getting in a fight. But something bigger and more substantial. Something you want to eliminate."

"Like the possibility of an undocumented student winning . . . someone you think isn't the right kind of person."

"Exactly." The captain stands up and paces back and forth in front of me. "So that exigent-circumstances clause allows the presiding officer of the process to write an emergency provision into the bylaws on the day of the process, provided they sign their name to it."

"Are you kidding?"

"I'm not."

"Then that's our ticket, right? I'm the presiding officer now. I can write a provision that says . . . that says whatever we want. That ends the process now—"

But the captain is shaking his head. He points. "Check it out. Page twenty or so . . ."

I flip through the pages, scanning the handwritten words. I squint because some of it is so hard to read. Finally, I catch the word "exigent."

"Okay," I say, "here it is. . . ." I scan through the provision and say, "Oh, I see."

"Yup. You're only allowed to pass one exigent provision per year. Checks and balances."

"I guess you could call it that."

"Back to our friend Natalia. I started to put this together when I was reading those bylaws and saw that note."

"It's never a good idea to make that kind of assumption—"

The captain looks at me like I'm stupid. "Don't you think I know that, sir?"

"Sure, go on."

"See, I resisted my initial assumption. I questioned it. Then I heard you and Natalia talk in the aftermath of her interview. She indicated she had admitted something to you. Something private she didn't want anyone else to know. She seemed very upset by it, so I started to think back over other things that have happened today."

"How would Nicholas have known?"

"That's what I thought about." The captain stops his pacing and scratches his chin. "During tea this morning, Mr. Hyde and Milo were talking about climbing. In fact, they talked about climbing in *Mexico*. You and I started to go out in the hallway to talk, which was very generous of you, by the way. But before we left, Natalia walked toward them, and I heard her say something about birth or being born. I can't be sure which. I didn't think anything of it, but when we came back, Natalia had moved away from them and was talking to Emily. Maybe Natalia told them where she was born and then more about her status. Before the exam, you'll recall, Natalia was talking to Nicholas Hyde and talking to him rather passionately. She said something like 'Why should that matter?' Remember?"

"She could have been talking to him about anything."

He extends his hands, palms up, and holds them there like he expects to collect rain in them. "Okay, here's what we know. Natalia didn't like Milo. She thought he cheated to get ahead and cheated to beat her in class and in a writing contest. She's undocumented, and our friend here"—he points at the body—"clearly *doesn't* like that and wants to keep the rewards from anyone with her status. Have you seen his Twitter feed? It's odious. Now, Natalia was in proximity to both of them. She had the bag of powder in her pocket, which could be poison. She's the most unassuming, the quietest, of all of us, so she can fly under the radar. That's the perfect cover if you want to kill someone." He points again, this time at the pocket doors. "And we're locked in here. And she's out there. With everybody else."

64

WE REACH THE DOOR, and the captain looks ready to charge through the heavy wood.

But I raise my hand, silently asking him to slow down. And he pauses and nods, accepting my leadership of the situation. At least for the moment.

I put my ear to the door again, straining to hear anything. Silence.

I knock with the bottom of my fist, three knocks meant to summon someone to the door. Then we wait.

Nothing.

I knock again, a little louder. "Hey. Hello. Who's out there?"

Floorboards squeak outside the door. At least I think that's what I'm hearing. I hope. The steps come closer.

"Hello?"

"Mr. Gaines?" A small voice from the other side.

"Natalia? Will you unlock the door and let us out? We should all be together. It's safer that way."

"I already told you we want it *this* way," she says. "Did the captain explain what happened to Duffy yet? He's in bad shape out here. I think he's saying someone came up behind him before he got hurt. That's not good."

"You think?"

"Sir, you're not going to listen to that junk they're saying, you of all people. . . ."

"See, Mr. Gaines," Natalia says from the other side of the door. "We're just not comfortable—"

"These accusations, sir . . . they're getting to me."

"I understand that, Captain," I say, managing to keep my voice much more level than I feel. "But I need to know if I can continue to defend you. What happened in the cellar?"

Some energy has drained out of the captain, leaving him more limp in posture and attitude than I've seen all day. "Would you accept it if I said I don't really know, that I'm not sure?"

"On another day, I would. Today . . . I've about lost the ability to give anyone the benefit of the doubt."

The captain purses his lips like he just ate a lemon. "Fair enough, sir. You're a good man, so I'll tell you what I know." He scratches his chin again. "It's dark down there, and I couldn't see very well. I followed that path in the cellar. Heck, I even banged into that pipe you banged into. I got closer to Duffy and saw he was working on that bulkhead door with something. I'm not sure what. But he was trying to work on that opening and get out. And I told him to wait."

The captain stops his story. He looks into the distance, replaying the events he's describing in his mind and not giving voice to them anymore.

I clear my throat, try to bring him back to the parlor in Hyde

House instead of the cellar. "If you were just defending yourself and something went very wrong, you can tell me. You and Duffy had some tensions running both ways today. I'll see you're treated fairly."

He blinks his eyes a few times, returns to our conversation. "Are you trying to lead me into a confession?"

"I'm trying to understand what happened, that's all."

"Duffy was holding something in his hand. A crowbar. A screwdriver. I'm not sure." The captain lifts his hands in the air. "Maybe I should just keep my mouth shut so I'm not misunderstood."

"Captain—James—don't shut me out of this."

"I was going to convince him to stay—*or come clean*—and that's when you showed up. We got him out together."

"How did he get hurt?"

"Didn't you assume the worst when we were down in the cellar together? When you approached me in the dark?"

I don't answer, which serves as an answer.

"There you go," he says. "If your mind is made up, I can't change it. I've learned that much in life."

My mind bounces from one side to the other like a metronome. It can't stop or settle. "Let's hope Duffy ends up being okay."

"I hope the same thing," he says. Then pauses. "I guess I hoped you would believe me. Nobody else does."

His gaze hits me hard.

"We're united in a common purpose right now, Captain." I tilt my head toward the locked pocket door. "We need to get out."

The captain raises his index finger again. "I'm way ahead of you on that."

He walks across the room, stepping gracefully over Nicholas's body like he's a sleeping dog. He gets to the far wall and the fireplace. He reaches up, stretching his body to its full length, and starts tugging on the major's cavalry sword in its scabbard, which has been mounted there for over one hundred years. It takes a few tries, but he gets it down.

Looking as at ease with the weapon as one of the three musketeers, the captain draws the blade from its scabbard with a flourish and stands in the center of the room like a vision of nineteenth-century soldiery.

"Sir, I know the college is in some dire financial straits. It took you a while to try to break a window. Can the school bear just a tiny bit of property damage to that door?"

"It can. But just . . ."

I go closer to the door and make a last attempt. "Hey? Hello? Natalia? Anyone?"

Only silence. The captain is coming toward me, sword raised.

There's no choice, so I step out of the way, and the captain raises the sword like he's Abraham and the door is Isaac and he brings it down against the lock with a sharp crack like an ax hitting a tree in the woods.

It takes a moment, but he works the blade loose from the wood and prepares to swing again. I'm not sure how many hacks it's going to take to get the lock open, but I'm willing to go for it.

The captain prepares to swing again, but I lift my hand. "Wait."

He cuts his eyes my way, and for a moment, I think he's going to swing anyway and slice my hand from my body.

But he stops. "Sir?"

I keep my hand in the air. I move back to the door and press my ear against the wood again. For a moment, I believe I've imagined things, that nothing is out there.

Then the voice again.

"Mr. Gaines?"

Faint and weak. A man's voice.

"Duffy?" I ask.

More silence. How warped has my mind become that I'm hearing the voice of a man who can't even move?

The lock starts to click. It takes nearly thirty seconds, but then the door slides an inch, making a small opening.

I seize the moment and work my fingers into the opening and pull. The door slides all the way open, revealing Duffy, his arm draped over Sydney's shoulder. He looks like a ghost.

"Mr. Gaines . . ."

65

DUFFY LIFTS HIS EYES.

The movement appears to cost him a great deal of energy. Like he's a dying man carrying out his last wish.

"Duffy, you should be lying down."

"He insisted," Sydney says. "It's some kind of macho thing."

Duffy's eyes look glassy, like they have a film pasted over them. He blinks rapidly. Someone repurposed a hand towel and wrapped it around his head as a bandage. Blood seeps through, a red spot the size of a half dollar. And growing.

"Mr. Gaines . . ."

"Duffy, this can wait, I'm sure. Why don't we—"

His eyes focus on a spot just past my left ear. The captain stands behind me and to that side, the sword still clutched in his right hand. My feet rest on pieces of the splintered door.

"I want to tell you . . . about the cellar. . . ."

"He's not coherent, sir."

"He might be." I slide next to him, lifting his free arm over my shoulder so that Sydney and I can guide him into the room. "There's a sofa in here, okay? Lie down on it."

Duffy moves his feet. Tentative half steps like an old man's. But he moves forward. Slowly.

The captain backs out of the way, the sword held across his chest like he's an Arthurian knight. Duffy catches sight of it and freezes.

"Why does he have a sword, Mr. Gaines?" His breath comes in frantic puffs.

"No one's going to hurt anyone, Duffy. Okay?"

My words hover in the air between us, as empty as a deflated balloon. What does it mean for me to make any promise to anyone in this house? Two people are dead. One is seriously hurt. How can I make promises about safety?

We get Duffy moving again, but the captain makes him stop with his next words.

"What about what we talked about, concerning Natalia?"

"Leave her alone," Duffy says.

Sydney keeps her body supporting Duffy but manages to move a little closer to the captain. "She's been through enough already. She thinks you're going to turn her in for her status. She's scared—"

"Sydney. We said—" Duffy coughs, cutting off his words.

"You said what?" I ask.

Sydney clamps her lips shut. Duffy clears his throat but doesn't speak.

"I'm not turning anyone in," the captain says.

"Come on."

We maneuver Duffy to the sofa and ease him down. Sydney lifts his feet and swings them off the floor while I adjust the pillows behind his head, trying to get him comfortable.

Duffy's eyes are closed tight. It doesn't seem possible, but more color drains out of his face. His skin looks see-through.

"Okay, we'll let him rest," I say. "But where is Natalia? We do need to talk to her. In fact, let's just get Natalia and Emily in here. We can all talk."

"Duffy and I haven't been interviewed," Sydney says.

"There's time for that, if he can even talk. But for right now, where are Natalia and Emily? Can you go get them, Sydney? I'd like us all to be together. To be safe."

She remains in place, arms folded across her chest.

"We'll keep an eye on Duffy. And you can come right back."

"The captain will keep an eye on him?"

"Will you go get them?" I ask.

"I'm here."

It's Emily standing in the doorway. She leans against the jamb, her tattooed arms crossed.

"Where's Natalia? Is she in the hallway?"

Sydney and Emily exchange a look. Something passes between them, some understanding, but I can't hazard a guess about what it means.

"Well?"

Silence.

Except—Duffy groans on the sofa. His eyes remain closed, but his mouth works around like he's chewing something sticky.

"Duffy?" I say.

His lips move silently. He groans again.

Then he says, "I told her . . . about the doors . . . the opening. . . . She's getting out. . . ."

66

AT THE PARLOR DOOR, Emily blocks my way.

She refuses to budge, even as I get closer.

"Just let her go, okay? She's scared. She's worried someone's going to turn her in for being undocumented. Or that she'll have to talk to the police and get busted. Can't we just respect her right to leave if she wants?"

"I just want to talk to her," I say. "To help her understand what's going on. It might be worse for her if she runs."

"What is going on, then?" Emily asks. "Besides Natalia's oppression because she doesn't have papers to present on your command."

"I just want to—"

"It's possible she's guilty, isn't it?" the captain asks. "She hated Milo, and she could have poisoned him to knock him out of the competition. And she found out that Mr. Hyde didn't approve of undocumented students. It's in the book right there. The bylaws. So she offed him too. With those pills we found."

"Pills . . ." Duffy's voice is a faint croak. "She had . . ."

"He's right. The crushed-up pills are kind of weird," Emily says. "But that doesn't mean— I mean, I don't know what's going on."

"What about the book?" Sydney asks.

The captain points to the book of bylaws and tells her to turn to the last page. Sydney does, and when she reads the note, she lifts her hand to her mouth and makes a choking sound, like a drowning person emerging from the water.

"This is sick." She walks over, holding the book out to Emily. "If Mr. Hyde wrote this, then he . . ."

"Deserved to die?" I ask.

Emily reads the note, shaking her head. She slams the book down against the floor with a loud splat, which makes Duffy flinch on the sofa.

"I didn't say that. . . ." Sydney kicks the bylaws out into the hallway. "I don't know."

"Can you excuse me, Emily?" I say. "I just want to go talk to Natalia."

"To harass her?"

"To let her know that no one—and I mean, *no one*—is going to jump to any conclusions."

"Mr. Hyde did," Sydney says.

"She's already in the basement," Emily says. "She's going to be gone."

"Shit," I say. "Where is she going?"

"Just let her go."

"Sir, those bulkhead doors open to the rear of the house. And the woods. If she gets through them, she can run. And the police won't see her."

The last thing I want to do is return to the cellar. To push my body through that dark space, following a scared young woman . . .

But she's making a mistake. Things will be far worse if she runs.

And we don't really know what she did—

"Stay here," I say. "All of you."

"Sir, I can—"

"All of you. Stay here. And if anyone else gets hurt . . . Just stay here."

Emily steps out of the way. I bend over, grab the bylaws, and quickly move down the hallway toward the back of the house and the kitchen. Silverware, cups, and a bloody towel litter the floor. A bloodstain decorates the table as well, like someone butchered a side of beef. But I know the blood spilled from the back of Duffy's head.

The cellar door hangs wide open, only darkness beyond.

And this time I hold no Sterno can or light of any kind. I stop in the doorway, lift my free hand to my mouth. "Natalia?"

The sound of movement reaches me. Scuffling footsteps. Metal clanging.

"Natalia? Why don't you come up? We can talk. . . ."

The movement continues, the sound receding. I have no choice.

I start down the stairs.

Step-squeak-step-squeak.

67

A DIFFERENT SOUND REACHES me when I step off the stairs and onto the dirt floor.

A pounding. Deep, steady. Desperate.

It comes from the far side of the cellar, where the bulkhead doors lead out to the rest of the world. Without the Sterno can, it's impossible for me to make out Natalia's shape over there. But something glows where the pounding is happening—the opening I'd seen earlier when I was down here with the captain.

It looks larger, like Natalia has managed to expand it by a good six inches.

And she continues to bash the doors.

"Natalia?"

Her response is to keep beating at the hinges of the doors.

My feet move toward her slowly. Carefully. My memory guides me slightly, but I'm flying blind, trying my damnedest to remember the path through the junk that fills the major's cellar. I bump into a pile of crates. They start to fall and so do I, teetering to my right. I reach out into black air, hoping to steady myself. When I reach the point where I know I'm going to fall and land on God knows what, my body finds an equilibrium point, and I stop.

Balance returns, and I straighten. I hold the book of bylaws in my left hand, sweat forming where my hand touches the leather cover. My heart pounds three times as fast as it should. And the crates finally go, falling over like a demolished building, the crash so loud it murders my ears.

When it's over, the cellar falls silent. My near catastrophe causes Natalia to stop her hammering. I seize the moment, hoping to convince her to stop.

"Natalia? Will you just talk to me for a second?"

"About what?" Her voice is small and distant in the dank space. "About turning me in?"

"No one's turning you in."

"The captain wants to, doesn't he?"

"He said he didn't."

"He thinks I killed Milo. And Mr. Hyde. Because of the bag of pills. They all think that."

"People are theorizing about a lot of things."

I start moving forward again. Half steps. Trying to be quiet. If I can't see her, she can't see me. After five feet, my knee hits the metal pipe again.

"Argh, fuck."

"Watch out for that pipe," she says. "I just missed it."

My eyes squint shut, a wash of red behind the lids. A bruise on top of a bruise. I start forward again.

"I have no idea what's really going on, Natalia. But I know that Mr. Hyde didn't approve of your immigration status."

"So you think I hurt Mr. Hyde? Will you stop walking toward me?"

I freeze. The air brushing against my face is warmer than before. Perhaps leaking in from the opening Natalia has worked on, a hint of the freedom that waits outside.

"He knew about your status, didn't he?"

The moment draws out. I stay in my place, feet planted to the cellar floor like weeds.

She starts pounding again, three quick swings of whatever she's using to bash the door. Wood splinters and cracks, a deeper, more fractured sound than has been made before. More light comes through, a shaft that cuts across Natalia's face. Sweaty, determined.

She speaks through huffing breaths. "When he and Milo were talking about climbing, Mexico came up. I mentioned that I was born there. I should have kept my mouth shut. But then Milo told him I was undocumented. That's what I was trying to explain to him before the exam."

My mouth is dry. "How did Milo know you were undocumented?"

"From honors class. Some of the students knew. He must have heard. He was trying to undermine me with Mr. Hyde by telling him my status. What does this have to do with Mr. Hyde dying?"

Lying to or hiding the truth from students never works. And it rubs me the wrong way. "He wrote a note in the bylaws that indicated he knew you were undocumented."

"He *said* he was thinking of making a change to the bylaws. I wasn't sure if he went through with it. What a shit."

"He meant to cut you out of the competition. It's wrong, Natalia, and I'll do anything I can to fight it. He was drunk or not in his right mind. In fact—"

"So if I remain, I don't get the scholarship. And if I leave, I don't get it. And I might get accused of murder too, which means dealing with the authorities and the attendant hassle that might come as a result."

"I think you should stay. I think we can—"

She swings at the door two more times. The second one punches through, opening a space more than a foot across. Past Natalia a fragment of blue sky, a puffy cloud.

She tosses her tool away and starts tearing at the boards, widening the opening.

Then the first half of her body is through, her legs digging against the wall for propulsion.

I move toward her, but before I get to the short flight of stairs and the door, Natalia slips through the opening and is gone—her heavy shoes disappearing along with the rest of her into the world that exists outside of Hyde House.

I move quickly, heedless of any obstacles.

A shaft of light comes through the opening Natalia made, illuminating the set of stone stairs, the splintered door. Even the bloodstain on the dirt floor where Duffy lay.

My foot mounts the bottom step. My hands go up, trying to find purchase without grabbing a fistful of splinters. I fumble around, get poked in the palm a few times, take splinters under my skin.

"Ow. Shit."

I toss the book of bylaws out through the opening. I search around, and in a faint sliver of light I see an old screwdriver with a wooden handle. I use it to chip away at the door, trying to expand the opening so I can fit. It's awkward work in the tight space, and I miss my mark more than I hit it. On my tenth chip, the screwdriver slips out of my hand and clatters back to the cellar floor.

"Crap."

The longer I wait inside, the farther away Natalia gets.

"Okay, okay."

I find a clear space where I can grab on and pull with both hands. My body braces, my knees bend.

But I don't go.

The captain's close reading of the bylaws pops into my mind. *If the presiding officer leaves the house before four o'clock, then the entire scholarship process is null and void. Forever.*

Forever. *As my dad always says, forever is a long, long time.*

But haven't we all bowed and scraped enough?

Two people are dead. Duffy is hurt. Possibly seriously.

And Natalia is running away—which puts her in greater danger.

What do I care about the most?

The burning pain in my arms and shoulders and back flares as I heave my body up, kicking my legs, digging my shoes against the stone wall in the same way Natalia did.

Splinters dig into my side, tear at my shirt. The opening presses against me, grabbing, clutching. My breath comes quickly, accompanied by the grip of panic, a stuck feeling like I might not make it out.

My mind conjures a picture of a grown man stuck in a cellar opening, waiting for someone to come and rescue him.

"No. Nonononono."

The words may have been spoken out loud or shouted in my brain. But they inspire me, push me like a mantra.

My arms push against the opening. Push and push. My teeth are gritting, grinding against one another so hard they might crack.

Then a hint of relief, pressure easing against my body. My arms burn and shake, but I keep going. More relief. The opening scrapes against my thighs, my knees.

I grab fistfuls of grass, dig my nails into the dirt as I keep pulling. And pulling.

My feet kick free, clearing the opening. My body collapses against the ground, my heart throbbing in my chest like a ringing alarm. Cold sweat against my skin, beneath my clothes.

I open my eyes. Blue sky. One fat puffy cloud. A flock of birds. I'm out.

68

MY CHEST RISES AND falls for a few moments.

I smell grass and dirt, hear birds singing somewhere in the trees. The rear of Hyde House is an imposing wall of faded brick and chipped mortar. The bulkhead doors look splintered and rotten.

Where's Natalia?

I push myself to my feet and wobble a bit. My upper body hurts. My knee stings. The trip through the basement and out the hole has stained my clothes like I've been in a fight. I search in the grass, notice the bylaws sitting like a fat toad. I gather them up.

Thirty feet away the woods begin, the trees just coming into the fullness of their spring greenery, but not yet thick enough to hide someone. I jog that way, each step jarring my body and heightening the pain. I reach the trees, crunch over twigs and old leaves. The scent of loam and pine grows stronger.

"Natalia?"

I stop, tilt my head to listen. The breeze picks up, shaking the branches overhead, stirring the grass. At any other time, I'd marvel over the beauty of the spring day. I'd want Rachel and the girls here with me, walking through the woods at a leisurely pace together. Relaxed.

No such luck.

I lift my free hand to my mouth again. "Natalia?"

A twig snaps on my left, causing me to spin that way. A squirrel scampers across the ground and then up a tree.

My heart pounds more and more. It must be pumping sweat out of my body with each beat. I swipe my arm across my forehead.

One more time: "Natalia?"

But she's gone. No sign of her.

I try not to think the worst—the crushed pills, the disdain for Milo, the hateful note written by Nicholas Hyde.

The running away . . .

I can't dwell.

I can save the others, so I sprint.

Around the side and out toward the front. In the distance, cops and protestors remain at the barricade. Chief stands to one side, a phone pressed to his ear. I run and run, my chest on fire.

The protestors see me, start to jeer and shake their signs.

I ignore them, keep going. Chief sees me, checks his watch, ends his phone call. He starts my way, moving faster and more gracefully than I am.

When we reach each other, I can't talk. Can barely breathe . . .

"Chief . . ."

"What the hell is going on, Troy? You're supposed to be inside."

"Trouble, Chief. Big trouble . . ."

"Where?"

The other cops come our way as the protestors increase their volume.

"People are dead, Chief. Inside the house. Hurt too. Call . . . call for help. . . ."

Without hesitating, he's on his lapel radio. And moving at the same time. All the police are moving. And so am I. Toward the house, trying to help.

PART 4
AFTERMATH

69

ONE ADVANTAGE OF LIVING in a small community—it never takes long for help to arrive.

The chief's concern runs in two directions: First he called for help for Duffy. Then he began treating the house as a crime scene and everyone emerging as a suspect.

Within five minutes, an ambulance *whoop whoops* its arrival, turning down the drive and arriving at the front door, accompanied by two Bluefield town cruisers and a Kentucky State Police car that must have heard the call and decided to come along for the ride.

While the paramedics unload their gear—a stretcher, black equipment cases, a defibrillator—and haul it all up onto the portico and into the house, the chief herds the ambulatory students—and me—out the front door and onto the lawn, all the while barking orders at the officers.

"Lord," the chief says, "who on earth could have seen this coming?"

Sydney asks to stay with Duffy while the paramedics attend to him, but the chief shakes his head and informs her that she has to leave along with everyone else, that Duffy is in the best hands possible, and that it's an encouraging sign that he's conscious and able to communicate.

"Besides," the chief says, "we need to get statements from all of you while it's still fresh in your minds."

"Can I have my phone back to call my mom?" Sydney asks.

"I'd like to make a call too, sir. By the way, did you find Natalia?"

"She ran off. Chief, there's one missing. Natalia Gomez. She ran out the bulkhead doors and took off. That's how I managed to get out. . . ."

"We'll look for her," Chief says.

"Chief? She's scared. Okay?"

"I hear you."

"Can I get my phone?" I ask. "Can we all? Word will spread quickly through the campus community and the town. Rachel and the girls will hear about trouble at Hyde House. A lot of people will. Can we just tell our loved ones we're okay before the rumors start to fly?"

The chief rubs his forehead. "Sure." He calls one of his underlings over. "Go get those phones out of the car. One call each. *One.* To their parents or guardians. And make it a fast one."

The officer jogs back to the barricade, the equipment on his belt jangling. The three healthy students and I stand around in a loose grouping. Everyone wears a shell-shocked look, like we've all been hit over the head with shovels. The sun is bright and warm, mocking us with the beauty of the spring day.

"We're safe now," I say because I have to say something.

Chief comes over and starts pointing. "Separate. Stand apart. We need to talk to you all individually. Spread out. One of you knows something."

The captain's eyes follow the officer heading to the barricade. "That's odd."

"What is?" I ask.

"The protestors. They're all leaving."

He's right. About fifteen or twenty remain, and they're all wandering off, taking their signs and chants with them. But they don't appear to be dispersing out of boredom or hunger or exasperation. They walk off—march off—as though they have somewhere else to go.

"Maybe they can tell there's been trouble, and they don't want to add to it," Sydney says.

My eyes pull toward Emily, but I force myself not to look. No one else needs to be singled out. No one else needs to be suspected. Not by me. It's in the chief's hands now, so I keep my eyes on the dispersing crowd.

"I don't really care why they go," I say, "so long as everyone leaves peacefully and safely."

"Amen," the captain says.

"Spread out," Chief says, his voice rising.

So we do. We drift apart under the watchful eyes of the police.

But as if the protestors hear me and want to prove me wrong, two of them at the rear of the pack stop and come back toward the house. It's impossible to make out their faces or anything about them from this distance, but they stand at the barricade. Waiting. Watching.

"What gives?" Sydney asks.

One of them, the figure on the right, turns toward the other and reaches into a pack strapped to their companion's back. Maybe hunger is exerting its influence, the need for a sandwich or a granola bar.

The protestor pulls something out of the pack, extending it from their body, and then the protestor wearing the pack extends their hands as well and starts moving their arms around.

"It's a weapon of some kind, sir."

"No way," I say.

The police officer pays them no mind. He pulls the locked and zippered canvas bag out of the back of the cruiser and starts to jog toward us at the same jangling pace. I try to find Chief, but he's going back inside the house in the wake of the paramedics, who are tending to Duffy.

"Then what is it?" the captain asks. "Another brick?"

"If it's a brick, it's no threat to us," Sydney says. "No one could throw something that far."

"You're right," I say. "See?"

The officer reaches us with the bag. As he does, something flashes between the two protestors. A dim spark in the afternoon light. The protestor on the left continues to move their arms in that herky-jerky way, almost like—

The flash again.

"Is that a match?" Sydney asks.

"Too bright for that," the captain says. "They're lighting something."

The protestor pivots to their left, moving closer to their partner. Then a burst of sparks erupts between the two of them.

"Is it an incendiary of some kind, sir?"

Sydney gasps.

"Officer?"

The cop turns, takes two steps toward the protestors, the zippered bag in his hand. *"Move back, move back."*

We all retreat, stumbling backward toward the safety of the portico.

The protestor on the right lifts the sparking, flaming device in their hand, raising it toward the sky like they're the Statue of Liberty.

"They can't reach us," Emily says. "Even if it were—"

The protestor's hand erupts.

It shoots a flaming burst into the air. Red. Then another. Blue. Then another—

"It's a Roman candle," the cop says. "Just a firework."

Three more flaming balls shoot out of the tube. They rise high in the air, making a soft *whoomp*ing noise that we can hear across the lawn, and when they reach their apex, they pop into a starburst pattern and sparks before falling harmlessly to earth.

"My God," Sydney says, "I'm sick of this shit."

When the candle tube empties, the protestor tosses it to the ground, spins on their heel, and starts walking off after the rest of the group, their companion at their side.

"Is that it?" the captain asks. "They just wanted to set off an inane firework and leave? Why?"

"I don't know," I say, my breath rushing like a gathering storm again. "I just don't know."

The cop turns to us with the bag. "Well, they're gone," he says. "We can forget about them for now."

Something rattles at the door behind us, causing us all to turn.

The paramedics are coming out—with Duffy on the stretcher between them.

70

THE STRETCHER CLATTERS OVER the threshold and then down the one step leading from the portico to the sidewalk.

A sheet covers Duffy all the way to his chin, and his eyes are closed. When the paramedics come abreast of us, Duffy mutters something, and the paramedics stop.

"Is Mr. Gaines there . . . ?"

"I'm here, Duffy. But they need to get you help."

"Oh." He swallows hard. His lips look painfully dry and chapped, but some color appears to have returned to his face. "I just . . . I don't think the captain hurt me in the basement. . . . It wasn't his fault. . . . He wanted me to stay and not run away. He said that. . . . But then I fell when I was swinging that crowbar at the door. . . . It's a tight space. . . . I fell back. . . ."

"Just don't worry about it, Duffy. Okay? The police are going to question everyone. They'll examine Milo and Mr. Hyde. They'll get to the bottom of it."

"I just . . . We all left. . . . Is the scholarship over?" Duffy asks.

I sense everyone else, all the students, looking at me, waiting for the answer. I choose my words carefully.

"I'm not sure. But we all kind of left together, and I'll do whatever I can to see that somebody wins."

"But we didn't—" Sydney says.

"And I know you and Duffy didn't do the interview part. We can try to take care of that too."

"But, sir, the bylaws say—"

"Yeah, well, fuck the bylaws. Okay?"

Duffy manages a small laugh, and the paramedics carry him over to the ambulance. They load him in while we all watch.

"Hold on one second," the chief says. He uses one of his two million keys to open the canvas bag as he walks to the back of the ambulance. "Which one is yours?"

"Android," Duffy says.

Chief fishes around and brings out the right phone. He hands it to the paramedics and then turns to the rest of us.

"Here you all go," he says as he opens the bag.

Like a school of piranhas jumping on a wounded fish, the students descend. It takes seconds for them each to find their device and pull it out of the bag. They all step away, ready to call whoever they need to call.

"Just one call," the chief says. "And make it fast. Okay?"

I grab my own phone and turn my back on the small crowd, tucking the bylaws under my left armpit. My fingers quake as I call Rachel, and it takes forever for her to answer.

"What's wrong?" she asks instead of saying hello. "It's only— it's just after three."

"I know, I know. I wanted you to hear it from me. And I don't have much time."

I give her the rundown of the day. As quickly and succinctly as I can.

She listens without saying much, but when she does interject, I can tell how scared she is. I'm scared as well—my hands shake the whole time we talk. But it's so good to hear her voice, to know she knows I'm okay.

The chief claps his hands at all of us and makes a hurry-it-up gesture by winding his hand in the air.

"I have to go," I say. "The police need to get statements from everyone."

"Okay. I get it."

"Look, I figured something out today. And . . . I know it's hard for us with the kids getting close to college and everything, but I don't think I want to do this job anymore. I've never liked kissing up to these donors, and after today . . . Well, despite everything, it's nice to spend time with students and get to know them as human beings."

"I can tell how much you miss teaching," she says. "We'll figure it out, okay? Remember, I can take on more clients. With the kids older, we can make it work."

"Rachel, you and the girls are all that really matter to me. The rest is . . . Nothing else matters. That's it."

The chief claps again.

"Okay, I'll call when I'm coming home. I love you."

"I love you too. I'm sorry about everything that went down, but I'm glad you're safe. Stay that way, okay?"

"I will. I promise."

When I finish, I head toward the chief. Sydney sniffles as she tells her mom she loves her. The captain speaks a highly formal good-bye to someone, then asks them to give Tanya a kiss on his behalf.

Emily continues to speak into her phone in a voice so low we can't hear anything. The chief takes a step toward her, about to hurry her along, but then he turns and looks the other way, toward the main drive.

"Oh," he says. "See that, Mr. Gaines?"

"Oh."

Two vehicles head our way, coincidentally arriving at the same time. The first is a white van with one word emblazoned on the side: CORONER. Behind the van comes a vehicle we all recognize—the white Ford sedan driven by President Chan.

"Looks like you have someone else to tell your story to," Chief says.

"Looks that way. Chief, can I ask you something?"

"What?" He fixes the laser stare on me.

"Did you have any idea there would be this kind of trouble? Inside the house, I mean. You said people are disgruntled, the workers on campus."

"What are you saying, Troy?"

I'm stepping through a minefield. "Just . . . did you know or suspect? You all were in there this morning, and the food . . ."

He looks like he doesn't understand me. Then he shakes his head. "Fuck you, Troy."

Emily continues to talk, her voice growing louder. "Yes . . . Yes . . . Yes, I'm ready."

"Ma'am?" Chief says. "We really need you to wrap that up. You can call your parents again later."

She ignores him and steps farther away. "Yes . . . Yes . . . I saw it. . . ."

"Emily?" I say. "Chief needs you to—"

With a loud huff, she says, "Good-bye, okay?" and ends the call.

"Can you just come over here?" Chief says. "All of you?"

They start to gather—

—except for Emily, who surprises everyone by turning and making a mad dash across the lawn, up onto the portico, and back inside Hyde House.

71

THE CHIEF AND ONE of the other cops—the one who brought the bag of phones—start to go after her. I run along behind them, and when we reach the portico, I call out.

"Easy, easy."

They stop at the doorway. The chief looks at me, his brow furrowed, his hairless scalp glistening in the bright daylight. "Stay back, *Vice President* Gaines."

"Hold it," I say. "Can you let me— She's probably scared out of her mind."

"That's a crime scene," the other cop says.

"I know. That's why I want to get her out of there," I say. "I feel responsible for these students, okay? Can I just get her out? Talk to her and get her out of there? Safely."

The chief studies me, brow still wrinkled like a mussed bed. He looks like a man just realizing how long his day is going to be—and it's going to be a long day and evening and night for him as everything gets sorted out.

I'm trying to make his life a little easier.

His posture remains ramrod straight, his muscles taut as wire. "You'd *better* get her out of there fast. And the only reason I'm allowing you to do it is because we have to start interviewing these other students."

He holds up his hands, every finger extended. "*Five minutes.* Then we're coming in and dragging her ass out. And you with her."

"I promise." I hand him the bylaws. "Hold this for me."

Chief takes the book and nods to his underling, and the other cop, who's scowling to show his displeasure with the chief's decision but is still going along with it, nods back.

"Let's go get these statements started," Chief says. "*Five minutes.* And don't touch anything."

"Chief, I want to be done with that house forever."

They leave, their gear rattling as they walk away.

I'm face-to-face with the opening to the house. I don't want to go back in. My skin prickles with gooseflesh at the thought. A wave of unease spreads through my stomach. I reach out, place my right hand on the jamb as I step through, hoping Emily is right there inside the door, ready to leave.

The foyer sits empty.

The staircase stretches out ahead of me. In the distance, the faint ticking of the grandfather clock continues. To my right, Milo's body rests in the music room. To my left in the parlor, Mr. Hyde. Even though I spent the day inside here, my mind struggles to process all that happened. It's already like a haunting dream, the kind that hovers over our heads for an entire day with a creeping unease. I'm not sure I'll ever shake it.

"Emily?"

It's so quiet, so hushed, she must be upstairs. But no sounds come from above. No squeaking floorboards, no steps.

"Emily? You need to come outside. If you don't, the police are going to—"

Metal strikes metal in the parlor. A sharp ringing sound. Once and then twice.

"Emily?"

I go that way, enter the parlor. Emily stands by the far end of the fireplace. She holds the sword—the major's sword, which the captain dropped—over her head. The blade extends nearly to the ceiling and appears to be as long as she is. Determination twists her face as she swings again, brings the sword down against the gas sconce.

Clang!

The sconce sits at an odd angle. The stem attaching it to the wall twists like a slithering snake, and the screws anchoring it in place are popped loose.

"Emily. That's gas. *Real gas.*"

The flame reflects off her glasses, obscuring her eyes. She ignores me, sucks in a deep breath, and takes one more giant swing like she's a miniature Paul Bunyan.

Clang!

The blade sends the sconce flying off the wall and across the room, where it clatters against the hardwood and comes to rest at the side of Nicholas Hyde's body. Gas pours directly out of the wall with a whoosh.

"Emily, my God—"

She digs in the pocket of her dress and brings out a lighter. "I brought this with me. I kept it to myself when you went downstairs with the matches."

Her thumb strikes the wheel once and then twice, but the flame doesn't catch.

"Emily, stop." I hold out my hand. "Think about what you're doing. The criminal charges."

"It doesn't matter."

"You're with the protestors. They *did* call your name during the day. The phone call outside, the Roman candle. It was a signal."

"They're all marching now," she says. "They're going to tear down the statue of Major Hyde, wipe any trace of him off the face of the earth. A polluter and a mass murderer. A genocidal maniac."

"Emily, we need to—"

"I can't believe I thought about staying and taking his blood money. I did. I was ready to stay until—"

"Until you found out about the job. And working for a year."

"Exactly. That was a bridge too far."

"Did you fake being sick so we wouldn't suspect you?"

"I didn't fake it, but I overplayed it. I haven't eaten meat in years. They don't give out much good meat at the food pantry, so I tried the rabbit here. I think it disagreed with me, and that was my chance to throw suspicion off myself. The whole thing makes me sick. Really. And I hate myself for being tempted by the handouts, the crumbs. That's what always happens. I'm always tempted off the true path by some vestige of privilege. This house has to go too."

"Did you kill them? Did you kill Nicholas as part of this plan?"

She looks down, the lighter in her hand. She studies the body as though she's seeing it for the first time. "Fuck him. He's small potatoes compared to all of this and the college."

She shakes the lighter, runs her thumb across the wheel. The lighter ignites.

Without hesitation, Emily lifts her hand. She looks like a smaller version of the Statue of Liberty—with Virginia Woolf's face painted on her arm.

The flame from the lighter reaches the gas jet from the wall—

An orange flash as big and bright as the sun—

I'm in the air, suspended for a moment above the furniture. My feet rise as high as my head.

I'm leaving my body, leaving the earth. Rachel and the girls flash through my mind, my parents and my friends—everything I know and care about flying by—

Then I slam against the floor. My body rolls, a reverse somersault with my feet swinging back over my head and hitting the parlor wall underneath the window. I'm crumpled in the corner like a pile of old clothes. Heat and flame grow in intensity above me.

72

THE RINGING IN MY head brings me back to life.

Everything burns, and the air glows. My lungs pump and gasp but can't find enough air to breathe.

I get on all fours, look across the room. The walls, the ceiling, are all aflame—and the flames dance and spread.

"Emily?"

The word barely escapes my throat. My throat burns, and I choke. The heat blisters my lips.

"Emily?"

Something moves across the room. Illuminated in orange, Emily stumbles to her feet. I do the same, start toward her. Smoke fills the space in thick gray puffs. Emily comes toward the center of the room. As she does, a portion of the parlor ceiling falls and lands where she was standing, sending up an eruption of flame and spark.

"Let's go," I say. My words are lost in the crackle of the flames.

I take Emily by the hand, feel the grit and dirt on her skin. We start for the hallway, but she stumbles, goes to her knees with a grunt.

"I can't. . . ."

"Come on."

With all my strength, I pull her up, keep my arm around her back to make her go. We enter the hallway. The flames jump out here, igniting the walls and the staircase.

A coughing spasm takes hold of my chest, sending me to my knees. I can't breathe, can't force any air into my lungs. Giant bands of pressure squeeze my chest like I'm underwater.

Emily goes to her knees as well.

I can't move. Strength drains out of my body.

"Go, Emily. . . ."

"I can't. . . ."

Smoke fills the space so I can barely see her right next to me. I just want to close my eyes, go to sleep—

A figure appears before us, emerging from the outside.

"Sir?"

"Captain . . . take . . . her. . . ."

Something grabs me, a giant hand. Like I'm a toy in one of those claw vending machines. I'm moving toward the light— toward the door—

Then daylight surrounds me and other hands take me. I'm dragged off the portico steps and into the grass. Dragged and dragged, my shirt pressing against my throat.

But the oxygen flows into my lungs, clean and clear. I inhale it greedily.

The chief leans over me, undoes my tie, loosens my shirt. "You're okay," he says. "Just breathe."

"Emily . . ."

"She's okay too. Breathed a little smoke like you, but that's it."

"The captain . . ."

"Well . . . he went back in."

"Back in?"

I struggle to rise. Chief places his hand against my chest gently, trying to keep me down in the grass. I can't do anything. . . .

I rise to a sitting position. Hyde House is a cauldron of flames. They shoot out the windows and chimney. Smoke pours from every opening.

Two police officers and a paramedic stand on the portico but can't enter. More sirens wail in the afternoon, approaching fire trucks and ambulances—but none of it can help the captain.

Painful moments pass. Everything inside me feels scorched and raw. My eyes water. Yes, because of the smoke, but also for the captain. He saved us—Emily and me.

And he didn't get out.

"Chief, you've got to—"

A figure emerges from the smoke, hunched and carrying a large burden. He stumbles across the portico and out onto the lawn. The cops and paramedic rush to his side as he goes down on his knees, the body on his back flopping onto the ground beside him.

"It's the captain," I say.

He's surrounded by help. I stumble to my feet, Chief by my side. I make it to the captain's side, fall to my knees. The paramedic places an oxygen mask over his face. He's breathing. His clothes are dirty, his hair is scorched, but he's breathing.

"Captain, thank you."

His eyelids flutter.

I see what—*who*—he carried out of the house on his back. It's Milo. Milo's body rescued from the flames.

"Captain . . ."

He lifts his hand, moves the oxygen mask aside. "I couldn't let . . . His mom will want . . ."

"I get it," I say. "I do."

The paramedic slides the mask back over the captain's face.

"Is he okay?"

"He should be fine. Smoke inhalation and some burns on his hands and arms. But it doesn't look too bad."

The same can't be said for Hyde House.

Flames engulf every inch of the structure, foundation to roof. It's a total loss.

73

HYDE HOUSE BURNS. AND burns.

Two fire trucks arrive, but by the time they pull up to the front of the building, it's far too late. They drag out their hoses and spray the flames, but they might as well be spitting on it for all the good it does.

The paramedics load both Emily and the captain onto stretchers and wheel them to separate ambulances. A cop walks alongside Emily's stretcher, asking her questions she refuses to answer. She says only one thing:

"I waited until the house was empty. I waited. . . ."

More police arrive, and the chief redirects some of them to the entrance of the college to try to stop the protestors from bringing down the statue of Major Hyde and Lancer.

I cough and cough. My mouth tastes like an ashtray. My lungs burn like someone has taken a blowtorch to them. Chief and Grace Chan approach.

"Let's get you to the hospital," Chief says. "I can get one of my officers to drive you."

"I'm okay. I want to stay."

"You trying to get more hero points?"

I blink and blink, trying to ease the pain in my eyes. "I don't know, Chief."

Grace takes a step closer. "Chief's right. Why don't you go to the hospital? We can handle it all here. It's pretty obvious what happened, isn't it? These protestors had a grand plan to bring down the Hyde family and all they represent. The house, the statue. And yes, even to kill Nicholas Hyde. I just can't believe one of our students could commit murder in such a way." Grace struggles to find the right words and fails. "I just . . ."

"They're likely not all students from Hyde," Chief says. "Most of them are outside agitators. That's the way these things go. This Emily fell in with a bad crowd."

"And she murdered one of her classmates in the process," Grace says.

The chief rubs his forehead. "I suspect she didn't want to do that. She probably intended to poison Mr. Hyde and was sloppy. Nerves cause mistakes." He points at me. "We heard this Milo and Mr. Hyde were standing next to each other during teatime."

"They were." I blink and blink. The day's events run through my mind like a sped-up film. A horror film. "But Emily wasn't near them . . . and she just said she waited until the house was empty to burn it down, which is true. She could have done it anytime during the day. . . ."

"I know you want to figure out a way to let her off the hook," Grace says. "It's tough to accept any of this."

"How are they picked, Grace? These students. How are they picked to go in there?"

"It's financial need and—"

"Grace, I know that song and dance. But the students who were in there today—they were desperate. Utterly desperate. It's like the Hyde family and the board found the students who were the most vulnerable, the most needy. Students with sick children and murdered parents. Undocumented or broke or homeless. Is that how they guarantee obedience and compliance? Is that how they make sure no one talks about the process? No wonder it ended up like a viper pit."

"We have to cooperate with the family, Troy. You know that. If they want to pick certain students . . . If they want us to tell them what we know about their personal lives, we do. Or people find out. Professors. Advisers. It's a lucrative scholarship. The family needs to know that the student values it."

"Damn, Grace. It's like they're lab rats."

A coughing fit seizes me. I bend over, place my hands on my knees until it passes. Chief pats me on the back, repeats his offer to take me to the hospital.

I attempt to speak and can't. The words won't come without coughs. Chief walks off to one of the police cars, comes back with a fresh bottle of water. "Here."

I guzzle it. It cools like rain in the desert.

When I can speak again, I say, "Thank you."

"Don't mention it."

"Listen," I say, straightening up. "These deaths. They happened hours apart. First Milo and then Nicholas."

"What's your point?" Grace asks.

"Why did it happen that way? If you're Emily and you want to kill Nicholas, why do it first thing in the morning or in the middle of the day and then stay until now and burn the house down? Something doesn't add up—"

Chief's phone starts to wail on his hip.

Not ringing. An alarm. He uses his thumb to silence it and smiles wryly. "Four o'clock. The time I'd be opening Hyde House and letting you all out in a normal year." He sighs, the sound carrying the weight of all the day's losses.

"It's a tragedy any way we cut it," Grace says.

A police car slowly rolls up, stopping fifty feet away from us. An officer climbs out and comes toward the chief, her thumbs hooked in her belt. "Chief?"

"What is it?"

"I found that student," she says, jerking her thumb toward the car. "The one who was unaccounted for."

"Natalia?" I say.

"That's her. She was on one of the footpaths, just wandering around. She said she was coming back here. I'm not sure."

"Did she say anything?" Chief asks.

"Is she hurt?" Grace asks.

"She's okay. She says she wants to talk to Vice President Gaines. And *only* Vice President Gaines."

Chief looks over. "What do you know about this, Troy? Do you have reason to suspect her of something?"

"No—I mean . . ." Suspect her? The pills? The xenophobic note about her? The running away? Her hatred of Milo? "Can I talk to her?"

Chief nods, and the cop goes to the car to get Natalia. "Do you think Natalia and Emily were working together? Maybe Natalia is with these protestors too?"

"I don't know."

"Let's take this slow, Chief," Grace says. "The kid's scared."

"Troy, you said things didn't quite add up," he says. "The gap between the deaths. Could Natalia have killed someone as well?"

Natalia stares at Hyde House, her mouth slightly open. The flames reflect off her dark eyes. "What happened?"

"Emily—"

Chief cuts me off. "What do you know, Natalia? Why did you run? Are you and Emily friends?"

Natalia looks at me, then at Chief. "I ran because I was scared. Because I'm undocumented, and I thought I was going to be reported. To the police."

"We don't care about that, Natalia," Grace says.

She goes on. "But I really was coming back because . . . well, I wasn't sure where to go. And I was worried about everyone getting out."

"Did you do something?" Chief asks. "We heard you had pills crushed into a powder. What were those for?"

She swallows hard. "I told them why."

"Did you hurt Milo Reed? Or Nicholas Hyde? It's better if you just tell us the truth now. Get it all out. We can try to help you, but only if you tell the truth as soon as possible."

"Natalia," I say, "what did you want to tell me?"

She looks at the house again. "I didn't do anything. I didn't. I ran because I was scared."

"But the pills," Chief says. "Did you do something with them?"

She repeats herself. "I didn't do anything. I don't know why anybody died."

Grace's phone buzzes. She makes a face and reaches into her pocket. The chief looks down at his phone.

"Shit," Grace says. "We're all getting alerts. The news is spreading. I need to get in touch with the board. We need to put out a statement of some kind. No, no, not that. I need to call Milo's parents. I have to do that *first*. Then Mr. Hyde's next of kin if he has one. I think there are some cousins somewhere. . . ."

"President Chan?" Chief raises his phone.

"Chief, will you help me coordinate with the authorities from town? I don't want to step on any toes about how they handle things, but we have to tell Milo's family about—"

"Grace? Troy?" Chief says. "You both need to see this."

74

I CHECK MY OWN phone.

Grace says the alert comes from Twitter. It takes me a moment to understand, but months ago, I set the alert to notify me whenever Nicholas Hyde tweeted. It made sense at the time as a way to keep abreast of what he—and the Hyde family—was thinking and doing.

The result was that Nicholas tweeted so much—and such distasteful—content that I turned the notification off.

But now, today, four hours after he died on the floor of the parlor in Hyde House, Nicholas is still tweeting. Has someone hacked his account? Is it an assistant? An employee?

"Sweet Jesus," Chief says.

I start to read, squinting to make out the text on my phone. It's a thread.

By the time you read this, I will be dead. And the process, carried out by my family for one hundred fifty-two years, will be complete. Truly complete.

As the result of a series of bad investments I have made since gaining control of my family's fortune, we are now bankrupt. A company teetering on the brink of financial ruin when I took the reins has now completely fallen. And it can't get up. I'm just glad my dad and especially my mom aren't here to see it.

I decided to end my life where my family's life—and fortune—began. Hyde House. And just to save the coroner a little time—it's an extract of an Aconitum plant. Ingested during teatime. I decided to get it out of the way at the beginning of the process today.

"What's an Aconitum plant?" Grace asks.

"Monkshood," Chief says. "Wolfsbane. It grows around here. It's highly lethal. People are using it for suicide more and more."

"Could you easily dilute it in tea?" I ask.

"Yup."

I don't know if the college will go on with the process after my death or not. I hope you don't. It's not worth it with no money for the awards.

I apologize to my few remaining family members, my few friends, the employees of the Hyde Corporation, the board of Hyde College, and anyone else I've hurt or offended. I also apologize to my substance abuse counselors and sponsors. This is my fault, not yours.

My family had a glorious run that stretched from the late nineteenth century to the beginning of the twenty-first. But that torch is now extinguished. Farewell!

The events of the day run through my mind again. This time through the lens of Nicholas's tweetstorm . . .

Nicholas and Milo standing next to each other and talking about climbing during teatime. Demonstrating grips and techniques. Their cups placed down on the table next to each other's . . .

Nicholas referring to himself as the big bad wolf . . .

Nicholas so distraught over Milo's death . . .

Nicholas sitting alone upstairs . . .

Nicholas distraught over his mother's death . . .

Nicholas promising me the moon and the stars for the 100 More Initiative when he knew there was no money for it . . .

Nicholas insisting we all stay, thereby delivering a giant middle finger to his family's signature event . . .

Nicholas going upstairs after the toast, glass of bourbon still in his hand, claiming to look for the briefcase, which was sitting in the dining room . . .

Is that where he drank the poison? By himself upstairs, away from everyone else so another accident wouldn't happen?

And collapsed in the parlor right after that . . .

A cop runs over. "Chief, they just pulled down Major Hyde and Lancer. They're trying to drag them out into the highway and block traffic."

"Aw, hell. Call the state police for more backup."

We all turn and watch Hyde House burn.

"What are we going to do, Troy?" Grace asks. "If the Hyde family has no money, then the school has no money either."

"I was going to tell you that I wanted to give up my position and go back to teaching."

"We might all be looking for new positions."

Sydney comes over and stands next to Natalia. Sydney asks, "Did you all see these tweets?"

"We did," I say.

"Are they true?" Natalia asks.

"We believe so."

"Wow."

We stand, watching the flames lift toward the sky.

"So is there, like, no scholarship either?" Sydney asks. "No job or loan forgiveness?"

"I'm sorry, but I don't think there is. We can try to figure something out, but . . . it's not looking very promising. I'm sorry. I know you both went through a lot today."

The silence draws out, fills with the crackling of the flames, the sound of timber snapping and glass shattering.

"I just wanted to say something, Mr. Gaines."

"What's that, Natalia?" I ask.

"I just wanted to thank you for . . . you know, for everything you did for me. Really, for everyone inside the house. You did your level best to take care of us and make sure everything went okay. And you tried to give us all a fair shot."

Is it corny to say that her words reach me deep down inside? That my eyes mist—and not because of the smoke and the burning?

"Thank you, Natalia. I appreciate that."

"Same goes for me," Sydney says. "I'm glad you were there for us. And you were so understanding and stuff."

"I'm sorry the day went so poorly."

"I'm sorry too," Sydney says. She looks at me, her mouth pressed into a tight line.

"Did you want something else?" I ask.

She shifts her weight a little, then says, "My mom says she's probably going to sue the college because of everything we went through today. Her boyfriend is going to go to the media."

"Do what you have to do," Grace says.

"Cool," Sydney says.

"What happened to that book I handed you, Chief?"

"Oh." He looks around, turning his body one way and then the other. "I set it down on the edge of the driveway over there."

I walk over and pick it up. Its cover feels warm to the touch from the sun, the black leather having absorbed the heat.

"Is that what I think it is?" Grace asks.

"Is it true there's only one copy?" I ask.

"That's right."

"So . . . I mean, if this were to happen to . . ." I walk toward the fire.

"Troy, you shouldn't. Let's think about this. And all its ramifications."

I look back, the heat brushing my face. "Is there enough money somewhere to at least give these five—or, I guess, *four*—students their fellowships? Five thousand each?"

Sydney and Natalia look from me to President Chan. She meets the students' eyes and then turns to me. "I think we can do that."

"Great." I move closer to the fire, holding the book out. The heat washes over me in waves. "We could write our own rules for the future, right? I mean, if this book were to go away. And maybe the Hyde family with it."

"There might not be a Hyde College if that happened, Troy. At least not the one we know now."

"Maybe there shouldn't be. Or maybe if it can start over and become something else, it should. Think of the college changing in that way as . . . collateral damage. A consequence of doing the right thing and getting the Hyde Corporation and family out of our lives."

"Troy, stop."

I get as close as I can, so close I think my skin might blister. I heave the bylaws into the fire. The black book disappears into the hellish orange wall, never to be seen again.

I back up, join the others. We watch a few minutes longer. The roof of Hyde House collapses. Within fifteen minutes, the entire structure is burned to the ground.

ACKNOWLEDGMENTS

Thanks once again to all the talented folks at Berkley. I want to give special thanks to Loren Jaggers, Jin Yu, and Bridget O'Toole, who have worked tirelessly and creatively for so many years on behalf of my books. And thanks to Eileen Carey for the amazing cover design.

Thanks to Kara Thurmond for her web prowess. Thanks to David Hale Smith for his wisdom. Thanks to Tracy Bernstein for guiding the book to the finish line. And big thanks to Ann-Marie Nieves and everyone at Get Red PR for their endless efforts.

Massive thanks to Laney Katz Becker for years of loyal friendship, wise counsel, and psychological support.

Big, big thanks to my editor, the wonderful Danielle Perez, for her attention, thoughtfulness, and patience.

Special thanks as always to my friends, family, readers, and fellow writers.

And thanks to Molly McCaffrey for everything.